Cheyne moved closer to Miss Bright, but she sprinted for the door. He spun around and lunged, catching her around the waist and quickly pulling her against him. And then Cheyne realized his mistake in not holding her at arm's length.

They were pressed against each other like tinned sausages, and he could feel her breasts heave against his chest. Every movement, every squirm and writhe brought curved parts of Miss Bright in contact with his body. The righteousness of his purpose disappeared from his thoughts. Arousal burned away his vexation. It raced to other parts of him as well, making him want to howl with the tension of it. Unable to endure the agony, Cheyne suddenly let go of his partner.

The abruptness of her release caused Miss Bright to lose her balance. She dropped to the floor on her bottom.

"Hey!"

Cheyne retreated to the window, grabbed a handful of velvet curtain in his fist and pressed his forehead against the glass. "Go away."

JUST BEFORE MIDNIGHT

Just Before Midnight

Suzanne Robinson

BANTAM BOOKS
New York London Toronto Sydney Auckland

JUST BEFORE MIDNIGHT
A Bantam Book / March 2000

ISBN 0-553-57961-4

Published simultaneously in the United States and Canada

Bantam Books are published by Bantam Books, a division of Random
House, Inc. Its trademark, consisting of the words "Bantam Books" and the
portrayal of a rooster, is Registered in U.S. Patent and Trademark Office
and in other countries. Marca Registrada. Bantam Books, 1540 Broadway,
New York, New York 10036.

PRINTED IN THE UNITED STATES OF AMERICA

OPM   10 9 8 7 6 5 4 3 2 1

This book is dedicated to Joan Robinson,
an English lady whose beauty, manners, and
appreciation of elegance are reflected in
this story of Edwardian opulence.

Acknowledgments

Early cars figure prominently in this book, and I would like to thank Mr. David A. Kolzow, Sr., for his generous help on this subject. Mr. Kolzow has restored many cars, among which are a 1894–95 Benton Harbor and a 1899 Panhard-Levassor. He is one of the few experts in this country to have restored cars of this early date. For further information on this subject readers can refer to the Antique Automobile Club of America (http://www.aaca.org), which has an excellent library and research center.

Just Before Midnight

1

London, 1899

If she didn't escape before dawn, she wouldn't get away at all. Mattie Bright tiptoed through the darkened house, her boots clutched in one hand, her skirts lifted in the other. If she was discovered, the consequences would be terrible—another morning of lessons in elocution, manners, and the peerage from Mademoiselle Elise; more fittings for her new Worth gowns; and after that, more calls. If she had to sit through another afternoon listening to Society ladies and their daughters gush about gowns and lace, calling them "deevie," which was their private word for *divine*, she'd squall like a bobcat in a pickle barrel.

"Deevie indeed," she muttered.

Such affectations irritated her intensely, causing her to slip in her determination to improve her character. For Mattie was engaged in a great endeavor to reform, to become more tolerant, more even-tempered, calm and, above all, sweet-natured. These were the qualities of the great lady Papa had always wanted her to become. Sadly, she lacked most of them. Closest to her heart was the desire to be like other young women. Other young ladies seemed to glide along with sweet smiles and kind words, never growing angry at things like women not being allowed to vote, never losing their tempers or wishing they could take charge because some man was making an all-fired mess of things.

Mattie hurried down the stairs, through the drawing room and past a table on which were scattered her mother's books on conduct. Her resolve to improve vanished. Glaring at Mama's copy of *Titled Americans*, Mattie cursed every girl in it who had married an English lord. Ever since her parents' efforts to conquer New York society had failed so embarrassingly, their hopes of establishing social preeminence had fastened on their twenty-three-year-old daughter.

Ordinarily she would have refused to have anything to do with such carryings-on, but just before he died, Papa had asked Mattie to do just one thing for him. Marry a titled Englishman. It would make all his hard work, all his efforts to give them a better life, worth it. And he and Mama hadn't been satisfied with low standards like the Jeromes, whose daughter Jennie married Lord Randolph Churchill. Papa and Mama aimed high, and Mattie must set her cap for the best, like Consuelo Yznaga, who became Duchess of

Manchester, or her goddaughter, Consuelo Vander-
bilt, the new Duchess of Marlborough.

The path to gentility had been a rough and long
one for Mattie. It had begun as soon as Papa grew
wealthy, with many a rebellion along the way. But
over the last few years Mattie had come to realize
how different she was from most girls, and after a
while she'd begun to suspect there was something
wrong with her. Otherwise she wouldn't find inventions and new ideas more fascinating than Paris fashions and marriage offers. Her character was flawed,
or she would long to be as sweet, loving, and giving
as her mother and her friend Narcissa. Just when she
thought she'd turned herself into a lady, she'd forget
to control her tongue or her temper, or both.

With a sigh Mattie shut the door to the drawing
room. Avoiding the kitchen, where the maids would
be starting fires and heating water, Mattie left the
house through the conservatory. She stopped to pull
on her boots, wiggling her foot into the aged leather.
These were her old boots, the ones she wasn't supposed to wear because they were Texas trail boots
rather than fine English riding ones. But why wear
anything fancy when no one was going to see her?

Mattie stood and luxuriated for a moment in the
soft wrinkled and scratched leather. Then she stamped
her boots to settle her feet in them comfortably and
set off for the stables. With every step away from the
house, her spirits rose. She was wearing her long, loose
coat that covered her from neck to boots and fastened

tightly at the cuffs. Her hair was covered by a hat and veil, and goggles hung about her neck. Letting herself out the garden gate, she crossed an alley with eager steps and met Trimble, the coachman, on his way to feed the horses.

"Good morning, miss."

"Mornin', Trimble. You haven't seen me."

"No, miss. I never do."

Trimble opened the stable doors, and Mattie went to a canvas-covered mound opposite the stalls. The coach horses stuck their heads out and nickered at her. Mattie waved at them as she hauled the canvas off her new motorcar. The gray hue of dawn lit the black metal body and polished brass headlamps of the Panhard-Levassor. A shiver of excitement whipped through her as she reached over and flipped the lever on the steering wheel to retard the spark. Hurrying to the front, she gripped the crank and turned it once. The engine burst to life with a steady metallic hum. It was unlike anything else heard on the road, those tiny, muffled, rapid-fire explosions that blurred into one continuous purr. The brass carriage lamps rattled against their glass. Mattie grinned over her shoulder at the horses, who had become used to the noise of the car.

"One crank every time, fellas. It's a caution." Equine ears pricked. One of them snorted and kicked his stall.

"Dang, Trimble. I think they're jealous."

The coachman was filling a bucket with oats.

"More like they wish that foul machine to perdition, begging your pardon, miss."

Pulling her goggles into place, Mattie jumped into the Panhard and released the brake. "Don't worry, we're leaving. Come on, Pannie, before the poor creatures have conniption fits."

Mattie drove out of the alley at a sedate pace. No sense in waking Mama with engine noise. These drives served as a refuge from the trials of being in Society and trying to catch a titled husband. Essentially American in her outlook, Mattie had trouble giving up her ideals regarding men, women, and marriage. She didn't want to get married at all, but if she was going to do it, she wanted to marry someone she loved. Of course, that was no longer an option. Among the English aristocracy, marriage was an alliance between families for financial and social advantage. Love had nothing to do with it. Love was what happened after an heir had been provided— then the partners went their separate ways to find it, the husband sometimes getting a head start on his search.

"Mattie Bright," she said to herself as she turned a corner, "you got as much chance of finding a lovable man in Society as an armadillo does of going to a tea party."

Besides, how was she ever going to know for sure whether a man valued her or her money? If she married the kind of man she'd promised Papa she would, the answer would be obvious. Sighing, she reminded herself that she'd given up on finding someone who would love her for herself. She liked all the wrong things, like motorcars and finding ways of employing her money for the good of others. English ladies weren't supposed to finance the education of the poor or advocate the vote for women.

Of course, she'd had to leave all of that—except the motorcars—behind in America. Which meant she was bored when not corresponding with friends like Mr. Roosevelt or the administrators of her various projects. And she wasn't going to fool herself. A beauty she wasn't, so her greatest asset was her money. It would be at home as well as in England.

"So there's no point in not doing as Papa asked," she muttered.

Practical, that's what she was. Finding true love, like in Mama's old bedtime stories, was a dream. But every time she reminded herself of this, something inside her ached. Usually she could distract herself by recalling how much Papa had wanted her to succeed and how desperately she wanted to make him proud. Papa had died ashamed of his inability to conquer high society, and now he was depending on her to do what he couldn't.

"Don't get all blubbery. Pay attention to your driving."

Mattie watched carefully for early pedestrians as she entered St. James's Street and stopped at Piccadilly. Then she positioned herself in the middle of the deserted street. A passing flower seller eyed her with alarm when she pressed the gas. The Panhard's engine whirred, and the car jumped into motion. Wind hit Mattie's face, taking her breath away. Her worries vanished as the brick pavement blurred and the Georgian and Regency buildings on either side sped by.

Exhilaration pumped through Mattie's veins with the speed of fuel through the engine. She laughed and whooped, keeping her eyes on the road. Ahead loomed Hyde Park Corner and Wellington Arch. Slowing only a bit, she turned the wheel and accelerated into the curve. The Panhard hugged the pavement and spun onto Park Lane, startling a chimney sweep and a maid cleaning a wrought-iron gate. The maid shrieked and covered her ears, but Mattie zoomed by, her eye on Marble Arch at the end of Park Lane. She would race around the arch, down Bayswater and into Hyde Park by the Ring. There she could circle the park via Rotten Row.

As she sped past Stanhope Gate, Mattie fed the engine more gas. The ends of her scarf flapped wildly, and she gulped in deep breaths. She was going to make this stretch in record time! She was approaching Grosvenor Gate, her pedal foot almost on the floor, when a dark flash appeared in the corner of her eye. Her foot came off the gas pedal, and she grabbed the outside brake with one hand. Mattie and the Panhard swerved, barely missing a chestnut Thoroughbred as its rider hauled on the reins. She heard the horse scream as the motorcar continued its careening circle, jumped a curb and stopped. Mattie was thrown against the steering wheel. Her hat and veil slipped over her face, and the engine stalled.

Mattie fell back in the seat while she caught her breath and her vision cleared. Her shaking hands pushed her hat back and pulled the knot in her veil loose. Behind her she heard shouting and the clatter of hooves on pavement. Somewhat recovered, Mattie tore her hat from her head and jumped out of the Panhard. A continuous stream of curses greeted her. She was relieved at the sight of a costermonger rushing after the Thoroughbred. The horse was dancing down the street with alarm but was unhurt. The cursing rider, however, was buried under a cascade of lettuce, squash, melons, and tomatoes—lots of tomatoes.

What she could see of the man seemed whole. She must have missed him completely, if only by an inch or two. Mattie folded her arms over her chest and watched him flail at a rain of peaches and strawberries that were sliding from the top of the costermonger's cart onto his head.

Had his hair not been seeping with squashed tomato, the stranger would have been blond. His riding outfit had the elegant cut of Saville Row, but the effect was marred somewhat by lettuce-leaf epaulets while tomato pulp stained the starched purity of his shirt. Mattie forgot her outrage at the man's carelessness and chuckled. The swearing stopped. The rider paused in the act of wiping his face and gave her a look of outrage that belonged on Banquo's ghost when confronting Macbeth.

"Bloody hell, woman, you should look where you're going. You almost killed me. You must be a blithering fool." Mattie opened her mouth, but the rider held up a hand, noticed it was holding a squash and dropped the vegetable. "No, don't answer. I can see you're one of those ghastly New Women. Driving infernal motorcars, probably screeching about the vote and other absolute rot. It's obvious you're a blithering fool."

Tossing a lock of jet-black hair over her shoulder, Mattie drew her brows together. "What are you so all-fired huffy about? You're the one who doesn't look where he's going. You must be blind as a post-hole not to have seen me coming, and I'm not fixin' to let you cuss at me for something that's your own blamed fault."

The rider was staring at her, open-mouthed. "Dear God, what kind of beastly accent is that?"

"I don't have an accent. You're the one with the accent. You sound like you've been eating lemons for breakfast, all pinched and tart."

At this the rider lunged to his feet, only to slip on a melon rind and crash to the ground on his posterior. Mattie clapped her hands together and laughed, which elicited another colorful blasphemy from him.

"You look like a piglet in a mud hole!" Mattie chuckled again, but her mirth ended abruptly when something wet and cold smashed her in the face. "Ugh!" She wiped her eyes and looked at her hands. They were covered with tomato. "Why, you ornery priss-pants, I'll . . ." Words failed, but Mattie took action. She scooped up a handful of red melon pulp and hurled it at the rider's newly cleaned face. He ducked, but Mattie followed with the contents of her other hand. This time the melon hit him in the ear.

The rider lunged at her, keeping his footing. He would have had her if the costermonger hadn't rushed up with the Thoroughbred in tow.

"Sir, I caught him, I did. He's all right."

Mattie's opponent clenched his fists, gave Mattie an acid glare and took the reins. His face lost its harsh lines the moment he turned to the horse. His voice took on the quality of a father soothing a lost child.

"There, old chap, you're all right. Yes, you are. You're just fine. Pay no attention to the harpy and her infernal machine."

"Harpy!"

The horse tossed his head and widened his eyes while the rider turned on Mattie.

"Damn it, woman. Will you be quiet? Only a savage spooks a horse like that."

"What in Sam Hill do you mean calling me a harpy, you no-account skunk?" Mattie scooped up a tomato and aimed.

"Here!" The costermonger rushed to her and snatched the tomato. "Who's going to pay for me cart and vegetables? Look at it. There ain't a whole piece of fruit nor nothing in the whole lot."

"The harpy will pay," said the rider as he led his horse around the cart.

"Ha! The accident was your fault, not mine," Mattie said. She glanced at the costermonger. "The dude will pay."

The vendor looked from Mattie to the rider. "Someone's got to pay, or I'll be getting a copper, I will."

"An excellent idea," the rider said as he mounted his horse. "When he comes, just explain to him that the harpy was motoring on Park Lane over thirty miles an hour and caused the whole thing."

"Why, you—"

Elegant brows raised. "Do you deny you were going that fast?"

"I'm not in the habit of telling tales. I know how fast I was going, but you just trotted right into the street without looking."

Ignoring her, the rider leaned down and handed the costermonger a card. "Cheyne Tennant is my name. Should you need my testimony, you can reach me at that address."

"Where are you going?" Mattie demanded. "Come back here!"

She sprang across the space that separated them and grabbed the reins. The horse shied, but she hung on. Tennant swore and grabbed her upper arms. Hauling her against his leg, he steadied the horse and bent down to spit out each word.

"My dear young lady, I have no intention of allowing you to shriek at me in the middle of Park Lane. If I were you, I'd pay this poor man and go home where you belong."

For a frozen second they stared at each other— a Montague and Capulet stare. Then something changed. His gaze faltered, darted to her mouth, her neck, lower. When his glance lifted to her eyes, Mattie felt a strange warmth kindle in her chest and spread through the rest of her body. Never in her born days had she seen eyes like that. If a magic spell took shape, it would take the form of those eyes— a sapphire charm, one moment blazing, the next freezing. Then Cheyne Tennant blinked rapidly, as if coming to his senses from unconsciousness. Mattie felt his hands loosen their grip, and she plummeted to the ground. She landed on her ass, her skirts flying up to her knees.

"Ow! You idiot, that hurt."

"Then I would suggest we're even."

Tennant kicked his mount lightly and trotted off before Mattie could think of a sufficiently nasty retort. She scowled at him as he vanished down Grosvenor Street, even contemplated jumping into the Panhard and chasing him. What if she caught him? Recalling the results of her last attempt to accost him, she thought better of the idea.

"What about me cart, miss?"

Mattie retrieved her purse from the motorcar and paid the man a sum that would allow him to buy a new cart and several loads of vegetables and fruit. Tennant had her; she'd been going far faster than motorcars were allowed in England, and no one would question his word should she quibble. Despite his disheveled appearance, Cheyne Tennant was a gentleman, she was sure of it. Even though Mattie had been raised in Texas and New York, his rank screamed at her—in the refinement of his language, in the way he rode a horse as if he lived on one, in the spare elegance of his clothing and most of all in his manner. Cheyne Tennant had the air of someone born to privilege, that unstated but nevertheless unquestioned assumption that he had a right to command. And beneath the refined elegance lurked a trace of ruthlessness that persuaded Mattie she shouldn't confront him on her own.

So she was left to fume at the injustice of his accusations. Mattie closed her purse, then hesitated, turning back to the costermonger.

Holding out a pound note, she said, "The dude gave you his card?"

The vendor eyed the note, snatched it, and handed her the card. "It don't do to mess with his kind, miss. No profit in it."

Mattie wasn't listening. She was staring at the card. In expensive embossed printing it read, "Mr. Cheyne Tennant, 23 Sussex Place." Nothing else. No title, no initials after his name.

"Dang. The way he acted, I thought he was at least a sir."

Mattie tapped the card against her teeth for a moment, then slipped it into her purse and started the Panhard. She got in, backed it off the curb and drove slowly back to the town house. No sense hurrying. She was already dreading her next important engagement, the Duchess of Bracewell's dinner. When was that? Next Thursday. Dang. She wasn't looking forward to spending endless hours in the company of people to whom ideas, books, music, and art were little more than props on the stage of their useless, frittering lives.

As she turned a corner, she slowed the motorcar and cursed silently. She'd done it again. Another lost battle in her war to improve. Why couldn't she have reacted in a more ladylike manner? Because Mr. Tennant had been so blamed ornery, that was why. Still, there had to be something wrong with her. Every impulse, every instinct she had seemed to be wrong.

"I guess I'm just naturally unladylike," she said to herself as she steered down the street.

Otherwise she wouldn't find it so hard. The trouble was that only part of her wanted to reform, for her papa's sake. The other part wanted to drive fast and speak her mind. She grinned as she remembered how exhilarating it had been to zoom down the road this morning. By the time Mattie sighted the tall plane trees of Green Park, she'd forgotten her ire. She was late, and Mama would be up. Sighing, Mattie wished, as she had countless times before, that she hadn't made that promise to her father. If she hadn't, she could be at home in New York right now racing her Panhard and pursuing her interest in politics, and she probably wouldn't care about her lack of good character.

But she had promised, and she would have to do her best to keep her word. She was old enough to remember the early days on the ranch in Texas. The sultry, brain-frying heat, the dust that got into every pore, the vast distances to anywhere that made a body feel so blamed lonely. Papa had punched cows for years as a rancher, enduring the heat, the bone-jarring work, and the bad trail food. But when he came home, he'd show up on the doorstep with a grin and a joke to make her laugh. He'd sweep her up in his arms and whirl her around in circles while she laughed.

"That's my little mockingbird. Give your pa a hug, Mattie girl."

Mattie drove the Panhard into the stable, shut off the engine and lowered her forehead to the wheel. She missed Papa so much her heart hurt. He was worth a million fancy-dressed dudes like Mr. Cheyne Tennant. She missed Papa so bad it seemed there was a hole in her, a bottomless shaft of pain, and emptiness that had become a part of her so that she'd never be whole again. The idea of fulfilling Papa's last wish seemed to assuage the pain when nothing else would. How long had he been gone? Almost three years now.

It wasn't fair. A fine man like Papa died, but useless fops like Tennant would live to be a hundred. And if she ever saw him again, she'd tell Mr. Cheyne Tennant just how poorly he measured up to Marcus Bright. Papa might not have worn clothes like he was royalty, but he could at least look both ways before he crossed a street.

2

Still dripping with tomato and melon, rigid with anger, Cheyne marched up the steps to his front door in Sussex Place north of Mayfair and pressed the bell. He ignored the stare of a passing cabbie, then caught a glimpse of himself in the beveled glass door and cursed the young woman who'd nearly killed him.

"The little savage," he hissed.

His valet and personal assistant, Alfred Mutton, opened the door, raised his eyebrows and snorted. "You're a sight. Fell off your horse into a bloomin' dustbin, din't you?"

"I'm in no humor to be mocked."

Cheyne brushed past Mutton and hurried up-stairs. He had thrown down his gloves and riding crop and was jerking at his cravat when Mutton sauntered into his dressing room. The valet pushed Cheyne's hands aside and began unknotting the material. Mutton was as far from the usual gentleman's gentleman as a mule is from an Arabian, but he suited Cheyne, whose requirements were hardly those of an ordinary gentleman.

Mutton was a big man, thick-boned and fleshy. His face bore the scars of a youth spent in the rookeries of Seven Dials and Whitechapel. Dark hair thinned on the top of his head to reveal a white dome. His cheeks ballooned out while his eyes sank into his skull so that he seemed to be squinting all the time. His size, his huge, knobby-knuckled hands and his rough face caused respectable visitors to hesitate on Cheyne's threshold, uncertain if so crude a person could possibly be in the service of a son of the Duke of Bracewell.

"You going to tell me what happened?"

"I was nearly run down by a motorcar driven by a she-devil," Cheyne replied. "A screeching little harpy with wild black hair, scarlet lips and a barbaric accent that would curdle wine. I think she was American, and if I ever see her again, I'll thrash her with that." Cheyne stabbed a finger in the direction of the crop.

"You ain't hurt." Mutton tossed the cravat aside and took Cheyne's soiled coat.

"She had the temerity to berate me for getting in her way." Cheyne swept away from Mutton, yanking at his shirt buttons and prowling the room. "And she called me a—let me see if I can recall the colorful phrase—an ornery priss-pants." He stopped undressing when he heard a guffaw from the valet.

"It's not funny. She caused me to fall into a vegetable cart, and then she threw melon at me."

"For no good cause, right?"

"Exactly." Cheyne poured water from an antique porcelain pitcher into a bowl and splashed his face. "Damned motorcar. Appalling little beast." He dried his face with a towel, then scowled at his hair, which was still matted with vegetable pulp. "She had eyes like volcanic glass. God! I never saw such a bold miss. She glared at me in the most direct and brash manner."

The sound of running water issued from the bathroom along with Mutton's cockney voice. "Right, gov'nor. Not like them young English ladies you're always telling me about. What was it you called them? Oh, yeah. Vapid. That was the word. And dreary. And washed-out."

"At least they haven't tried to kill me." Cheyne sat down and pulled off a boot. "What does God intend by allowing a dangerous madwoman like that to own a motorcar?" He dropped the other boot and stalked into the bathroom, where Mutton waited with wash-cloth and soap.

"Women should never have been allowed to ride bicycles, much less drive motorcars." He shed his clothing and sank into the tub.

"Right," Mutton said. "They should go back to being vapid, dreary, and washed-out."

Cheyne narrowed his eyes. "I don't appreciate your cheeky tone. One day you'll presume too much on the fact that you saved my life."

"Them were glory days, out in India and Africa. I was the best batman in the army, me."

"So you say."

Mutton folded a towel, then placed a hand over his heart and raised his gaze to the ceiling. "I never asked for nothing. It was the Lord's will that I was around when you got yourself shot and surrounded by them Boers. It weren't nothing, me sneaking out and dragging you back to camp in the middle o' the night."

"I'm not listening, Mutton."

"You don't owe me nothing, my lord."

Cheyne clenched his jaw and remained silent. Mutton only called him "my lord" when he wanted to annoy, for Cheyne didn't use his title.

"When are you going to get one of them motorcars? I'd look real flash behind the wheel of one o' them. You been putting it off for months."

Sinking under the water and bursting back to the surface, Cheyne sputtered and said, "It's clear that the streets are no longer safe for riders. I'll find out what kind the harpy was driving and buy one. It was fast, and it didn't fall apart when it jumped the curb. And if I ever see that girl again . . ."

Cheyne smiled at the idea of scaring the savagery right out of Miss Motorcar by racing up to her and coming to a stop at the last moment. No doubt she would berate him with her bizarre vocabulary. Her dark eyes would erupt with volcanic flame and her white-rose skin would flush. He expected she'd be wearing her voluminous driving costume that failed to hide her quick, lithe form. Miss Motorcar wasn't a beauty, but she had an altogether pleasing and dramatic appearance. What a pity she ruined it with her uncivilized manners and speech.

An uncomfortable pruniness of the fingers and toes reminded Cheyne of how long he'd been thinking in the tub. Mutton had left him there, and it was time to begin the day's business. He was the only member of his family who was "in trade," as those of his former set would have termed it. Having developed a distaste for the vacancy of mind fostered by an aristocratic life, Cheyne had chosen a profession that took advantage of his talent for logical thought. He was a private inquiry agent.

Not that any of his Society friends or family knew it. They only knew what he allowed the public to know, that he'd done something equally distasteful— gone into investments in the city. This ugly truth was enough to scandalize his parents and their friends. Gentlemen lived off income from vast estates. Only the lower orders actually set out to make money.

He got out of the tub, dried, and was dressing when Mutton knocked and came into the bedroom. "Got a visitor."

"How many times have I told you, you should say that Mr. So and So has called?"

"Right," Mutton said, rocking on his heels and causing his shoes to creak. "Superintendent Balfour has called. He's waiting in the drawing room, and—"

"I told him I wasn't interested in his case."

"Looks like you got to tell him to his face."

Cheyne turned away to examine his tie in the mirror. "No, you tell him."

He heard the door shut. Mutton had a way of vanishing before he could be told to do something he didn't want to do, and dealing with Scotland Yard was something he never wanted to do. Sighing, Cheyne took a last look at his frock coat, adjusted his cuffs, and went downstairs.

Stuart Balfour waited for him by the fire in the drawing room. He was looking askance at a Regency daybed across the room. The piece was upholstered in pale blue to match the walls, while the pattern of the brocade echoed that in the Robert Adam ceiling of blue, white, and gilded plaster. Cheyne paused by the harpsichord and smiled.

"It's an heirloom. There's a rumor that Empress Josephine wrote letters to Napoleon while reclining on it."

Balfour cleared his throat, "Quite. Now, see here, Tennant. This stubborn refusal to help out in this case won't do."

"I'm not going back into Society just to find some blackguard who's purloined the indiscreet letters of some foolish and spoiled debutante."

Balfour chewed his mustache, then pulled a photograph from his coat pocket and handed it to Cheyne. "I believe you know the young lady."

A girl of nineteen looked back at him from beneath golden hair pulled up and puffed out in the new style. She wore an enormous hat festooned with ostrich feathers, lace, bows, and a stuffed sparrow. She had the face of a porcelain doll, a small, prim mouth and little hands. She held herself erect in that impossible stance created by corset and padding, and somehow managed to look like a shepherd's daughter dressed in borrowed finery.

Cheyne shook his head in pity. English girls were kept ignorant of the world, cosseted and cloistered with nannies and governesses until they reached marriageable age. Then they were thrust into Society, paraded around London, Biarritz, and the Riviera until they caught the eye of an eligible young man. Their parents sent them, ignorant and full of rosy hopes, tripping blindly into marriage. This was the Honorable Miss Juliet Warrender, daughter of his father's old friend Lord Hubert Warrender.

"Tell Lord Hubert to pay what's demanded. You fellows at the Yard are quite capable of lying in wait when Warrender meets the blackmailer."

"A lovely idea, Tennant, but Lord Hubert's a bit busy at the moment, making arrangements for his daughter's funeral. She took laudanum last night."

It was like being rammed in the chest by a motorcar. Cheyne laid the photograph on the harpsichord and walked to the windows that looked out on Great Chartwell Road. Hansom cabs, coaches, victorias, a milk wagon, and an omnibus clattered in the street, while vendors added their clamor to the general din. He remembered Juliet as a schoolgirl, all teeth and legs. She'd been a shy thing, fond of flowers, toads and climbing trees. Her one claim to charm had been her voice. A soprano of operatic quality, she made a splash her first Season and captured the attention of the Earl of Hartfield's son.

Cheyne moved the sheers aside and contemplated the progress of a nanny and her three charges as they marched along the opposite sidewalk. Juliet hadn't been long away from such outings when she died.

"All right," he said, turning and indicating that Balfour should take a chair. "Tell the whole of it again." He joined his guest.

"The first we heard of this man was when Sir Thomas Folkestone vanished from his home in Shropshire. His wife and sons came to us for help, and we found the chap had absconded to Australia, of all places. Someone had gotten hold of the bills he paid for his mistress's house in Cheapside here in the city."

"Ah, yes, I remember."

"That was almost eighteen months ago," Balfour said. "Since then we've been keeping an eye out for further incidents. It's hard to know when someone of rank and position becomes a victim of blackmail unless something goes wrong. We suspect that old General Sir Michael Kent was being bled."

Cheyne's gaze sharpened, and he leaned toward Balfour. "Old Kent was supposed to have died in a hunting accident. His shotgun misfired."

Balfour shrugged, and Cheyne cursed under his breath. "What did you find out?"

"The general spent most of his life in the military. It seems his affection for his men went deeper than what one would expect." Balfour studied Cheyne's pallor for a moment. "So you see that we need someone familiar with the aristocracy, someone who'll be accepted. Whoever is blackmailing these people knows secrets that only someone moving in the highest circles could know."

Cheyne rested his arms on his thighs and lowered his head. "You think it's someone in Society. It could be a servant, you know."

"That's why we picked you. You know how to investigate, and you've got that appalling fellow Mutton who can handle the servants."

Looking up at his guest, Cheyne nodded. "Mutton will be glad to hear that he has such a sterling reputation at Scotland Yard. Leave what you have. I'll look at the files and contact you."

"The commissioner wants you to begin at once."

Shaking his head, Cheyne smiled. "It will take me a few days to convince my family that I wish to be included in their guest lists again."

Balfour didn't ask why. Cheyne hadn't expected him to. His estrangement from his family was common gossip. Luckily his mother still sent pleading letters several times a year begging him to "do his duty," give up practicing a trade and do nothing, as became the son of a duke. He would have welcomed her letters had they contained any hint that she missed him. He wasn't foolish enough to expect such expressions of fondness, however. The cold stone tomb of his mother's heart had barely enough space to contain a mild affection for her eldest son, much less anyone else.

Beatrice Maud Allington, née Seymour, was one of England's great Society hostesses along with the Duchess of Devonshire and the Duchess of Manchester. Her life was devoted to the pursuit of the traditional pastimes of such great ladies—grand balls in the Season, massive country house parties out of Season, and a little dabbling in charity and political affairs as long as these didn't interfere with her social engagements.

Balfour rose to leave. "I'm glad I was able to convince you. I couldn't face another call in the middle of the night to look at the body of a dead girl."

"I can't work miracles, old man. It will take time to reintroduce myself to Society and discover who's doing this."

"I know. We'll just have to hope the fellow is sated with money for a while." Balfour shook Cheyne's hand. "Thanks, old chap. You know I wouldn't have presumed on our acquaintance for any but the gravest reasons."

"You allowed me to prove my ability when I first set myself up in this little occupation of mine, Balfour. I'd listen to anything you cared to say."

Once his guest was gone, Cheyne picked up the leather document case Balfour had brought, crossed the drawing room and opened a pair of doors to enter the White Library. This was one of his favorite rooms because, like the drawing room, it had a wall of soaring windows that faced the busy street. The sun had burned the morning mists away, and shafts of golden light marched across the carpeted floor. The room took its name from the white plaster walls and coffered ceiling as well as the long series of inset bookshelves with their pediment tops. Beige and white chairs and couches surrounded the fireplace. Cheyne found the button set unobtrusively in the wall beside the marble fireplace mantel. He subsided in a wing chair, lay the document case on the floor, and drummed his fingers on the chair arm.

Mutton appeared immediately. "So, we're going to have ourselves a Season, are we?"

"Someday you're going to get caught listening at keyholes by someone who won't take kindly to your prying," Cheyne said with a scowl.

"Seeing as how Scotland Yard specifically asked for the services of yours truly, I think I'm allowed." Mutton hooked his fingers in the armholes of his vest and expanded his chest.

"They're familiar with your criminal past," Cheyne snapped. "That's why they think you'll do."

"Bloody smart thinking, that is."

"Cancel my appointments for the rest of the week."

"I got Smythe doin' that right now."

Cheyne glanced at the document case beside him, then turned his icy regard on Mutton. "Then you'll be so good as to get my dear mother on the telephone. I understand she has recently had one installed in Grosvenor Square."

Mutton whistled. "So you really are going back.

After what you said when you was delirious with your wounds that time, I'd of thought you'd keep clear o' them."

"I don't want to talk about it."

"This'll be a show, it will."

"Shut up, Mutton, and go do as I said. I believe Her Grace is giving an intimate dinner for thirty or forty people next Thursday. The perfect opportunity to commence."

"Right." Unperturbed, Mutton lumbered out of the room.

When he was alone, Cheyne went to the mirror and stared into his own eyes. He wouldn't mind seeing his mother so much. He'd grown used to her indifference. Sometime after he entered Cambridge he'd realized she couldn't help being shallow as a lake in a drought. The poverty of her mind wasn't all her fault, for her character had been pruned and trimmed from birth to fit the narrow boundaries laid out for women of her rank. It had taken him years to recognize this, and many more to admit it without his attempts at objectivity being overwhelmed with childhood pain.

No, Mother wasn't the problem. The problem had always been his father. *Father*—what an ironic appellation.

It had taken Cheyne quite a while to realize just how distasteful his existence was to his father. This was because, like all children of his class, Cheyne saw little of his parents until he was almost an adult. Raised by nannies, then sent to Eton and Cambridge, his contact with the duke and duchess had been limited to appearances in the drawing room at teatime. Even then Cheyne's tastes had irritated His Grace. Frederick James William Tennant Allington's ideal man was a sporting one. He remembered countless equine trivialities, such as the names of every Derby winner since 1870. He could recall hunt events in excruciating detail. But he couldn't abide five minutes of conversation about philosophy, science, music, literature, or art. This last word, upon the duke's lips, became an epithet, which he spat out as if it were the vilest obscenity.

Cheyne winced as he remembered the times he suffered his father's ridicule for daring to bring up a forbidden topic. The subject of Mr. Charles Darwin had earned him a beating. He worked his shoulders, trying to ease an imaginary sting. His back bore three crossed scars, the legacy of His Grace's riding whip.

And books. Books other than those on sport led a short life at Grosvenor Square. Cheyne learned to hide them, especially the Shakespeare, for if the duke found them, he would toss them into the fire. The day his father threw *A Midsummer Night's Dream* into the flames was the day he earned Cheyne's contempt.

The memory was bright, like a painting by Renoir. Cheyne had been hiding in his room reading instead of going for a walk in Hyde Park with his brothers. No loud footsteps warned him of the duke's approach. Suddenly he was there, looming over Cheyne like some fairy-tale giant.

"What's this? Shakespeare, that drivel!"

Father ripped the small leather volume from Cheyne's hands and hurled it into the fireplace. Cheyne yelped, jumped up and would have rescued the book had the duke not caught him and tossed him into a corner. Cheyne hit his head on the wall. With pain searing his skull, he curled into a ball and sobbed while the duke stomped out of the room. By the time Cheyne had recovered, the book was beyond saving.

That was the day Cheyne made up his mind to show his father. Show him he could be as great a sportsman as his older brothers. Show him that a boy who loved music and books could excel at riding, shooting, wrestling. Eventually he had shown the duke. What had hurt was that it hadn't made a difference. The fact that Cheyne grew into an expert marksman and rider only made his father furious. When Cheyne became a member of the Horse Guards, His Grace was nearly apoplectic.

Slumped against the mantel, Cheyne studied the glowing coals, his spirits black at the idea of spending perhaps months in the company of the duke. He'd rather face that absurd little barbarian and her motorcar.

Why did he think of her now? True, he couldn't seem to get her image out of his thoughts. Her midnight hair and black-flame eyes lingered in his memory, and he kept hearing her strong, low-pitched voice carrying those absurd phrases of hers— *dang, your own blamed fault, blind as a posthole,* whatever that was.

Cheyne turned and rested his forehead against the cold marble mantel. "God, she probably knows less than Father about Shakespeare."

The last thing he needed at the moment was to allow himself to become obsessed with a pretty savage. Far better to dwell on the coming ordeal than allow such a useless passion. Besides, he didn't even know her name.

3

Mattie stepped out of Spencer House into the cold March night and hugged her fur-lined cape around her body. The cool evening air filled her lungs, and she felt renewed determination to change, to reform her wayward character and fulfill Papa's dream. She *would* remember to be sweet, gentle, and good.

In the glow of the new electric street lamps she could see the tops of the plane trees in Green Park; their bare branches scratched at the night sky. Looking over her shoulder, she saw her friend Narcissa Potter being helped into her cloak by a footman. Mama was nowhere to be seen.

Going to the unveiling of the Duchess of Bracewell's portrait had been Mama's idea. Mattie had almost reached the limit of her endurance of Society. She'd been fed up since she'd been presented at court last month. The aged Queen Victoria had made one of her few public appearances. Mattie had been as

nervous as the dozens of debutantes being introduced. The one saving feature of the whole evening,
in Mattie's opinion, was that the queen had the right
idea about Society. Like Mattie, she thought there
was entirely too much of it.

Nearly running over that obnoxious young man in
Park Lane had made Mattie long for the freedom and
ease of New York. There people knew how to cross
streets without blocking innocent motorcar drivers.
In New York people didn't call each other savages
and look down elegant noses with aristocratic contempt. Mattie flushed as she remembered her adversary. His anger would have been easier to deal with
had he not been so handsome. Somehow, being
given a dressing-down by a man who looked like he'd
been born to wear royal ermine and a sword of state
made the experience downright embarrassing.

"Don't think about him." Mattie stamped her feet
inside their silk slippers and paced on the front
step. So far this command had failed to keep her
mind from dredging up the man's image at the
oddest times.

"No-account and self-important, that's what you
are, Mr. Tennant. I don't care how pretty you are,
I never met a ruder man in all my born days."
She turned and nearly stumbled over her train.
"Danged dress."

Preferring to wear simple skirts and blouses, Mattie disliked having to dress in gowns such as the one
she wore now all delicate Honiton lace from shoulder to train, with kid gloves of the same hue that

bore dozens of tiny pearl buttons. These matched the pearls sewn into the center of the lace flowers that made up the design of the Paquin gown. Her only consolation was the simple flowing lines of the gown; the infamous bustle was no more, and the skirt hugged her hips, then fanned out to leave her legs free. Mattie pulled her cloak closer, careful not to crush the white rose on the pearl dog collar at her neck. She didn't want Mama to see her gown until they arrived at Grosvenor Square.

The town coach appeared around the corner as the coachman walked the pair of matched Hanoverian creams. They snorted, blowing mist into the air and raising their hooves high. Mama had hired the vehicle along with a brougham from a London jobber, then had the coach repainted and polished. Mattie scowled at the brightly colored family crest, an invention of Mrs. Bright's. Ever since Ward McAllister refused to list her family among the four hundred who could fit into Mrs. Astor's ballroom, Elsa Jane Bright had become even more fervent in her quest for respectability and social acceptance. After all, Mattie needed to attract a nobleman, didn't she? Her recent campaign included commissioning a coat of arms—fictitious, of course. The Brights had never been anything but plain ordinary folk, which Mattie had pointed out to no avail.

Now Mattie folded her arms, snorted at the crest— a rearing black stallion on a field of gold—and muttered, "Never saw anything so all-fired foolish. Unless it's Mama in a tight-laced corset."

"Did you call me, dear?"

Elsa Jane hurried out of the house with Narcissa close behind. Mrs. Bright's coloring had been as vivid as Mattie's, but her hair was mostly silver now. Her figure had thickened with childbearing, but her bright pink cheeks and lively expression made her seem younger than her years.

"No, Mama. I didn't call you."

"It's Ma*ma*, dear. Pronounce it like the French do. The other way is so common."

"Aw, Mama."

"Please, dear. You have promised to employ the correct accent and diction when we're among people of quality."

Knowing her mother was right, Mattie glanced at Narcissa and sighed. Narcissa had been to boarding school in France and was a two-year veteran of the London Season. With curling gold-and-wheat-colored hair and an expression of impending mischief, she had captured the heart of St. John Everly, Earl of Millhaven. Mama constantly held up Narcissa as an example to Mattie. Mattie knew that Mama had no notion of the escapades at which Narcissa excelled, including riding her horse through Burlington Arcade. Half a dozen shopkeepers had complained to the police.

But there was no use arguing with Mama. Besides, if she was going to make Papa happy in heaven, she was going to have to improve herself. Luckily Mattie was good at accents. It was a simple thing to adopt the clipped flat tones of the upper-class Englishwoman. Indeed, aping the speech of blue-blooded Society ladies afforded both Mattie and her friend amusement during dull evenings among the rich and insipid.

"Very well, Mama. I shall endeavor to speak in a civilized manner," Mattie said through the top of her mouth. "I say, though, this evening promises to be perfectly appalling. You know I don't care a snap of the fingers for dukes and duchesses."

Mrs. Bright gathered her black lace train and entered the coach with the help of the footman. "There's no use speaking elegantly if your opinions are vile, Matilda Bright. Now get in this carriage, or we'll be late."

"I don't see why we couldn't take the motorcar," Mattie grumbled as she got in after Narcissa. "Mr. Theodore Roosevelt would take his motorcar. So would Mr. Edison."

"Mattie," her friend said, "the ride might be short, but our hair would come out of its pins before we got around the corner and you know it."

Mama sniffed. "And I don't see Mr. Edison or Mr. Roosevelt getting themselves invited to the Duke of Bracewell's."

"You wouldn't catch them at a party full of boiled shirts."

"I'll hear no more grumbling from you, Matilda. Remember your poor father."

A rush of longing caught her unprepared. Mentioning Papa was certain to force Mattie into compliance, and Elsa Jane knew it. When Mattie was little, if Papa wasn't too tired, she used to climb in his lap as he sat on the porch of the ranch house after dinner. Together they would gaze at the wide Texas sky, ever on the lookout for shooting stars. Each time they saw one, they made a wish. She remembered the way she'd felt, so safe and loved, as if nothing bad could ever happen.

She missed being able to talk to a man who wasn't secretly counting her money. The distance between ladies and gentlemen here seemed vast, and she had little hope of meeting anyone with whom she could be herself. And she missed her brother and sister. Her older brother was back home managing the family's assets. Her younger sister was in France being finished. Dang it. Being a Society belle was a lonely and miserable lot.

To cover her emotions, Mattie helped Narcissa arrange the folds of her train. Her friend's coloring suited the white silk gown covered with lace appliqué. Narcissa gave her a sympathetic smile and a wink. Mattie smiled back; Narcissa always knew when Mattie's spirits plummeted and was often able to bring her out of it with one of her silly facial expressions. A little mischief was allowed, since her fiancé was away seeing to his land interests in Africa.

The short drive to Grosvenor Square was filled with Mama's instructions on correct behavior. Mattie only half listened and got out of the carriage as soon as it stopped in front of the grand ducal mansion that lay behind a wall of stone and wrought iron. Gazing up at the facade, Mattie felt Narcissa poke her with her elbow and remembered that staring revealed how little she was used to grand surroundings. She followed her mother and friend into the imposing entry hall topped with a stained-glass dome. When Mattie handed over her cloak to a footman, she heard her mother suck in her breath.

"Matilda Bright," came the theatrical whisper, "where is your padding?"

"Left it off. Don't need it." Most ladies added pads to their corsets to create the necessary rounded effect and further reduce the size of their waists by contrast. Mattie thought she was padded enough naturally. Besides, the pads were hot and cumbersome. No sense trying to reform if she got sick from the heat and vomited in front of everyone.

Before Mama could object, Narcissa took Mattie's arm and swept her over to the line of guests waiting to greet the Duke and Duchess of Bracewell. Mattie had never seen two more oddly matched people. The duke, stocky and wind-burned, had bushy brown hair and side-whiskers. In contrast to his exalted station, his height was only moderate, but Mattie was amused to see that he had an unlit cigar clamped between his teeth—despite the fact that smoking at such a function and in the presence of ladies was against the rules of polite convention. As Mattie approached, she noticed that His Grace greeted with enthusiasm only those friends with whom he could discuss some sport.

Beatrice Maud Allington stood beside her husband, a delicately made porcelain figurine to the duke's leather-and-brass appearance. Her silver hair was piled high and bore a tiara of enormous diamonds. With her long legs and arms, high forehead and angular features, she was far more regal than her noble husband.

"Ah, Mrs. Bright," the duke bellowed. "About that stallion you said you owned . . ."

Mattie and Narcissa exchanged knowing looks. They had wondered how Mama had extorted an invitation from the duchess. They took advantage of Mrs. Bright's distraction to join the procession of guests mounting the stairs.

The portrait to be unveiled that evening stood at the end of the Long Gallery on the second floor. The gallery extended the length of the house and bore portraits of Bracewells from the Renaissance to the present on every wall. In the middle of this enormous room were arranged groups of chairs and couches, ferns and flowers in antique vases and urns. Upon their arrival in the gallery, Narcissa was snatched up by her fiancé's parents. Mattie had just enough time to glimpse Edward Allington's portrait by Holbein before being surrounded by young men.

"Miss Bright, my evening is complete at the sight of your beauty."

Mattie put on a polite smile. "Why, Lord Herne, you're so kind."

"He's not kind," said Harry Blinksdale, "he's boring. Herne, you rotter, can't you think of anything original to say about Miss Bright? I call her uncommon fair. Her beauty is the toast of the empire."

"And her voice," chimed in the Marquis of Eckleshire. "Her voice is that of a goddess singing in the clouds."

Mattie let the gentlemen babble and tried not to roll her eyes. It was amazing how the plainest of girls became exquisite when her fortune reached the millions. She happened to know of at least twenty young ladies far more presentable and certainly more charming than herself who rated no such attentions simply because they had but a few hundred pounds a year. Before the evening was over she would accept asinine compliments like this from almost a dozen titled men. And all of them wanted her money.

The marquis, for example, had to support three sisters, a widowed mother, and two aunts. Lord Herne's father had gambled away most of the family fortune, while Harry Blinksdale was in search of a lady who could support his expensive stud. When he looked at her, Mattie had no doubt he saw the face of his favorite racehorse. Blinksdale's highest ambition was to beat the Prince of Wales's entry in the Derby.

"I say," Blinksdale said in his high, wheedling tone, "did you hear old Allington is coming tonight?"

"No!"

"You're not serious."

"It's true. I heard it from the duchess herself. He's decided to reform."

"Good God."

Mattie glanced from one supercilious face to another, noting the alarm that they shared.

"Who's old Allington?"

The marquis sniffed. "An absolute rotter, my dear Miss Bright. An unsavory younger son of the duke's. Almost got himself kicked out of the family for his beastly manners, you see." He lowered his voice to a stage whisper. "Went into trade, in the city. Investments, of all things. Absolutely no conception of what it is to be a gentleman."

"Yes," said Herne. "You should be warned. More than one young lady has been blinded by his appearance, only to discover what an unsavory sort he is."

Harry Blinksdale elbowed Herne. "Shhh! The duchess."

Herne tried to whisper something to Mattie, but Her Grace's voice drowned him out. "Miss Bright, I'd like you to meet my youngest son, Geoffrey Cheyne."

Mattie disengaged herself from Lord Herne and turned to the newly arrived nobleman. Her jaw fell while he paused in reaching for the hand she'd extended for him to kiss. Time stopped while Mattie beheld the startled Geoffrey Cheyne Allington.

Without his dressing of tomato and melon pulp, Allington's effect on her was unexpected. He wore jet-black evening attire as easily as he had riding clothes. No Saville Row tailor had been forced to pad the shoulders of his coat or widen the waist of his trousers. He wore no jewelry, but no woman would notice once she'd glimpsed the Prussian blue blaze of his eyes. What was more startling was the aura of barely leashed force emanating from the man. Like some puissant mage in a fairy tale, a sorcerer, one expected powerful spells, the summoning of dragons or black enchantments.

"Lord Geoffrey," the duchess said as if to prod her son from his silence, "Miss Bright."

Allington blinked, as if startled awake. "Dear God, it's the harpy."

"Geoffrey!"

Mattie came out of her amazed trance and flushed. Her suitors bristled.

"I say, old man. What kind of tone is that?"

"Don't complain to me, Blinksdale. This young woman nearly ran over me with her motorcar last week, and then had the gall to swear at me like a drunken miner."

Caught off guard, Mattie tried to cover her embarrassment. "I beg your pardon, my lord—"

Allington gasped and gave a sharp laugh. "Damn. She has caught civility and a proper accent. When I last saw you, Miss Bright, you spoke as if you belonged in a Wild West show." He grinned at the suitors. "I assure you she made me blush with her rough speech."

"Geoffrey," the duchess ground out. "That will be enough. You've embarrassed Miss Bright and her friends."

"She deserves to be embarrassed," Allington retorted. "She nearly killed me and my horse, and then she blamed me for her actions in language that would get me chucked out of a music hall."

Crimson with fury and shame, Mattie glanced around to find that more and more heads were turning their way. With a stiff expression, the duchess turned her back on her son and announced that it was time to unveil her portrait. Everyone moved toward the end of the gallery where the painting stood. Allington gave Mattie a derisive glance and followed his mother.

"I say," Blinksdale said in a shocked tone. He eyed Mattie.

The Marquis of Eckleshire harrumphed and offered his arm to Mattie. "Not a gentleman, whatever his birth. I'm sure your accent is charming, Miss Bright."

"I—I have no idea what he could mean," Mattie said as she walked toward the portrait on the arm of the marquis. "I've never encountered such ghastly behavior."

"The bloke needs thrashing," Lord Herne said.

The marquis shook his head. "He'd grind you into pepper, old man."

"Please, gentlemen," Mattie said. "I've no wish to discuss this subject further."

Blinksdale bent over her hand. "Of course not, Miss Bright. Anyone who knows you understands that you're a young lady of delicacy and refinement."

Beside the portrait the duke was giving a speech. It was short, not surprising given his almost complete lack of interest in the topic, and he soon swept the velvet cover from the painting. There was a burst of applause, not just out of politeness but for the way

Sargent had captured the duchess's nobility of carriage and her air of snowy detachment. The artist himself was in France, but the duchess was more than happy to receive everyone's compliments in his place.

It was all Mattie could do to keep her composure. She had to preserve her dignity. Papa would be ashamed if he had witnessed that scene with Allington. Mama would hear of it and have a conniption fit. Mattie put a gloved hand to her cheek. It was still hot.

That horrible man had exposed her most grievous faults to the very people she had to impress with her refinement if she was to succeed. She disliked herself intensely for her shortcomings. Having them repeated in public was almost more than she could stand. Thank God no one believed him.

Narcissa appeared at her side. "Mattie, what happened?"

"That fella I told you about," Mattie whispered as she joined in the applause that came after the duchess finished speaking. "That Cheyne Tennant. Turns out he's really the younger son of the Bracewells, damn his hide. He doesn't go by his full name or his title. Just now he called me a harpy in front of everyone, including the duchess."

The crowd was breaking up now. Narcissa pulled her away and headed for the lady's retiring room. As they went, Mattie felt the stares of the guests. She tried not to look at them for fear of seeing Allington again. When they reached the retiring room, she flounced down on an ottoman and groaned.

"Papa would be so ashamed."

"Who cares for Allington anyway?" Narcissa said. "He's only a younger son."

"With a nasty way of making me look like a flea on an angel's wing."

Narcissa sank to her knees in front of Mattie. "Then you make him look like a bigger flea. Remember what you did to Pokey Depew back in New York?"

"That was a long time ago," Mattie said. "We were girls."

She stopped as she remembered how Allington had humiliated her. Yet there seemed to be no way of retaliating without appearing either spiteful or wounded. She was supposed to be above spite, and she had no intention of revealing her distress. Besides, maybe a child's prank was just the thing to assuage her and teach Allington proper conduct. Slowly Mattie began to smile. It was a smile at home under rocks in the desert, that basked in the sun and waited for small rodents to pass by.

"I'll need the fixin's."

"Leave that to me," Narcissa said. "It's almost time, so you go look at the place cards while I slip down the back stairs. I'll meet you in the dining room."

Her spirits restored, Mattie gave her friend a peck on the cheek and hurried downstairs. Dinner was to be held in the saloon, the oldest room in the ducal mansion. Mattie had learned from a book on great houses Mama had made her read that it was one of the finest remaining examples of a great chamber.

The old medieval solar had become, in Elizabethan times, the great chamber, the room in which lords entertained. In the Baroque and Palladian periods this became the saloon, and finally most of these enormous rooms ended up as picture galleries. Of high architectural style, the great chamber was still a nobleman's setting for great gatherings. The Duke of Bracewell's saloon was indeed a chamber fit for any such occasion. Its ceiling rose over thirty feet high, and no fireplace broke its symmetry. The doors were set in alcoves surrounded by marble arches, topped by carved shells that reached fifteen feet above Mattie's head.

Mattie avoided the gallery, walked across a drawing room and opened one of the saloon doors. They were so heavy she had to use both hands and lean against them. Life-size murals of spectators leaning on balconies decorated the walls, making Mattie feel as if a crowd of seventeenth century dandies and ladies were spying on her. She hid in the alcove while two servants brought in covered dishes and left. Then she raced to the dining table set for thirty and found Allington's name near the middle, all the while whispering imprecations against titled Englishmen. Not that American men were much better. After five years she still cringed at the memory of Samuel Pinchot.

She'd been eighteen, fresh from a ladies' finishing school in New York, the pride of Marcus and Elsa Jane Bright. Mama and Papa had organized an enormous coming-out party for her. Oblivious to social protocol, they invited every last one of the four hundred, plus as many other notables as they could squeeze into their new stone mansion on Fifth Avenue. Mattie got all dressed up in her gown by Paquin, but nobody came. No, that wasn't true. None of the four hundred came because Mrs. Astor hadn't called on Mrs. Bright. Since she hadn't, the Brights weren't known to the Astors in the social sense, and thus weren't among those eligible to receive the honor of Mrs. Astor's company. Labeled parvenu by this social demigoddess, the Bright family might as well have lived in a tugboat for all the recognition they got from the American aristocracy.

So Mattie had stood in the middle of the marble-and-gold ballroom in her gem-studded gown with the extra-long train, waiting to receive people who never came. She'd shivered with humiliation while the dozen or so people who showed up talked loudly to one another in an attempt to make the cavernous room seem filled. Just when she thought she'd burst into tears and complete her disgrace, Samuel Pinchot, the son of one of the oldest Knickerbocker families of New York, was announced. To the Pinchots, the Astors and Vanderbilts were vulgar newcomers. Burly, bumptious, and shortsighted, Samuel bounced over to Mattie and rescued her from mortification.

"My dear Miss Bright," he chortled, grinning at her through his wire-rimmed spectacles. "They didn't want me to come, but I told them all to go to the devil. I said that there was nothing that would keep me from meeting the lovely Matilda Bright, not even Mrs. Astor."

The weeks that followed had been a girl's fairy tale come true. Samuel had courted her in his energetic manner, and Mattie had loved every moment. She hadn't cared that Pinchot's appearance failed to measure up to her romantic ideal. He made up for it with his love of life and his adventurous spirit. It had been Samuel Pinchot who had introduced her to motorcars.

Samuel asked her to marry him exactly three months from the day they met, and Mattie accepted. Two weeks later she learned the truth when she overheard her fiancé's remarks to one of his friends.

"Just in time," he had said. "My creditors were hounding me, and the only thing that kept them out of court was the loan I got from Father. But the second she accepted me I let them know I was marrying the rich Miss Bright. Not a word from them since. Once we're married, I'll pay the whole lot of them. Say, Joe, what do you think about this new landau? Pretty elegant thing, isn't it? I've ordered one, and it'll be delivered when we get back from the honeymoon. Damn. I can't wait to build another house in the Hudson Valley. One in Paris, too, by God."

Mattie had broken the engagement the next day, after a night spent in tears. It had taken her a long time to get over Samuel Pinchot. Mattie wasn't one to lie to herself. She knew she wasn't beautiful, but she had still hoped to find a young man who might care for her—and make her parents proud. After Samuel, Mattie made sure she never fell prey to hope again. Now she had a realistic view of the world and men. Practical. None of the English gentlemen she'd met had behaved in a way that would prove anything to the contrary existed.

Every so often Mattie would stand in front of the mirror and give herself a good talking-to. "Mattie," she'd say, "don't go dreaming again. You're pleasant-looking, but that's about the limit. You keep your eyes open and your heart protected. Never believe a gentleman's fancy compliments. The money is always going to be what they see when they look at you. Don't be fooled, or you'll get hurt again."

So far she'd remained true to her discipline. No English aristocrat's smarmy ways were going to fool her, and no skunk of a duke's son was going to make her look ridiculous. Pushing aside memories of old hurts, she scurried around the table and to the door as her friend popped inside. Narcissa handed her a pastry confection that resembled a pink custard pie.

"Don't let anyone come in," Mattie whispered. She raced to Allington's chair, put the custard on the seat and ran back to Narcissa. Just then they heard voices outside the drawing room.

Mattie whispered, "Quick, act like you're helping me button my glove." They rushed to the middle of the drawing room and posed as the duchess entered on the arm of a royal minister.

As Americans of no rank, she and Narcissa featured near the end of the procession with gentlemen of no title but good breeding. Her seat was directly opposite her adversary, and Mattie watched Allington closely as he engaged in conversation with the lady he'd escorted. He hadn't sat down yet.

Mattie scooted closer to the table, clasped her hands in her lap and waited.

4

In the cavernous and drafty saloon Cheyne stood beside his chair making conversation with his dinner partner, the eternally fatuous Lady Plimpton. The woman was over thirty, but her character had frozen during her first Season, and she preserved the girlish enthusiasm and trite conversation of the schoolroom. Cheyne kept up his end of the light banter while he tried to see where Miss Bright was seated.

If it had been possible to lash his own tongue for his rudeness upon meeting Miss Bright, Cheyne would have done it. But it wasn't all his fault. His mother had dragged him over to introduce him to a likely young lady—likely in the sense that she was young, wealthy, and in search of a titled husband.

No matter how many times he corrected her, Mother persisted in believing he would relent in his decision to go into "trade." She also assumed that he was poor. Her greatest wish was that he marry and settle down to the life of a gentleman, which meant living on a great country estate and doing little else. She concluded that he needed to marry wealth in order to fulfill the destiny she'd planned.

Thus when he'd telephoned, she had taken it for granted that he was ready to do as she wished. He'd allowed her to keep the illusion. He couldn't tell her about the blackmailer.

So far his work had seldom required him to move in Society, and he didn't miss it. So when the duchess brought him to the group of sycophants surrounding a vision in ivory lace, the last person he expected the vision to be was Miss Motorcar. He'd anticipated another dashing American girl fresh from being finished on the Continent, a girl who wore a Paris gown and ruled the gathering like an empress. As he'd drawn close to the heiress an extraordinary feeling had come over him. He took in the long neck and sinuous curves wrapped in priceless lace, and his body responded. He'd seen plenty of lovely women. Yet there was something about that long, elegant neck that enthralled him. It was so long that it looked unable to support those thick, smooth waves of hair.

And then she'd turned around. He'd recognized her, but it hadn't mattered. If he'd drunk an infusion of poppies or a full snifter of brandy he couldn't have felt the effect more. It wasn't that she was beautiful, for her nose was too short, her mouth too wide. But her face was one of those that captured the eye by its contrasts—the black hair and brows, the cream of

her skin, the tulip-pink lips all gave her a vibrancy
lacking in pale Englishwomen. Then there was the
way the lace gown molded itself to her figure, not
stiffly but naturally, lending her whole being an un-
contrived grace he'd never encountered before.

What had been in his mind at that moment? Ah,
yes. He'd been thinking that it would be incredibly
stupid to quarrel with a young lady who looked like
that. In a few moments he'd managed to conceive an
infatuation for a young woman he thought he de-
tested. How utterly callow.

Alarmed at the effect she'd had on him in spite
of his disapproval of her, Cheyne had blurted out
the first thing that came to his lips. Harpy. What
bloody lunacy.

He'd never have been rude had he not been so
upset at having to deal with his family, with having
to reenter a world he'd fled years ago. He was learning, however, that his antipathy toward the duke and
duchess faded in comparison to the havoc wrought
by his desire for Miss Bright. Damn her. She made
him feel infernally uncomfortable. His skin felt tight
and hot, and he was breathing like he'd run the
length of Rotten Row.

He had to control himself. He was here to do a
job, not to lust after a lovely savage. He would master
this absurd weakness at once.

All the while he'd been thinking, Cheyne had
been exchanging pleasantries with Lady Plimpton
and watching for Miss Bright. She entered on the
arm of some man he didn't recognize and took her

seat across from him, of all places. Cheyne helped
Lady Plimpton to her chair and pulled out his own
while trying not to stare at Miss Bright. As he sat, he
knew he failed to keep his gaze averted, and he was
looking at her as he made contact with the chair. He
hit something wet and squishy.

His gasp caught Lady Plimpton by surprise, but
he was still staring at Miss Bright, who showed
not only no surprise but much amusement. He remained still, taking in the glitter and satisfaction
in those dark eyes. His posterior felt clammy while
his face burned. Cheyne rose slowly, glaring at his
adversary across the table. He felt a suction, and the
silver plate holding the pastry plopped back to the
chair cushion.

"Oh, dear," Lady Plimpton trumpeted for all to
hear, "whatever have you sat on?"

He heard sniggers and saw ladies hide smiles with
their napkins. Miss Bright calmly smoothed her own
napkin in her lap and patted her hair.

His friend, perhaps his only real friend left in
this gilded world, the honorable Lancelot Gordon,
exclaimed, "Dear God, Allington. Your trousers
are pink."

The sniggering was louder now, and some of the
men were chuckling aloud. Cheyne forced himself
to smile.

"It seems I've found a misplaced pastry, old chap."
He managed a slight bow to his mother. "I'm afraid
you must pardon me, Your Grace."

He left the saloon as quickly as dignity allowed. As

he went, he silently cursed Miss Bright and vowed revenge. Hurrying to the entry hall, Cheyne donned his coat while he waited for a footman to summon his barouche.

"Evil little beast," he muttered, feeling the wetness of his trousers. "Bloody colonial." Everyone had laughed at him. His father had roared the loudest, just like when Cheyne was a boy and he'd made some embarrassing mistake. Bristling with suppressed outrage, he stepped outside and breathed in the damp, foggy air.

Mutton appeared out of the mist. "Wot's this about us leaving?"

"Shhh!" Cheyne glanced at the footman standing inside the doorway and shut the front door. "You can't speak to me that way when I'm working."

" 'Pears to me you done a bit more than me to ruin your dignity." Mutton eyed the back of his coat. "Sat inna pie, according to Daisy."

"Who's Daisy, and how did you find out so quickly? Never mind. You were supposed to be getting information from the servants."

"That's what I was doing, until the butler came down and said you got your trousers ruined."

"Damn her!"

"Who?"

"Miss Motorcar—Miss Bright, that is. She put that pastry on my chair. I know it. You should have seen her. She knew it was there, and she was waiting, just waiting to see me sit on it." Cheyne stalked down the steps and paced back and forth in front of the circular drive. "God, I wish I could get my hands on her. She was smiling so charmingly, the little ruffian, looking so elegant, all lace and ivory roses, with her damned tulip lips and damned midnight hair and damned graceful neck."

"Blimey, she's got you proper, she has."

The barouche rumbled out of the fog as Cheyne cast a look of supreme disgust at Mutton. "She's not going to get away with it."

"T'ain't a good thing, you making a spectacle of yourself over a bit of a joke."

"I'm not the one who's going to be a spectacle," Cheyne snapped. He jumped into the carriage.

Mutton climbed in after him. "Wot's wrong? You look like a dog's dinner."

"Have you ever sat in trousers caked with strawberry pastry?"

"Nah. I don't usually squat in pies, me."

Through grinding teeth, Cheyne said, "I'll thank you to abandon your humor at my expense, or you can bloody well pack your things and get out of my house."

"Have it your own way," Mutton replied, unperturbed. He pounded on the roof of the barouche to speed the coachman. "We got to get you out of them trousers. If I don't clean them and the coat quick, I'll have to order new ones from the tailor."

"Damn the tailor."

Mutton sighed. "Did you find out anything before you decided to scrap with the lady?"

"I talked to Elland Capgrave. He told me Sir

Archibald Preston has been nervous and distracted lately. Perhaps the blackmailer has got hold of him. I was going to try to speak to Lord Randolph Latimer, but my mother waylaid me and dragged me off to be introduced to that woman."

"What woman?"

"Miss Matilda Bright, the most annoying, rude, uncivilized witch in all of England. I tell you, if she isn't taught a lesson, she'll be a thorn in my side the whole time I'm trying to work. Everyone was laughing at me, and I can't stick it. She's appalling, and a blight on my existence."

"Yeah, all that midnight hair and them tulip lips."

"Oh, shut up, Mutton."

❦

The next morning Cheyne had recovered his dignity and his good humor. He whistled as he plucked a new tie from a dresser drawer. Mutton was in the sitting room laying out Cheyne's breakfast. He appeared in the doorway.

"You got to hurry if you're going to call on the countess by eleven o'clock." Cheyne had decided to talk to several people he knew were rabid gossips in order to get a hint of the most likely next victim.

"There's time," Cheyne said. "What's the matter? You look like you just smelled rotten fish."

"Beggin' your pardon, gov'nor. You going to wear that tie?"

Cheyne looked at himself in the mirror. He'd admired the tie at his tailor's and purchased it last week. "What's wrong with polka dots?"

"Gents wear black ties with their coats."

"This tie is black, with white polka dots."

"Won't do." Mutton went to the dresser and began inspecting Cheyne's ties. "Here, this one'll do a treat." The valet held out a simple black length of silk like half a dozen others in the drawer.

Cheyne drew himself up. "Mutton, this is the tie I wear."

"Awright."

"Indeed."

"Course, you look like a ponce."

Sighing, Cheyne turned back to the mirror. He studied the bright piece of material around his neck, then yanked it loose. "I suppose I'll never have any peace if I don't listen to you."

"Prob'ly not," Mutton said, and he handed Cheyne the black tie.

"You'd never know I was an officer in the cavalry from the way you behave," Cheyne said as he tied a new knot.

"You was a right proper gentleman even then," Mutton said, "but you wore uniforms what was already designed for you. Never had to choose any ties. Least, not where I could see you."

Mutton stood back and examined his master. "Splendid. Nice starch to the collar, good crease on the trousers. I like that new frock coat."

"God, you're so fussy."

"I'm not lettin' you out o' here without you lookin'

sharp. It reflects on me, and I got me reputation to think of."

"If I remember correctly, your reputation extends no farther west than Cheapside."

Cheyne forestalled more argument by quitting the dressing room and wolfing down his breakfast. On the drive over to Belgrave Square, Cheyne passed the time by designing his revenge on the detestable Miss Matilda Bright. For once he hardly noticed the din in the streets, the clatter of horse-drawn omnibuses, the shouts of street vendors and shopkeepers chasing urchins from their stores. In Belgrave Square he presented his card and waited to be admitted to the Countess of Ixworth's drawing room.

The countess, Rose Marie Seton, lived in a grand house built in the new fashion. It was a hodge-podge of Renaissance, medieval, and classic features— turrets, friezes, frescoes, towers, and stained glass. The indiscriminate clash of styles bothered Cheyne, but he felt nothing but pity for the countess.

The lovely Rose Marie had been, before her marriage, Rosie Leech, a music-hall entertainer. She'd fascinated Guy Seton, and the old buster had married her, to the horror of his family and all Society. Rosie had tried hard to remake herself into a lady. For years she worked on improving her speech, her manners, her education. Yet it was her humor and generosity that had won over the men of rank and position; twenty years after her marriage, neither had won over the women.

Poor Rosie was still ignored by the leaders of Society. Seldom did she receive an invitation to the most select gatherings such as Lady Lutterworth's ball, which the Prince and Princess of Wales attended every year. Ever cheerful, Rosie hovered about the edges of select groups at public gatherings. She attended the opera, the theater, and the ballet. She entertained lavishly those who were kind enough or brave enough to accept her invitations, and she hoped.

Cheyne would have given up long ago, having less patience than the countess. His estimation often plummeted upon learning that a friend had refused to call on Rosie. A man who couldn't brave the disapproval of people like his mother wasn't a man.

The countess's butler reappeared to escort him across a long hall decorated with medieval fan vaulting. He mounted the stairs as two ladies came down, and at the turn in the staircase he found himself looking up at Miss Matilda Bright. Everyone stopped. The butler, several steps ahead, paused silently.

"Miss Bright, how lovely to see you." Cheyne bowed and heard one of the ladies snigger. He straightened to cast an electric stare at the two.

Miss Bright met his challenge with a tranquil smile, a quite appropriate, refined smile such as one mastered and employed when making calls. It was a smile with no sincerity, no meaning, no depth, but Miss Bright's eyes snapped with merriment.

Cheyne might have countered with a sneer, but he was distracted by his own senses. They seemed to be befuddled by a cloud of lavender. Not the scent, but Miss Bright. She was lavender. Her visiting gown, her wide, graceful hat shrouded in netting and her gloves were lavender.

Most women would have faded beneath the dramatic effect. Miss Bright dominated it. Cheyne heard the whisper of kid gloves against her gown. That delicate sound stabbed through him. Clamping his teeth, he fought a wave of craving mixed with anger. Appetite won, for the moment, but Miss Bright saved him embarrassment by nodding to him and sailing down the stairs.

Gritting his teeth, he took a step, and the butler went on. Before he reached the landing, Cheyne heard the other young lady speak to Miss Bright.

"Your mother will be furious if she finds out you called on the countess."

"Narcissa, Rosie's the only interesting person I've met in London. Mama will have to get over it."

Cheyne heard Narcissa giggle. "Who would have thought we'd see your Lord Geoffrey?"

"Dang," Miss Bright said with amusement suffusing her tone, "he turned as pink as that pie he sat in." Then there was a chuckle. "I reckon he won't go around acting like he's the biggest toad in the puddle for awhile."

Cheyne's hearing failed as blood rushed to his head. He followed the butler across the landing and out of earshot of the abominable Miss Bright.

The dowager Countess of Ixworth crossed the morning room to meet him, her copper-gold hair a fiery halo in the sunlight that lit the chamber. His friend Lance Gordon was there, as well.

"My dear Cheyne, what's this I hear of your coming to your senses and going about in Society again?" The countess offered her hand.

"It's true, Rose Marie." Cheyne kissed the lady's hand and addressed Lance. "Hello, old chap."

Lance, who resembled a confused and starving trout, didn't wait for Cheyne to elaborate. "I say, Cheyne, I must tell you about this absolute stunner I met last week. I was in the Strand looking for a present for my cousin for her birthday when I tripped over a young woman selling oranges. She was the most beautiful creature I've ever seen."

"Lance, only a month ago you told me you were in love with a girl you'd met in Whitechapel. A young person who, if I recall, was more interested in gin than you."

A look of vacant adoration overcame Lance. "She was nothing compared to my darling, exquisite Bertha."

The countess and Cheyne exchanged glances and said together, "Bertha?"

"Yes, Bertha." Lance nearly danced on his tiptoes in ecstasy. "Isn't that a lovely name? Bertha Snaith. It just rolls off the tongue, like pure, sweet wine."

The countess smoothly changed the subject, inviting her guests to be seated. "I've rung for tea. Now tell me, dear Cheyne, what has brought about your change of heart?"

"I supposed it's my age. It's time I settled down, became respectable. After all, I am thirty, you know. An age at which one should acquire the trappings of a noble life."

Rose Marie stared at him, and Lance shook his head. "Impossible. Not after the things you've said about Society. If I remember correctly, you once scoffed that no one with brains could remain in Society without risking their atrophy."

"But age gives one a certain moderation. I've become more tolerant of the idiosyncrasies of others."

"Does that include the delightful Miss Bright?" the countess asked with a slight smile.

Cheyne frowned. "I don't know what you mean."

"It's rumored that you insulted her over some little contretemps having to do with a motorcar. Did you see her as you came up?"

"I did," Cheyne snapped. He noticed the interest his reaction caused and lightened his tone. "A trivial incident not worth discussing. Dear Rose Marie, are you going to the opera tonight?"

"Of course, one always goes to *Aida*. And speaking of the opera, do you know who I saw there last month? Sir Archibald Preston. So distressingly upright and stiff until one gets to know him. Then he's an absolute dear."

Lance abandoned his goggle-eyed trance over the divine Bertha. "By Jove, I knew there was something I wanted to tell you."

Rose Marie clapped her hands and scooted forward in her chair. "Oh, good. I do so look forward to your delicious stories."

"Well, a little bird told me that the upright and proper Sir Archibald isn't quite so proper anymore." Lance lowered his voice to a stage whisper. "I have it on good account that old Archie has become something of a roué."

Cheyne watched his two friends put their heads together like conspirators in a play. This was what he had come for.

"Not in love with his wife, I take it," said the countess.

"You'll never guess," replied Lance. "His carriage has been seen drawn up at the woman's house at an hour when the lady's husband is at his club."

"Who is it?" the countess asked. "Do tell, darling. I'm simply atwitter."

"Florence Drummond!"

Rose Marie covered her mouth with her hands and giggled. "Delicious."

Cheyne remained silent. Rose Marie was amused because Lady Drummond had had more lovers than people cared to remember, while Archie Preston was a dedicated prude. Cheyne noticed that the countess's mood shifted suddenly.

"It's really too bad," she said. "I never behaved in such a manner when I was on the stage, and yet I'm excluded from gatherings while Florence Drummond goes everywhere." Her hazel eyes grew glassy, and her lower lip trembled.

Rising, Cheyne distracted her. "Why do you think I'm so cynical, dear Lady Ixworth? It's because I found out long ago that the motto of Society is, 'Thou shalt not be found out.' One can do as one likes as long as one's indiscretions don't appear in the papers, or the courts, or come to the attention of the lower orders."

"But we must set an example for them," Lance said.

"That's just it, old fellow. We don't."

"Exactly," chimed in Rose Marie. "I abhor that kind of hypocrisy. My poor Lord Ixworth would spin in his grave if he were to witness the kind of behavior that goes on in good Society. I know I've never even considered such behavior. It would demean my dear husband's memory."

Lance changed the subject again. Allowing the countess to alight upon the topic of her sainted husband was a mistake, for she would detail his virtues for half an hour without stopping. Seton had been dead for six years, but Rose Marie still wore black. Of course, black suited her coloring, setting off her hair and fair skin. But she would have worn it had it made her look like a Tower raven.

"I say, Cheyne, old man, Miss Bright seemed quite interested in you."

"What are you talking about?"

"True, Lance," said the countess. "When she was here she asked all sorts of questions. The poor girl has no idea how to behave properly on a call. It just isn't done to ask so many personal questions about an acquaintance, especially a gentleman."

Cheyne raised his brows. "Do you mean she fails to confine her conversation to the fascinating topics of weather, balls, and sport? What did she want to know?"

"Oh, why you've dropped your family name on your cards, what you are like, why you behave like an arrogant—what was the word she used?—ah, yes, skunk," Lance grinned.

"I hope you took the opportunity to enlighten her as to my fine qualities."

Rose Marie laughed. "He did. Lance said you were a gentleman of infinite wit."

"And intelligence," said Lance.

"To which the lady replied that she doubted poor Lance's veracity. She said that in her experience you behaved like a—how did she put it?—a no-account, stinking rotten dog."

Hands clasped behind his back, Cheyne rocked back and forth on his heels. "Miss Bright should learn to keep her uncivil thoughts to herself."

"But Cheyne, dear, she was most specific in her account of your rudeness to her at the unveiling of your mother's portrait."

"That was a mistake. And anyway, did she also tell you about that so-called little incident with the motorcar? She almost ran over me and my horse with her infernal machine, and then she played a damned trick on me!"

They were staring at him, eyes wide.

"I say, old boy. Do you know you're almost shouting?"

Cheyne looked away from them. "I beg your pardon." He cleared his throat. "Perhaps I should take my leave." He bowed to the countess. "With your permission, I'll call when I'm better able to contribute to the delightful conversation that's always to be had in your company, dear Lady Ixworth."

Fuming, Cheyne left the house and jumped into his barouche. On the drive home he lectured himself. There was no reason for the annoying Miss Bright to dominate his emotions and make him lose his temper. He'd gained valuable information about Archie Preston and would have gotten more, no doubt, had he not made an ass of himself.

He had several more calls to make on his collection of gossipy acquaintances. His vulnerability to Miss Bright's insulting remarks must vanish. No brazen colonial was going to impair his ability to deal with a dangerous criminal.

But what was the remedy for Miss Bright? Cheyne's disgruntled mood lightened. Of course. Once he'd gotten back at her, the insulting remarks would cease. After Lady Lutterworth's ball tomorrow night, Miss Matilda Bright would be in no position to poke fun at anyone.

5

❧⦿❧

Mattie limped down one side of the double stair-case at Lutterworth House to the tune of a waltz. Her last partner had stepped on her toes so many times that she feared her feet would swell and become too large for her slippers. She had excused herself and sat out two dances. Mama would be wondering where she was.

The next dance was taken by yet another titled young man, one of several new to her who had sought an introduction tonight and begged the honor of a dance. Mama was so pleased she nearly vibrated with glee, for each came from a family of ancient lineage and no financial embarrassment that would force him to seek an upstart American heiress as a bride. So far Mattie's suitors had been driven by inspirations other than her charm.

Holding on to the mahogany, Mattie stopped

halfway down the stairs to admire the gilt bronze balustrade embellished with Grecian foliage. The two wings of the Carrara marble staircase met on a landing and continued down to another floor. Beyond the landing Mattie saw the foot-stomper headed her way.

"Land sakes," she muttered and skittered down to the lower floor, ducking into a white marble hall that had been the main room of the house in the eighteenth century.

At the end of the hall opposite the grand staircase was an ornate chimneypiece. Along the walls were arranged niches with rounded arches in which rested modern copies of Greek and Roman statuary. Beside the niches stood various works of art, including several gilded ceramic pedestal clocks as tall as Mattie was. She limped to the carpeted steps in front of the chimneypiece and sat down.

At least she hadn't encountered Lord Geoffrey, Mr. Tennant, or whatever he called himself. No one had been able to give her a satisfactory reason why he insisted upon not using his title. She had caught sight of her nemesis across the ballroom at various times during the evening, always in conversation with people Mattie knew to be great talkers.

Having suspected that he might try to retaliate for her little trick, Mattie had kept an eye out for him. She was ashamed of herself for reverting to her old bad habits, but it had been so gratifying to watch his face as he sat down. With Tennant around, it was going to be even harder to remember to be genteel. If he tried to pay her back with some meanness of his own, she wasn't sure she could restrain herself. So far he'd danced only a couple of times and seemed intent on conversing the whole night. Which was fortunate, because Mattie wasn't having a good time and having to spar with Cheyne Tennant/Lord Geoffrey would really foul her mood.

It seemed that every partner she'd had tonight was a bad egg. First there had been that condescending young earl who seemed to think all Americans lived in log cabins and fought Indians daily.

"Damn fool," Mattie said to herself as she took off a slipper and rubbed her toes. She groaned as her corset bit into her ribs. She'd had to wear it because her dress was cut exactly to the proportions she assumed when encased in the uncomfortable contraption.

She was wearing one of the gowns she and Mama had ordered in Paris. It had an underdress of pale rose silk and an overdress of spangled net. Mama had wanted the spangles to be diamonds, but Mattie had balked at such a display of bad taste. The spangles were rhinestones. Mattie realized she was sitting on the train, got up and shoved it to the side. The darned dress required fourteen yards of silk.

Mattie kicked off her other slipper and sighed with relief. Soon she would have to go back to the ball. The dance card on her wrist was full for the rest of the evening. What a misery. She'd already put up with a young man who couldn't follow the rhythm of a tune if someone held a gun on him. Then there had been that fellow who was sensitive to roses. A spray of pink buds nestled in her upswept hair. Her partner had sneezed on her with every beat of the polka they were dancing, and they ended up stumbling off the dance floor while he wheezed and tried to draw a complete breath. As the attacks continued with the ferocity of a runaway train Mattie had felt like she was in one of those new Kinetoscope moving pictures in which a man sneezes the same sneeze over and over again. The poor man had finally thrown up his hands to ward off her concerned attentions. Everyone had stared at them.

Mattie turned as pink as the roses in her hair at the memory. People had stared at her and whispered when her feet got stomped and she yelped, then they stared at her during the sneezing spectacle. People were probably thinking she was a lunatic or, worse, gauche and unrefined. She'd failed yet again to be the charming young lady Papa had wanted her to be. If she continued in this manner she'd never attract the admiration of a duke's heir.

Papa had worked so hard to get her here—to give her his dream. There had been times when she cried to see him so weary from ranch work that he could barely stand. Later, when they went east with his small savings, Papa had found himself a profitable business selling coke to the steel mills. That had been Papa's big risk, and success had come only with more long hours of work. But Marcus Bright had been clever. By the time Mattie turned fourteen, they were rich. No more living on nothing but potatoes so there'd be more savings for the business. No more going barefoot in summer like they did in Texas. Papa had succeeded beyond imagination.

But what Mattie remembered about becoming rich was what it meant to her father. The day he got that first big contract with the steel company, Papa had come home with his arms full of packages and tears in his eyes. He'd thrown the packages on the settee, produced a small box from his pocket and held it out to Mama.

"Here, Elsa Jane. It's what I promised you when we got married. I kept my promise, honey. Just like I always said I would."

In that box had been Mama's first diamond ring. Papa gave everyone in the family presents—Mattie's older brother Jimmy, her younger sister Pearl, and Mattie, of course. He even bought presents to send to his relatives in Ohio even though they never visited. That was Papa, always thrilled to buy things for folks and never buying anything for himself.

"Mattie!"

She jumped, startled at the sound of her name. Narcissa hurried into the hall and sank down beside her.

"I've been looking everywhere for you."

"I had to rest my feet."

"I know. I saw you with that clumsy man. Everyone saw you. That's what I've come to tell you."

Mattie put her hands on her hips. "Don't you think I know the whole ballroom was staring at me, Narcissa Potter?"

"No, no. I've been hearing talk." Narcissa scooted closer and looked around the room as if fearing the statues were listening. "I was sipping a cup of punch and overheard that silly Lancelot Gordon talking to Cheyne Tennant. Mr. Tennant had just asked Lady Hortense Nash to favor him with a dance."

Mattie frowned and said, "I'm not interested in anything that no-account had to say, not by a jugful."

"You'll be interested in this," Narcissa whispered. "From what I could hear, it appears that Tennant has been arranging for you to dance with the most odious partners he could find all evening so that you'd end up a spectacle."

Mattie's heart began to race as Narcissa continued.

"It was he who asked that clumsy Baron Hay-whithy to partner you, and he found that young man who sneezed all over the place, and the one who was so rude about Americans."

Now Mattie was as red as the carpet on which she sat. "Confounded, mangy skunk. Land sakes, why couldn't he leave things be?"

"I'm afraid several people overheard Mr. Gordon," Narcissa said with a rueful look. "The story will be all over the place."

"Faster than a prairie fire in a hot wind."

Mattie chewed her lower lip, her face hot with misery at the thought of these highfalutin blue bloods laughing at her. There were plenty of jealous debutantes and irritated mamas who would enjoy her embarrassment, embellish the story, and make sure it was all over London by the end of the week.

She had to give them something else to talk about. Mattie put her slippers on and stood.

Narcissa stood up, too. "What are you going to do?"

"Do you think Mr. Tennant has danced with Lady Hortense yet?"

"No, they're engaged for the next galop."

"Good," Mattie said. "I never did like Lady Hortense. She dismissed her lady's maid for burning a gown with an iron. I know how heavy irons are, and a second's inattention can get you a bad burn. It can happen to anyone. Fussy old cow."

Mattie lifted her skirt and withdrew a small packet of brown paper from where she'd lodged it in her garter.

"What's that?"

"Boot blacking." Feeling guilty, Mattie went on, "I kinda suspected I might need it." Giving in to her devilish streak, she grinned. "You ever notice how Mr. Tennant always stands real straight and stiff, like he was a soldier in a parade? Never looks at himself, like he's sure he's neat and proper." Mattie whispered her plan in her friend's ear.

Narcissa gave her a startled look, then giggled. "All right. Give me a few minutes."

Mattie passed the time applying gobs of boot blacking to the inside of her gloved fingers and palms. Then, taking care not to touch her dress, she went to the ballroom. She craned her neck to peer over the heads of the guests and spotted Narcissa talking to Lancelot Gordon. Standing with his back to his friend was Cheyne Tennant. Mattie skirted around the dancers on the floor until she approached the group. Part of her knew she was descending to childishness again, but she couldn't seem to resist the desire to get even.

Slowing down, she walked past Narcissa and winked. As she came alongside Gordon, Narcissa moved quickly, appearing to stumble against Mr. Gordon. Gordon lost his balance and knocked Tennant into Mattie's path. Mattie cried out and dropped to the floor at his feet.

Tennant recovered his balance and looked down, his eyes wide. "What happened?" Recovering from his surprise, he seemed to remember his manners and knelt beside her. "Are you all right, Miss Bright? You're not hurt?"

"No, I'm quite all right, thank you. I just slipped when you stumbled against me."

"Please, allow me to assist you," he said with formality.

Mattie gave him her most charming smile, the one she used to beguile a reluctant motorcar into starting. "Thank you, my lord."

She held out her gloved hands, and he grasped them. Beneath the skin-tight kid she felt the tensile strength of his hands. He lifted her effortlessly, but kept hold of her hands as she met his gaze with her smile. His own gaze faltered, then returned hers as if finding something new and unknown, something foreign and fascinating. A moment passed in which the music and din of the crowd faded.

Stray, dazzled thoughts flew about Mattie's head. *He could pick me up without any effort at all. When he's not sneering and scowling, his eyes are the color of wild hyacinth.*

Cheyne Tennant blinked, stepped back, and released her. His features smoothed into a chilly mask. "I do beg your pardon again for my clumsiness, Miss Bright. Pray excuse me."

Jolted out of her magical trance, Mattie hardly heard Narcissa's solicitous remarks. She was too busy giving herself a scolding. *Serves you right,* she told herself. *Think a man as pretty and elegant as that's going to notice you when he's got all the golden-headed English ladies he wants? I bet he likes the kind that cling and droop and prattle. He probably measures a lady's refinement by how many times she faints in a day. The skunk.*

Mattie glanced over her shoulder to see the skunk bowing to Lady Hortense. Waltz music began. "Excuse me, Narcissa."

She hurried to a corner behind a giant silver font filled with punch. Stripping off her soiled gloves, she dropped them in an ancient Chinese vase and pulled on a new pair she'd concealed in the same manner as the bootblack. Then she returned to Narcissa, who was talking to Mama.

"There you are, Matilda," Mama said. "Here is Lord Isidore Chelmer come to claim his dance."

A fence-post-thin man bowed to Mattie. He wore his hair in the new style, slicked down with scented pomade, and since his forehead was as prominent as his eyes, the effect was as if he wore a hair hat too small for his head. When Chelmer straightened from his bow, Mattie saw with dismay that he was several inches shorter than she was. He offered his arm, and they stepped onto the dance floor. When they came together, Mattie realized too late that Chelmer's eyes were level with her chest.

A gentleman would have kept his gaze fixed on her face, but Chelmer stared straight ahead, transfixed by Mattie's bosom. Mattie could have endured the rudeness had it not been the fashion in Society for ball gowns to have extremely low necks. The rose silk and spangles barely covered her, and the longer Chelmer goggled at her chest, the more uncomfortable Mattie grew. As they swept around the ballroom her face, neck, and chest turned the same rose color as her gown. At each turn in the waltz she glimpsed people watching and concealing smirks behind gloved hands.

She could endure a little embarrassment, but this particular incident struck at a sore spot. Ever since Mattie had begun to mature, she'd been warned by Mama that she had an "embarrassment of riches" in her figure. While rejoicing in her daughter's good fortune, Mama constantly warned her of the evil intentions that men harbored toward women with such endowments. The result had been to make Mattie wish she'd never matured.

After Mama's remarks, Mattie began to notice how men stared when they thought themselves unobserved. After a few months of this, she realized that to some men she would never be more than her endowments. A black melancholy ensued from which it took her a long time to recover. It took even longer for Mattie to learn to ignore the stares. Isidore Chelmer's stare, however, was impossible to ignore.

Mattie clenched her jaw. "Excuse me, my lord."

Chelmer remained oblivious, enchanted with her bosom.

"My lord."

Chelmer swallowed and pointed his nose at her chest, evidently in order to get a better view.

"Isidore Chelmer, you lummox! You keep gawking at my chest, and I have a mind to knock out your teeth and stuff 'em down your throat."

Chelmer dragged his gaze upward, and Mattie held his stare with one that would have singed the metal fenders on her Panhard-Lavassor. A few seconds passed before Chelmer looked down. This time Mattie stepped on his foot. He yelped and fixed a stare over her shoulder.

It was Tennant again. He'd sent this crude ass her way deliberately.

The waltz seemed to last hours, with Chelmer dropping his gaze to her bosom and Mattie retaliating with a stomp, a pinch, or a threat. At last the music stopped. Mattie turned her back on Lord Chelmer and swept off the floor.

As she went, she heard Lady Hortense giggle and say in a nasal voice, "Really, Cheyne, you are too bad."

Cheeks flaming, Mattie turned and approached Cheyne Tennant and Lady Hortense. "Dear Lady

Hortense, I couldn't help noticing your gown is soiled." Mattie turned her tormentor around and pointed to the black smears on the lady's pearl-studded dress.

Hortense shrieked as though she'd been stabbed. "My gown! And my gloves. What—who—where . . . ?"

Guests crowded around to watch as Hortense tried to see the back of her gown. She twisted her neck and turned around in circles.

"Careful," Cheyne warned and caught her arm before she tripped over her train.

Hortense squawked, jerked her arm free and tried to wipe off the black smear that had resulted from his touch. "It's you! What have you got on your gloves? Look at me."

Mattie moved out of the crowd as Cheyne turned his gloves over and examined them. His expression of disbelief and chagrin assuaged Mattie's humiliated soul. She grinned when Lady Hortense inadvertently touched the front of her gown with a soiled glove and blackened it even further.

Taking a seat beside Mama, she removed the dance card from her wrist. Mattie hummed to herself as she proceeded to mark off all the strange names on her list. For the rest of the ball she was going to dance only with men she knew. They might be fortune-hunting dogs, but at least they wouldn't stare at her chest. Mattie stopped humming and grinned. Lady Hortense bleated recriminations at Cheyne Tennant so loudly that the musicians behind their screen of foliage at the other end of the room began to chuckle. The group around the couple scattered, leaving Cheyne to face the furious lady alone in the middle of the dance floor.

Mattie glanced at her startled mother. "Sakes alive, Mama, such a fuss about one little gown."

6

Cheyne retreated into the shell of frosty discipline that had served him well during his years in the cavalry. The restraint was necessary. Lady Hortense's nasal whine reminded him of a goat that had swallowed a trumpet, and the comparison did nothing to control his urge to snap at the woman. But he couldn't risk giving vent to his usual sarcasm if he wanted to remain on the guest lists of Society. So he had to stand here, wondering how his gloves got boot blacking on them, and play the repentant horror-stricken gentleman.

Fortunately Lady Hortense's mother arrived.

"Mother, just look at my gown. It's awful, and I'll never recover from this. Never."

"Oh, hush, Hortense. No one wants to listen to you."

"But Mother!"

Cheyne fixed his gaze on a chandelier before his sympathy for the mother began to show. Then he looked at his gloves again. Sighing, he pulled them off and glanced around the room. Nearby he saw Miss Mattie Bright, a pleased-with-herself expression on her face. In that instant he knew what had happened. Fury exploded in him, but he couldn't do anything about it. Boiling with frustration, Cheyne made his apologies to Lady Hortense and her mother, made a graceful offer to replace the gown and excused himself.

Turning on his heel, he marched straight for Matilda Bright, who sat amid her spangled rose silk and complacency. The moment he took a step, however, Miss Bright rose and glided away from him through the thickest part of the crowd. He knew he should return to the business of hunting for the blackmailer, but he was too angry. Besides, he reasoned, how could he continue to move through Society unobtrusively with this mischief-making little savage making him look like an idiot at every function? She had to be stopped. And it would be his pleasure to do it.

Cheyne glimpsed Miss Bright's spangled gown as she fled across the ballroom and went through the French doors that opened onto the terrace. He darted after her into the cold April night. He was in time to see her race down the terrace and vanish into one of the rooms on the other side of the house. He ran after her and found himself in the Silk Tapestry

Room, so called for the woven Renaissance tapestries that hung from its ceilings.

He heard a door slam somewhere and hurried out, but stopped in a picture gallery with half a dozen rooms off it, uncertain. Light footsteps sounded above him and he plunged up the west staircase to another gallery. There he hesitated and caught a whiff of perfume—lilacs and spice. He followed the scent through several rooms, but it faded. Cursing, he started down the stairs. He'd been gone from the ball too long. As he made the turn in the staircase, he sniffed and smiled. The little devil had doubled back.

He slithered along the picture gallery, taking care to stay on the carpet that muffled his steps. He paused beside a pair of doors carved of mahogany, slowly turned the gilded handle and slipped inside the Music Room. Miss Bright stood at the floor-length windows and peered at the terrace through the wine-colored velvet curtains.

She really was a stunner. As he watched, she bent over to remove her slippers, giving him an interesting view of her posterior. Cheyne smiled and approached her while she rubbed her foot. He was near enough to deliver a good swat to his tempting target when she gasped, whirled around, and threw her shoe at him. The silk object hit him in the chest.

"Ouch! That hurt, you little harpy,"

Cheyne grabbed for her, but Miss Bright darted

around the grand piano. Cheyne dashed around the other side so that he was between the piano and the doors.

"You put boot blacking on my gloves, blast you."

"You've got no call to get wrathy. You made me dance with that passel of mangy oafs." Miss Bright turned the color of the curtains. "That Isidore Chelmer gawked at my—he stared at—I've never met a more repulsive fella in all my born days. Except you."

"Miss Bright, if you wish to marry a title, and it appears that is your quest, shallow though it may be, then you'll have to learn to put up with a few inconveniences." Cheyne moved around the piano. "Come here, Miss Bright. I want to give you a lesson in etiquette. It will help you remember not to make a gentleman look like a fool in front of the best families in England."

"Can't be the best, if you're one of 'em." Miss Bright circled around the piano and darted behind a harp that stood near the doors.

Cheyne leaped across the room to place himself between the harp and escape. "Never have I met a more tiresome, ill-mannered person. You seem to have been educated on the Continent, but it didn't do any good. So I'm going to teach you that running over people with motorcars and playing tricks at balls have no place among refined persons."

"You're the one who started this, blaming me for things that are your fault and bellowing insults at me at the portrait viewing," said Miss Bright. "You got no call to get uppity and accuse me of being uncivil when you're worse than a grizzly at Delmonico's."

"Will you please speak English? I understood only half of what you said."

"You mean you want me to sound like I've been soaked in vinegar and stuck on the shelf."

Cheyne moved closer to Miss Bright, but she tossed her remaining shoe at him and sprinted for the door as he dodged it. He spun around and lunged, catching her around the waist and quickly pulling her against him. Spitting colorful insults at him, Miss Bright pounded at his arm until he managed to wrap her in a hold that brought them face-to-face. And then Cheyne realized his mistake in not holding her at arm's length.

They were pressed against each other like tinned sausages, and he could feel her breasts heave against his chest. Every movement, every squirm and writhe brought Miss Bright's curves in contact with his body. The righteousness of his purpose disappeared from his thoughts. Arousal burned away his vexation.

Miss Bright tried to pry herself free by shoving his chest with her trapped arms. This forced her bosom back and her hips forward so that Cheyne glimpsed temptation while his most intimate body parts received stimulation to the point of pain.

"Stop that!" Cheyne squeezed her so that she couldn't move.

"I can't breathe, dang it."

He loosened his grip, and Miss Bright took a

deep breath. Through a haze of desire Cheyne watched her fill her lungs. She was still close to him, close enough to make those deep breaths torture. Blood pounded in his ears, and his heart raced. It raced to other parts of him as well, making him want to howl with the tension of it. He noticed the way she bit her lower lip as she struggled to regain her equilibrium. His gaze narrowed so that those lips filled his vision. The pounding in his ears, the beating of his heart, the discomfort of arousal all grew until he thought he would explode. Unable to endure the agony, Cheyne suddenly let go of his prisoner.

The abruptness of her release caused Miss Bright to lose her balance. She dropped to the floor on her bottom.

"Hey!"

Cheyne retreated to the windows, grabbed a handful of velvet curtain in his fist and pressed his forehead against the glass. "Go away."

Behind him he heard Miss Bright get to her feet and pick up her shoes. "What in blazes do you think you're doing, tossing me around like a sack of sweet potatoes?"

"I said go away." Cheyne gritted his teeth and closed his eyes, trying to will away the urge to throw her on the floor.

"Now, listen here, Mr. Tennant, if you think you can handle me like that and then just—"

Cheyne's fist jerked in the curtains, making the

rod jangle and startling Miss Bright. "Bloody hell! Get out."

Miss Bright narrowed her eyes and folded her arms across her chest. Cheyne's gaze dropped to her arms, and he winced again.

"What's wrong with you?"

A pained laugh burst from him, and Cheyne gave her a twisted smile that cost him much. "Miss Bright, further conversation between us is impossible. Are you really so innocent?" When she furrowed her brow, he closed his eyes and swore.

"*Christ.*"

He turned away from her and stared blindly into the darkness. "If you value your honor, Miss Bright, you'll do as I ask. Otherwise, it's quite likely I shall throw you on the floor and—"

"Dang."

"Dang indeed," Cheyne said wryly.

Before he could continue, he heard the rustle of silk and the sound of a door opening and closing. After a while he saw a figure in rose silk walk along the terrace. Miss Bright passed the window where he stood and hesitated. Their gazes met, but she broke the contact and disappeared into the ballroom. Cheyne remained where he was and rested his burning face against the windowpane.

He heard laughing and realized it was his own. What irony. To conceive a lust for that barbaric creature, and in the midst of this hunt for the black-mailer. Not only was it unprofessional, it was absurd. He could have any woman he wanted. Had he wished, he could have begun an affair this evening with any of half a dozen married ladies who'd made their interest plain. Women had always made their interest plain to him.

Once, he'd taken advantage of this power. For years he amused himself by making conquests of the most beautiful and unattainable women. Then he'd gone to war and learned that life was too precious to waste in pursuit of meaningless encounters and ephemeral gratification. He'd spent too much time fighting a Boer army that vanished into the bush, leaving him and his men to suffer in the heat and dirt. For a time after he came back to England, his wounds and the ugliness he'd seen caused a grief too deep to admit the presence of a woman. Now that the nightmares had faded, he had sought out a few ladies who had become friends as well as lovers. These women knew the rules—Cheyne's rules. Nothing serious, no promises, yet mutual respect and courtesy.

These rules enabled him to maintain a safe distance, a distance Miss Bright had just destroyed. How in the world had he lost his detachment? His anger. That was it. His anger had thrown him off guard. Well, it wouldn't happen again. He knew his weakness now, and he'd guard against allowing his ire free reign around Miss Bright. The whole incident was simply a result of too much emotion. Of course. He should have realized this at once. It wasn't Miss Bright's beauty. She was hardly a beauty.

Pleasing. He would admit she was pleasing. Especially her figure, and her face, and her midnight hair.

But he'd been with women far more beautiful. And certainly he hadn't been aroused by the lady's charming manner. Matilda Bright had the charm of a Boer and the manners of a fishmonger's wife. Her language was atrocious and her attitude disrespectful.

Exactly. So there was little chance of a reoccurrence of this evening's lapse. The whole incident was an aberration.

Cheyne straightened and left the window. Having convinced himself of his invulnerability to Miss Bright's allure, he was straightening his tie in order to return to the ball and elicit more gossip when Mutton opened the door.

"What are you doing here?" Cheyne asked.

"Been looking for you gov'nor. The superintendent wants you."

"Why?"

"There's been another death."

❦

Half an hour after being summoned by Mutton, Cheyne walked into a town house in Eaton Square and past a pair of policemen in the marble foyer. He could hear the sound of a woman weeping in a room upstairs, and distraught servants in various states of undress hovered in the doorway behind the staircase. He went into a room off the foyer where several more policemen had gathered and found Superintendent Balfour questioning a hastily dressed middle-aged man.

"That will do for tonight, Mr. Denton. Sergeant Notting will go with you and question the rest of the staff."

Balfour finished writing and closed his notebook before he saw Cheyne. He motioned silently and stepped aside to reveal a man in a leather chair slumped over a heavy walnut desk. An empty bottle of cognac lay beside him. Cheyne had noticed the reek of alcohol the moment he came into the room.

"That's Sir Archibald Preston," Cheyne said quietly. "Didn't you contact him when I gave you his name?"

"I had an appointment with him tomorrow morning," Balfour said, his expression solemn. "It appears you guessed right."

"I have several sources whose chief delight in life is keeping abreast of the latest gossip." Cheyne looked at the body. "Hell."

Sir Archibald had been a bushy-browed man with skin the color of vellum. He'd also recently become a connoisseur of music-hall singers. An unremarkable habit among society men that wouldn't have interested Cheyne ordinarily. Until he learned that the once prudish Sir Archibald was rumored to have indulged in assignations with several women at one time. Even this tidbit hadn't alarmed him enough to tell Balfour that contacting Sir Archibald was urgent. Evidently at some time during his excursions in the music halls Thurgood had left incriminating evidence of his activities, something that could be held over him.

"Don't blame yourself," Balfour said, regarding

Cheyne with severity. "Believe me, there's no way to know if a man will break under this kind of pressure."

A man who had been talking to one of the detectives picked up a leather bag and came over to them.

"I'm finished, Balfour."

"Very well, Doctor. It's suicide, then."

"Well, the poor man drank an entire bottle of cognac in the space of a few minutes. He poisoned himself, Superintendent. That much alcohol would kill anyone, but I don't know if he was aware of it. Unless I can prove otherwise, I shall have to record it as an accident."

"Very well," said Balfour. "Thank you and good evening, Doctor."

Cheyne looked at the body again. He could see a bald spot on the top of Preston's head. Somehow it made the man seem too human, too real to be dead. A muscle twitched in Cheyne's jaw as he recalled what he'd been doing while this man drank himself to death.

"You'll find a series of large withdrawals from his bank account," Cheyne said.

"Probably." Balfour glanced at him. "Sorry to drag you into this, old man, but I've little choice, as you see."

"I've done you little good so far."

"You've just begun. If there's any good to come out of this, it's that we can chalk the death up to accidental overdose of alcohol. No suicide to attract the attention of the papers."

Cheyne nodded and glanced around the room. It was a man's study, full of leather furniture and books on history, the military, and science. These books had been used; they were not kept for show. Sir Archibald had been a complicated man, who had left behind a grieving family.

After a few more words with Balfour, Cheyne went home. Striding into his entry hall, he whipped off his coat and threw it at Mutton. His hat followed as he headed for the brandy decanter in the drawing room. Pouring himself a large drink, he gulped down half of it. Then he looked at the crystal glass in his hand and hurled it at the fireplace. The glass shattered, and Cheyne had already picked up another to pitch after it when Mutton walked in with the air of an alert bloodhound.

"Here, here, here, wot's all this?"

The second glass splintered against the grate, and the coals hissed. "Bloody hell and damnation!" Cheyne cursed.

Mutton hurried to the table and picked up the tray of crystal. "No, you don't, gov'nor. You leave that Waterford be."

Cheyne slumped down on the couch in front of the fireplace and buried his face in his hands.

"Go away."

Mutton set the tray down, found an antique Minton dish and began picking up shards of glass. "Wot's got into you?"

"A man died tonight, in case you failed to grasp the message."

"Nah, I got it first time around," Mutton said companionably.

Lifting his head, Cheyne glared at his valet. "He drank a whole bottle of cognac, and it killed him. I knew he was in trouble, but I couldn't stop him."

"Cor blimey, squire." Mutton laid his dish of shards aside. "Don't see as how you could've helped, 'less you was one of them mind readers."

Cheyne lay back on the couch and laughed. It was a distraught sound, so he stopped. He smiled painfully at Mutton.

"Do you know what I was doing while Archibald Preston drank himself to death? I was chasing Miss Matilda Bright all over Lutterworth House like some demented colt, and when I caught her—" Cheyne realized he was breathless and talking too loudly.

He thrust himself to his feet and walked away. He paused by a sideboard over which hung a painting he'd bought last year. It was a landscape by Turner. Cheyne gazed at the hills covered with grass and wildflowers and wished he could somehow dive into that scene and stay there forever. He closed his eyes.

"What'd she do to you this time?"

He turned swiftly. "That's hardly important now. What's important is that I allowed myself to be distracted. It won't happen again, no matter what the temptation."

Mutton's brows climbed his high forehead. "Temptation?"

"Damn you, leave me alone." Cheyne went back

to the side table and poured himself another brandy. This time he sipped it.

Mutton picked up his dish and started collecting glass shards again. Silence reigned for a while.

"You're barmy if you think I can't see what's happened."

Looking up from his study of the brandy in his glass, Cheyne snapped, "What? What do you see?"

"She's took your fancy. More'n that. You're bleeding sick with it. Got her alone, you did, and found out what I knew all along."

"I am not sick with it, as you so eloquently put it," said Cheyne with deliberate calm. "I intend to have nothing to do with Miss Bright in the future. I've no time to waste on her. She's a title-hunting colonial witch, and she deserves the misery she'll get by marrying one of our self-important worthless English heirs. My only regret is that she seems to have little experience to see her through the coming ordeal, but that's hardly my affair."

Cheyne made a show of placing his glass on the tray quietly and marched out of the drawing room. Mutton followed him into the entry hall and to the foot of the stairs.

"Not your affair?" Mutton asked.

"No," Cheyne said as he climbed the stairs.

Mutton watched him go up. "Right, gov'nor." He paused. "Only thing is, if she means nothing to you, how come you know she has little experience? Unless you've give her some yourself."

Cheyne almost stumbled. Twisting around, he

gave his valet a look that would have frightened Jack the Ripper.

"Leave it, damn you. I'll hear no more!"

He went into his room and slammed the door. Too bad he couldn't shut out the thoughts that came in with him.

7

A week after the Lutterworth ball Mattie slipped out of Spencer House and went to the mews carrying a basket. Once in the stable, she switched on the gaslights and greeted the horses. She gave each a carrot and a pat on the nose before finding her box of polish and dust cloths. Cleaning her motorcars always made her feel better, and right now she was about as happy as a saloon owner at a temperance meeting. The Panhard-Levassor already gleamed, so she turned her attentions to the older Benton Harbor.

The Benton looked more like a carriage, with its curved sides and black roof. It had far less power and dependability than the newer, more elegant model, but it had been one of her first motorcars. Taking a clean cloth from her box, Mattie began to dust the body of the motorcar. It was yellow with black leather seats. As she dusted, she talked to it.

"Well, Bennie, it's true. I've conceived some kind

of horrifying fascination for that skunk Cheyne Tennant. It's humiliating, seeing as how he's treated me worse than dirt." She ran the cloth along a fender and shook her head. "It's 'cause he looks so good. Can't be his character, because that's rotten."

She stepped on the running board to dust the front seat. Her campaign to reform herself was failing in the grand manner of Napoleon's march to Russia, all on account of Mr. Cheyne Tennant. No matter how firm her resolve, she couldn't seem to control herself around him. He just made her too angry. The experience was beginning to worry her. What if she couldn't change? Maybe she was just too full of meanness and shortcomings. The idea shamed and frightened her. She never should have given in to that impulse to retaliate against his high-and-mighty lordship. And now it looked as if she'd never reform as long as he was near.

She'd never expected Tennant to come after her at the ball, and once he caught her, his behavior had been incomprehensible. Until he'd said those last words. *If you value your honor, Miss Bright, you'll do as I ask. Otherwise, it's quite likely I shall throw you on the floor.*

Then she'd understood, and something in her responded. In that second while he gripped the curtains and tried to master himself, she'd experienced a strange compulsion. Had she given in to it, she would have gone to him. And ended up on the floor.

Mattie had lived on a ranch. She understood what happened between males and females; she'd just never felt the kind of urgency that seemed to go along with relations between men and women. She'd met some likable gentlemen at home, but none had evoked this craving in her. And she couldn't get rid of it.

Since the ball she had taken care not to go near Cheyne Tennant. If she had, no doubt he'd have made her mad with his highfalutin ways and his waspy tongue. Besides, he was just too blamed pretty to ignore.

Unlike many men, Tennant had the height to carry off long frock coats or evening coats. His lean face bore no disfiguring mustache that so many gentlemen sported these days, and he moved with confidence and grace. She'd seen that kind of confidence in men who survived weeks on the range dealing with rattlesnakes and rustlers. Few men in Society possessed it. Oh, they acted as if the world had been designed for their enjoyment, but Mattie knew that, faced with real danger, most of them would have no idea how to face it and come through sitting straight in the saddle.

She sighed and moved to dust the back seat of the Benton Harbor. She was tired after having awakened from a dream about Tennant. It was galling to admit, but she couldn't forget the sight of him clutching that curtain, his entire body rigid. His hand, tangled in the velvet, had been elegant, the long fingers white with the strength of his grip. The sight of that hand had brought back the memory of it against her flesh when he held her. No gentleman had ever touched her so intimately. Oh, at first he'd intended something far less friendly, but something had happened to him once he touched her.

"I don't understand it, Bennie," she said as she stepped out of the motorcar and went around to the rear to run the cloth along the back end. "It's not like I'm irresistible. There's plenty of ladies prettier'n me. Look at Consuelo Marlborough, or Daisy Warwick."

So, she was in a quandary. She was losing her fight to become more admirable and ladylike, and she had a weakness for the very man who was helping her destroy Papa's dream.

Mattie shook her head in disgust. She stepped back and admired her cleaning job, then glanced at the horses. "What do you think, fellas?" One of the carriage horses snorted.

"A lot you know," Mattie replied.

She gave the Panhard under its dust sheet a look of longing and put her cloth back in the polishing box. No drive in the park today. She had a fitting this morning and then she'd promised Narcissa and Mama she'd go look for art and antiques. It was to make up for refusing to go to a dance last night, to Mama's great frustration. The Marquess of Stainfield was showing interest, and he was the heir to a dukedom. Stainfield was all right. He couldn't help it if he was a snob, Mattie supposed. But she was too upset with herself to go.

No matter how much she tried, she couldn't keep herself from wanting to go back to America, where she could talk to people about photographic cameras and electric lights and how telephones worked, and what these new things called X rays were. And better yet, if she went home, she wouldn't have to look at Cheyne Tennant and wonder if his hands felt as good as she remembered, or if she'd imagined them being so gentle and yet strong.

At home she wouldn't spend nights tossing like she had a scorpion in her bedroll just because she was afraid to dream about that skunk Cheyne Tennant. It was humiliating to be at the mercy of cravings for such an ornery man. The longer she was unable to master this attraction, the worse she felt. Narcissa had remarked upon her absentmindedness. Mattie longed to confide in her, but she was too ashamed of her weakness.

She had to talk to someone, though. The thought of the marquess touching her the way Cheyne had, revolted her. If she continued to feel this way, she would find it impossible to marry a nobleman, and everyone would be disappointed in her. Seeing her at the top of Society had been Papa's final wish. He'd wanted the best for her, and she was letting him down. All because Cheyne Tennant had threatened to toss her on the floor.

"Dang."

❧

Later that afternoon Mattie accompanied her mother to Catchpole's Antiques, a vast emporium divided into rooms and galleries. Each room housed objects that were related by period or function. Mama was anxious to acquire more fine art to fill the house on Fifth Avenue in New York and the cottage in Newport. While her mother visited the galleries containing old European paintings, Mattie wandered into a small room that held works by contemporary artists. She found paintings by Lucius Rossi, Julius Stewart, and Frederick Childe Hassam. There were even a few by Giovanni Boldini, who was going to paint Consuelo Marlborough.

Rain had kept most customers away from Catchpole's, so Mattie was alone. She was studying a view of the Luxembourg Gardens by Sargent when she glimpsed a familiar figure in dark coat and top hat. Cheyne Tennant stood in the china room, by a Sèvres display case of stained oak that was taller than he was.

Don't gawk at him like a maverick that's spotted a rattler, she told herself. She turned to the Sargent again, but a movement caught her eye. Tennant put his back to the display case and slid around it in a surreptitious manner. His attention was directed at something beyond Mattie's view, and he suddenly darted from the Sèvres case to a much taller one containing Coalport and Rockingham services.

Mystified, Mattie walked to the doorway in time to see Tennant affect a nonchalant manner by opening the catalog he carried and holding it up to his face. Thus he was concealed as a woman left the Staffordshire display and walked into the sculpture room. Mattie recognized her at once. She was Lady Augusta Darent, the wife of Lord James Darent, who held a post in the War Ministry.

Lady Augusta was one of those women who seemed to lead storybook existences. A fairy godmother had given her startling beauty and had bestowed upon her auburn hair that gleamed like silk in sunshine, summer-green eyes, and a height and figure that allowed her to wear the current sweeping fashions superbly. Lady Augusta had charmed Society from the day she came out, even casting her spell on the Prince of Wales. She had a unique ability to create amusement for those around her, which made her popular with an aristocracy cursed with too much leisure time.

Still beside the doorway, Mattie watched Cheyne Tennant lower his catalog slowly and peer over it at Lady Augusta. When she was well into the sculpture room he tucked the catalog under his arm and followed. Mattie frowned when he stepped behind a ten-foot statue of the Greek goddess Athena. Tennant was following Augusta Darent, and he didn't want her to know it. Mattie trailed after the two, wondering why her adversary was skulking after a woman in an antiques emporium.

When Lady Augusta stopped beside a row of sixteenth century bronze busts, light from a window turned her auburn hair to fire. Understanding broke over Mattie and, with it, a fury and disappointment she quickly denied to herself. Cheyne

Tennant was this woman's lover. He had reason to believe she was going to betray him with someone else, and he was following her.

The hypocrite. He'd been so contemptuous of her for trying to wed a titled gentleman when all the time he was carrying on with a married woman.

"Just like all the rest of them," Mattie muttered.

She ducked into an alcove beside a statue of the first Duke of Marlborough when the two turned in opposite directions. He was a blamed polecat, slinking after the woman like that. She stepped back as Lady Augusta walked past her and into the first of several rooms of furniture. Mattie's lip curled in disgust at the way Tennant now affected a casual air and strolled after his quarry. He knew how to seem like an interested customer and yet keep within easy distance of the object of his scrutiny. He must have done this often.

Mattie reddened at the thought of how many women he must have been with. Tennant was about thirty. He surely had had dozens of lovers—hundreds, for all she knew. It was disgusting. She didn't want to see any more. Tennant vanished behind a French armoire, and Mattie stalked away, headed for the painting by Sargent. She didn't care what he did.

But she did. "Land sakes." She spun around and hurried after the lovers.

They were still in the room with the eighteenth century French furniture. It was a vast place that smelled of dust and that distinct scent of age. An elderly lady in mourning garments lifted a lorgnette to survey Tennant, sniffed, and left the room. Tennant ignored her while he watched Lady Augusta from the shelter of the armoire.

Mattie crept to a boulle and lacquer cabinet from behind which she could see them both. Augusta appeared to be absorbed in her study of an oval table with a polished granite top. Then she suddenly moved around the table to a tall ebony and lacquer secretaire that concealed most of her body. Just as swiftly she left the secretaire to open the doors of an armoire and shut them again. Without another glance at the furniture, she strode out of the room.

This time Tennant didn't follow her immediately. He rushed to the secretaire and opened its drawers, searching in its slots and feeling around as if he expected to find something. Then he hurried to the armoire. He searched it, but evidently found nothing, for he scowled at it and bolted after Lady Augusta. Mattie had to walk quickly to keep him in sight. She followed him through rooms containing porcelain and tapestries, and one devoted entirely to candelabras, chandeliers, and sconces.

Mattie realized he was trying to catch up with Augusta Darent, and that she must have decided to leave Catchpole's. Mattie was almost trotting when she crossed the arms and armor room. Near the door that led to the reception hall she nearly impaled herself on the tip of a lance held by a model of a knight in armor. The knight was mounted on a stuffed horse. She sidestepped the lance, which was well over three times her height, and peeked around the open door. She almost yelped when she beheld Tennant rushing across the reception hall. He was headed straight for her.

Mattie scrambled around the mounted knight and took refuge behind an enormous suit of armor labeled as ceremonial armor of Henry VIII. It had what was called a tonlet, which looked like a metal skirt that flared out from the waist and ended above the knees. As she settled behind the wide bulk of steel, she saw Tennant plunge through the doorway and flatten himself against the wall beside it. With his back to the room, he watched Lady Augusta.

A few minutes passed during which Mattie grew more and more disgusted at having to watch him make a fool of himself. Mattie had almost decided to leave when Tennant moved. Removing his hat, he backed up while keeping his gaze fixed on the lady. She was talking to old Edwin Catchpole, the proprietor.

Folding her arms over her chest, Mattie waited to get a look at the expression on his face. Then she noticed he didn't seem to be aware that he was headed for the mounted knight. Another step would send his head knocking against the lance tip.

"Look out!" Mattie cried.

Tennant whirled around, nearly jabbed his eye on the lance and swerved. His movement brought him up against the horse, jarring the armor. The lance crashed to the floor, further unbalancing the whole display. The entire suit of armor toppled off the horse and onto Tennant, knocking him off his feet.

Several visitors who had come into the room as the accident happened rushed to him. Mattie was there first. She cast aside a great helm and shoved the cuirass off Tennant, who lay on his back. When he saw her, his eyes widened in shock. Then he glared at her.

"You again!"

"I tried to warn you."

Tennant struggled to his feet in time to confront Catchpole.

"Are you hurt, sir?"

"No, no. I believe the lance had become insecure, so when I brushed it, the whole contraption toppled."

"Oh, I do apologize, sir."

"It's nothing," Tennant said, staring at Mattie while he straightened his frock coat.

Lifting one eyebrow, Mattie picked up his top hat and handed it to him.

"Tennant?" Lady Augusta came toward them, all concern and grace. "I didn't know you were here. Has there been an accident? Are you hurt?"

Bowing, he kissed Augusta's hand. "Dear Lady Augusta, how kind of you. No. Just a bit of bad luck, I'm afraid."

The two conversed like old friends, in half sentences and with references to people Mattie didn't know. She felt excluded from their intimacy. Not knowing what to do with herself, she wandered over to a display of shields.

Determined not to look at the lovers, she forced herself to read the label on one of the older shields.

" 'Per pale or and gules, a chevron countercharged.' What the hell does that mean?"

"It means the shield is divided in half in gold and red and has chevrons on it," snapped Cheyne Tennant.

Mattie turned to find Lady Augusta gone and Tennant standing behind her with an air of righteous fury. "What are you so all-fired stirred up about?"

"You deliberately startled me."

"What?"

"How long had you been standing there spying on me? Never mind. It's clear you tried another of your childish tricks. I'll thank you to refrain from such absurd conduct in the future, Miss Bright."

Seething at the unjust accusation, Mattie planted her hands on her hips. "Just you hold on, Mr. Tennant. I'll have you know I got better things to interest me than your doings."

"Then why are you here?"

"I know it's hard for you to believe, but Mama and me like this stuff, and we're looking for some to take back to New York. Mama's going to buy a couple of Van Dycks and a Ruebens. Me, I'm partial to Vermeer and Rembrandt. Kinda like one by Albert Cuyp I saw back there, too. So, you see, I really don't have time to waste making you look foolish." Mattie looked him up and down. "Seems to me you got that figured out already."

Tennant turned a brilliant shade of red. His fingers gripped the brim of his hat. "If you weren't spying on me, why were you hiding behind that armor?"

"Wasn't hiding. I was looking at it."

"Do you know that when you're lying you bite your lower lip?"

Mattie compressed her mouth into a straight line.

"This absurd behavior must cease, Miss Bright. Please confine your attentions to other gentlemen. You've managed to interfere in business that doesn't concern you."

"Why, you uppity tinhorn. What in all creation makes you think I'd want your attention? And don't stand there and gibber at me about spying when you've been skulking all over this place after Augusta Darent. I never saw a more disgusting sight."

Tennant cocked his head to one side and frowned. "Skulking all over? By Jove, you have been following me."

"Have not." Mattie tossed her head, wishing she'd held her tongue. She'd revealed herself, and there was nothing she could do but lie her way out of it. "Dang it. I just happened to be going the same way you were, and when I notice you slinking around the place like a weasel, I got curious. You got no call to—"

Tennant made a slashing motion with his hand. "Spare me more ranting, Miss Bright. I suggest we refrain from discussing this incident further. No good can come of it. I simply ask that you also refrain from speaking of it to anyone else."

"It may surprise you, but I don't find your goings-on all that interesting, and I sure don't find them an entertaining topic of conversation."

"Miss Bright," Tennant said with exaggerated

patience, "is there any possibility that you might give me your word, and that I might trust you to keep it?"

He said it in such a chilly manner, as though his mind were on something much more important. Mattie flushed and realized how ridiculous she seemed, and again how utterly she'd failed to keep her promise to reform. He was used to Lady Augusta, the beautiful Aggie Darent with her cultured, sweet voice and witty ways. She, on the other hand, was a gauche little savage from America whose speech brimmed with countrified expressions and whose culture was a thin layer on top of a rancher's daughter's upbringing. Well, let him go to blazes if he was going to look down on her.

"You want my word?" she asked quietly.

"If you please."

"You got it. Now, if you'll excuse me, I must bid on a Reynolds that's a sight more pleasant to be around than you are."

Not waiting for him to reply, Mattie marched back the way she'd come. Tears nearly blinded her, but she found the doorway that led to the eighteenth century picture gallery. Luckily there was no one else in the room. She dabbed at her eyes with the handkerchief she'd tucked into her sleeve and stood in front of the Reynolds until Mama came to get her.

By the time they got into the carriage to go home, she'd made up her mind. She was going to ignore Cheyne Tennant for the rest of the Season. No matter what he did to provoke her, she wasn't going to retaliate. People were already talking about their antics and betting at the clubs on when the next explosion would take place. Well, they could just wait. She wasn't giving Tennant the satisfaction of thinking she was trying to get his attention. She wasn't going to have anything more to do with that rotten man.

8

Cheyne stalked out of Catchpole's, jumped in a hansom cab and barked at the driver to take him to his club. He was meeting Balfour there to report on his surveillance of Lady Augusta. Still fuming from his quarrel with Miss Bright, he spent the entire journey trying to calm down.

He didn't understand it. No other woman made him explode with fury, but coming within a few hundred yards of the young lady guaranteed disaster. Inevitably he ended up making a spectacle of himself, aided, of course, by Miss Bright. This time, however, his nemesis had witnessed him conducting surveillance. The last thing he wanted was to expose this grave matter to the scrutiny of the unpredictable Miss Bright. There was no telling what insanity she might produce should she blunder into his affairs again. The woman was an affliction upon his existence.

It didn't help that she had no respect for him, or

that she treated him like a wayward schoolboy. He had no regard for titles, but Miss Bright might at least respect his greater years, his experience, his knowledge of civilized Society. When she looked at him as if he were something that crawled out of a rubbish heap, he wanted to shake her.

What was so infuriating was that she looked at him that way while managing to appear like a dark-haired water sprite. All the time she was calling him a skunk her eyes flashed like jet, and she flushed just as he imagined she would under much more intimate circumstances.

The cab jolted to a halt, and Cheyne woke from his stew to find himself at his club. Forcing the image of Matilda Bright out of his mind, he paid the driver. Balfour was waiting for him, and they found a couple of overstuffed armchairs facing each other at one of the bow-front windows.

When a footman had taken their drink orders, Balfour said, "Any luck?"

"Sorry, old man. I don't think she was delivering the money at Catchpole's."

"Not your fault. I asked you to follow her because her husband wants to know the truth but fears a scandal."

"Don't they all?"

"True, but being in Her Majesty's government . . ."

"I know. Look, Balfour. We know the black-mailer must be bribing ladies' maids and valets. They're the ones in a position to see the victims hide incriminating letters and documents. The criminal is someone quite clever at sorting out the ones most afraid of exposure and scandal. That means he's too clever to risk being identified by the police."

"What can I say, old boy? My hands are tied by my superiors, none of whom want to risk their own hides by exposing the secrets of people who could ruin them."

The footman brought their drinks, and Cheyne took a long sip of whiskey. "That's why I think we're going to have to approach this business another way."

"We can't use a Scotland Yard man in Society."

"No," Cheyne said. He leaned back and gazed out the window. "No, but we can provide our own victim and set a trap."

Balfour gave him a surprised look. "You?"

"Not me. Given my well-known opinions, our blackmailer wouldn't attempt to threaten me. He'd know I'd tell him to publish the scandal and be damned."

"Exactly. And anyone with something to hide isn't going to help us."

Swirling the whiskey in his glass, Cheyne watched a lady and gentleman walk down the street and enter the premises of one of the most expensive jewelers in the city. "We need someone who's rich. Very rich. A wealthy person for whom respectability is essential and who therefore is vulnerable. I'd prefer a young lady. The blackmailer would hardly expect Scotland Yard to work with a refined and sheltered young lady."

"Tennant, I wouldn't work with a refined and

sheltered young lady. She'd make a mess of the whole thing."

Cheyne set his glass down and leaned on his knees while he regarded his friend. "What we need is someone known to value position, rank, and wealth above everything. Someone who appears vulnerable yet has the courage and daring to take the risk, and who won't mind if things get a bit rough. We need a young lady who's got some mettle."

"Tennant, old man, there are no bold young ladies in Society."

Cheyne glanced out the window again as a motor-car sailed by, its lamps clattering. He blinked and whistled quietly. "The little colonial."

"The who?"

"Miss Matilda Bright would be perfect."

Balfour was already shaking his head. "No. She's not a British subject, and she's known to the Prince of Wales. Besides, she's too young, and refined— What are you laughing at?"

Suppressing another chuckle, Cheyne said, "Miss Bright was raised on a ranch, Balfour. Her life hasn't been as refined and sheltered as it would appear from her demeanor."

"How do you know?"

"She calls me an uppity tinhorn and a skunk."

At Balfour's amazed glance, Cheyne stopped smiling. "Just take my word. Miss Bright is the perfect victim for us."

"Even if she is, how do you know she'll help?

Wait a minute. Is this the young lady you've been having quarrels with all over London?"

"Heard of that, have you?"

"She won't help you. She doesn't like you, old chap."

Cheyne picked up his glass and watched the sunlight dance in the amber liquid. "Leave Miss Bright to me. I'll manage her."

Several days later Cheyne alighted at Spencer House in St. James's dressed for a formal call. Mutton had provided certain vital information to him regarding the Bright household. The two ladies of the house were at home on Wednesdays, and today Miss Bright was certain to be there to receive a call from the Marquess of Stainfield, better known to Cheyne as Avery "Barmy" Richmond, the most supercilious and condescending of his old school acquaintances.

Barmy was all right as long as you didn't allow him to natter on and on about lineage and heritage and bloodlines. He even had a weightier side to him, having been responsible for an important effort to improve conditions in Her Majesty's prisons. But he approached his good works with an air of noblesse oblige that annoyed Cheyne.

He stopped to admire the eighteenth century town house. Originally built by the first Earl Spencer, it was an unparalleled example of neoclassical architecture. Cheyne admired its symmetry, the Doric portico on the side of the house that faced Green Park and its pediment crowned with statues of Bacchus, Flora, and Ceres.

He was admitted by a butler who took his card and begged him to be seated in the hall. Cheyne looked at the fragile antique chairs and remained standing. He'd presented his old private card, one he rarely used because it had his title on it. As he'd expected, the butler was back immediately to show him into the Palm Room.

As with all the rooms in the house, the Palm Room was based on classical themes, but at one end of the chamber rose four white columns set against rounded arches. The walls were painted a muted green, while each column was plastered and gilded to look like a golden palm. Behind the palms lay a series of coffered arches that led to a window. To his right through the French windows lay a sundrenched terrace. Mrs. Bright saw him enter and rushed over to him.

"Lord Geoffrey, this is an unexpected pleasure. How good of you to call."

Cheyne bowed. "My dear Mrs. Bright, I go by Cheyne to my friends, among whom I hope I may number you and your charming daughter." God, he almost made himself sick when he sounded like that.

As he engaged in small talk with his hostess, he looked for Miss Bright. She was seated between two palm columns talking to Barmy Richmond. There were two other callers with Miss Bright, Sir William Stellaford and his wife, Lady Julia. The Stellafords were known for their lively interest in America and their love of adventure, so Cheyne wasn't surprised that they'd made friends with the Brights. Mrs. Bright led him to join the others, and as he took a chair beside Lady Julia, Miss Bright eyed him with suspicion.

"Tennant, by Jove," barked the marquess.

"Hello, Barmy."

The Marquess of Stainfield sniffed. "I don't go by that name, and you know it."

"Sorry, Barmy, but you're stuck with it among the old Etonians."

He couldn't help it. The moment he came in and saw Stainfield sitting next to Miss Bright, something had gone wrong. He'd never felt one way or the other about Barmy, but suddenly the fellow irritated him.

Barmy Richmond was one of those young men who never seemed to grow into his head. Although he was tall, he was also thin, and his head was quite round, so that he looked like an upside down onion. It didn't help that he wore his hair slicked down with pomade or that his nose came to a decided point, like that of a pencil. Cheyne realized he was being harsh. Some women admired Barmy's looks. They said he was distinguished and refined, that his height was majestic and his features handsome in the manner of a Roman emperor. Disgusting.

"Lord Cheyne, we're planning a journey to America," said Lady Julia. "Miss Bright was just telling us all the best places to see in New York."

"I shall take photographs," announced Sir William.

"Hardly a surprise, old chap," said Barmy. "You drag that confounded box everywhere you go. I'm surprised you don't have it with you now."

"Julia wouldn't let me bring it," said Sir William.

While the others chatted about the new Kodak cameras that allowed anyone to take photographs, Cheyne turned his attention to Miss Bright and smiled at her. She stared back at him without returning his smile.

"What are you doing here?" she asked in a low voice.

"I've come to apologize for my conduct at the antiques emporium."

"Really?"

"Don't sound so skeptical, Miss Bright. I do have manners, you know."

"Really?" She turned to Barmy, dismissing him.

This was going to be difficult. He waited until she rose and went to the bell across the room to ring for tea. Joining her, he nodded at a statue standing in a niche, a Roman woman in a long robe and veil.

"Do you like classical art, Miss Bright?"

"What are you up to?"

Cheyne spread his arms. "I've been thinking about our encounter at Catchpole's, and I have realized how boorish my conduct toward you has been. We began terribly, and that one accident has colored all our dealings. Neither of us has benefited. Don't you think we should call a truce and begin again?"

"It's not my fault you don't look before you cross the street."

"You were going too fast," he snapped. Then he controlled his temper and forced a smile. "I beg your pardon. It's not done, correcting a lady, and I apologize."

"Why?"

Bloody hell, she was too distrustful of him. If he didn't get past her suspicion, his plans would fail. Mustering his most alluring manner, Cheyne tried to adjust his view of Miss Bright and treat her as he would any pretty young lady of his acquaintance.

"Why? Because I have found it most unpleasant to quarrel with such a lovely young woman."

He watched Miss Bright's mouth fall open.

"Oh, blast. I sound like a cheap music-hall actor, don't I? Why is it that one sounds so trite and foolish when one tries to be honest?"

Miss Bright closed her mouth. Then she said, "Thank you."

"For what?"

"It's only polite to say thank you when somebody gives you a compliment."

"Ah." Cheyne tried to remember what compliment he'd paid, but gave up.

A burst of laughter caused both of them to glance at the Stellafords and the marquess. Miss Bright made a move to rejoin them, but Cheyne stalled her.

"I say, Miss Bright. I didn't know you knew old Barmy."

"Haven't known him long. He's a good egg if you don't listen to all that talk about folks' families and such."

"Indeed." He wasn't listening with much attention because he'd noticed that Miss Bright rather resembled the statue by which she was standing. Her skin was as smooth, although certainly not as pale as the white marble. Cheyne must have drifted in his thoughts because Miss Bright was looking at him as if she were waiting for him to say something.

"Oh, yes. Um. I did want to ask you about motorcars, Miss Bright. I'm going to purchase one, and I'd like to know what type you recommend."

Matilda Bright lit up. "I love my Panhard-Levassor. It runs perfectly, starts on the first crank, hardly ever breaks down. Powerful engine, too. And fast."

"I'm aware of that."

She blushed and looked at the carpet on the floor. "Yes, well . . ." She cleared her throat. "Seeing as how you've been good enough to come here, I should admit I might have been going a bit fast." She appeared to make some decision. "Yes, yes, I was. I got carried away. Sometimes I just have to get out of here."

Miss Bright's gaze swept the Palm Room. "Sometimes all this elegance and stateliness is hard to live in, and Mama—sorry—Mama sets great store by elegance and stateliness. That's why . . ."

Seeing that she had lost her courage, Cheyne intervened. "Mrs. Bright has high ambitions, I take it."

"Papa, I mean, my father did, too."

Pain swept over Miss Bright's features and vanished so quickly Cheyne thought he might have imagined it. Then she smiled with pure joy.

"Papa—I mean P*a*p*a*—he and I used to go to galleries and museums together. The first time we went to the Metropolitan Museum of Art and saw the paintings, we both cried."

"Good lord, why?"

"All that beauty. Me and Papa had never seen any of those things except in books. It was better than magic."

Cheyne watched her ebony eyes take on the glassy sheen of unshed tears. Miss Bright had a sensitivity he hadn't expected. "I felt like that once, but it's been a long time."

"People who can paint like that, or make music the way Mozart did, they're the ones who deserve titles. Not folks who just got born into the right family."

"I agree."

She stared at him. "You do?"

"Yes. You're surprised." He grinned at her. "Don't allow your prejudices to color your view of all titled gentlemen, Miss Bright."

At last she smiled at him. "It's a deal, my lord."

"Let's make another deal, Miss Bright. Shall we agree for you to call me Cheyne?"

"Ma*ma* wouldn't approve, but I could call you Lord Cheyne."

"As you wish."

Having somewhat rehabilitated himself in Miss Bright's estimation, Cheyne excused himself and left Spencer House. His spirits soared, and he attributed the feeling to his success in convincing Miss Bright not to detest him. His plan was succeeding. She was well on her way to being his friend.

As he drove home, Cheyne congratulated himself. Miss Bright could be a pleasant person when she wished. She had taste to go along with her beautiful black eyes and hair. As long as she behaved, he could work with her. But he must see to it that there was no repeat of that chase at the Lutterworth ball. That way lay danger.

Two weeks passed during which Cheyne called several times on Mrs. Bright and her daughter. Each time he found Barmy Richmond there. Barmy was beginning to aggravate him more and more. He seemed a fixture at Spencer House, and Cheyne hated the way Mrs. Bright fawned on him. Cheyne's temper grew short, and he had to exercise great discipline not to ask Miss Bright why she wasted her time with such a git, as Mutton would have called him.

After the third week, Cheyne could wait no longer. Employing Mutton as a scout, he arranged to intercept Miss Bright as she was driving at Hyde Park.

He got up before dawn and rode for a while in St. James's Park while waiting for Miss Bright to drive to Rotten Row. He was north of the lake when he heard the mechanical purr of a motorcar and saw his quarry speeding down the Mall toward Buckingham Palace, her driving scarf flapping behind her.

Kicking his mount, Cheyne trotted into the Mall to watch her drive by. She saw him and waved.

As she passed him, he shouted, "Is that the Panhard?"

"Yes," she cried and whipped past him.

There was a loud explosion that made his horse shy. Cheyne's hands convulsed on the reins. The noise was just like gunfire, and it provoked images of the bloody plains of South Africa. Miss Bright's car swerved and stopped suddenly. He mastered his animal and trotted over to her. She pulled on a lever as he arrived.

"Dang it." Miss Bright slid out of her vehicle and walked around the far side to inspect a tire. "A flat."

"A flat what?"

"A flat tire. Must have run over a horseshoe nail or something."

Dismounting, Cheyne joined her and contemplated the squashed-looking tire. "Can't you drive it anyway?"

"Nah, I'd ruin the wheel."

"You mean this thing is stuck here?"

"Until I can get another tire. Don't want to ruin it."

Cheyne smiled. "So it's going to take a team of draft horses to move it. That's funny."

"No, silly. I'll bring the tire here. I usually have one, but I took it out while I was cleaning, and I forgot to put it back in."

"What luck," Cheyne said. "This means I shall be able to do you a service and take you home."

Miss Bright looked taken aback. "Oh. You don't have to do that."

"I should never forgive myself if I allowed you to walk all that way."

"It's not that far. Nothing's far in England. It takes about two weeks just to ride out of Texas."

Cheyne shook his head. "Please, Miss Bright. You'll distress me if you don't allow me to do my duty as a gentleman after my wretched conduct toward you."

"Well . . ."

He offered his arm. "Shall we walk across the bridge and visit the birds before we go? It's a shame to waste this lovely sunlit morning. Old Henry VIII built this park, and I'm sure he'd want us to enjoy it."

Miss Bright hesitated. For some reason she blushed as she consented and placed her hand on his arm. They walked to the bridge that spanned the lake and paused in the middle of it to look at the city in the distance, its spires and domes glistening in the rising sun. Mist floated over the lake, clinging stubbornly to the cool places before the sun chased it away.

Removing her driving hat and veil, Miss Bright leaned on the balustrade, her lips curled into a relaxed smile. Cheyne picked his moment.

"Miss Bright, you're a sensitive young lady, and a lovely one."

She turned to look at him in astonishment. "I never figured you'd be saying that."

"Why, when it's so obviously true?"

Miss Bright shrugged. "Lots of fellas say nice things, but you don't seem the kind of gentleman who—I mean—you and I haven't seen eye to eye."

"True, but that's in the past." He bent down to her and grinned. "Now, you're forbidden to hold that against me. Where's your Christian spirit of forgiveness?"

She smiled back, still flushed. "It means a lot to you, that we get along?"

"A great deal, Miss Bright. May I tell you why?"

9

Mattie couldn't believe that Lord Cheyne, the man who a few weeks ago was her idea of Satan's first assistant, had contrived to meet her alone and court her. Yet here he was standing beside her on the bridge in St. James's Park admiring the sunrise and talking about how lovely she was.

The past few weeks had brought about a sea change in her attitude toward Tennant. His generous effort to make amends had impressed her, especially since she'd been feeling so guilty about her behavior toward him. After all, he hadn't set out to annoy her. Their dealings had been cursed with ill luck and her failure to become a more sweet and gentle person.

So she'd been feeling kindly toward him. How could she not, when he paid her the compliment of admiring her sensitivity? Accustomed to noticing her faults, Mattie had never thought of herself as sensitive. Tennant had shown her an astonishing glimpse of herself. Who would have thought he'd admire her? After all, he'd called her a colonial and a savage.

Narcissa said he was a renegade. Her tales of his rebellion against his conforming parents had knocked little chips in the walls she'd erected against him. The fact that he refused to allow anyone to dictate the course of his life earned him Mattie's respect. She would love to embark upon her own path free of convention and duty, but that would be incompatible with the life of a great lady. And of course Cheyne Tennant had never made a promise to a dying father.

Still, it was a relief to realize that there was at least one man in the world who combined beauty of character with physical perfection. Narcissa said he was "in trade" as an investor in the city. A nobleman who insisted upon earning his living was a rarity. So when Tennant had offered a peace pipe and Narcissa told her a little of his background, Mattie had slowly relinquished her ire. And while she reserved judgment, he'd somehow sneaked into her good graces.

So here she was, talking pleasantly with Lord Cheyne. But she'd never expected him to start behaving like a suitor. Yet he'd just told her it was important to him that they become friends, and now he was going to admit why. Land sakes, what a turn of events. Evidently while they'd been scrapping and playing tricks on each other he'd come to admire her. Otherwise he wouldn't have suddenly made peace.

Mattie swallowed hard again. "I'm listening, my lord."

It was hard to look him square in the eyes, knowing what he was going to say. His profile was like one of those medieval effigies of knights she'd seen in cathedrals. What if she accepted his attentions? She wondered what would happen if he touched her again, the way he had wanted to at the ball. A shiver ran through her as she realized what might happen between them.

"Miss Bright, there's something important I haven't told you."

"Yes?" She'd never seen Tennant at a loss for words. He was much kinder, and at the same time much less self-possessed, than she'd realized.

"You see, I'm rather an odd bloke. Unlike most gentlemen in Society, I have an occupation. I'm a private inquiry agent, an investigator of crimes, and there's a case I'm working on that concerns many of our mutual acquaintances. It's sensitive, and I must ask you to promise not to speak of what I'm about to tell you."

No request to court her. No words of affection at all. Mattie stuttered, "A—A case. Th-that's what you wanted to talk to me about, a case?"

"Yes," Tennant frowned. "What did you think I wanted to say?"

Wake up, Mattie Bright. Don't let him know what a confounded fool you've been.

"Oh, I thought you might . . ." She gripped the balustrade and pretended to gaze at the ducks and swans on the lake. "I thought you might want to talk about motorcars some more."

"No, this is quite a grave matter. May I have your promise to reveal none of what I'm about to say?"

"Sure."

Stupid. Stupid, stupid, stupid. Thinking a fine gentleman like that would be interested in plain old Mattie Bright. He'd want a great lady, which is something it appears you're never going to be. The only fellas that want you are those that need your money. You knew that. Besides, why are you so upset? You don't care anything about Lord Cheyne Tennant.

Mattie struggled to master her confusion and pay attention to what Tennant was saying. When he told her about the blackmail and the deaths, she forgot her embarrassment and disappointment. By the time he'd finished, she was alarmed.

"What a helluva stinking rotten way to treat folks."

Tennant gave her a pain-filled smile. "Indeed, Miss Bright. Most rotten, and I need your help to stop the blackmailer."

Slowly turning to face him, Mattie stared. "Me? What can I do?"

"Help me set a trap for the criminal. I need someone to pose as a victim, someone who has enough tin to tempt the blackmailer, someone whom he'll believe is vulnerable."

"I'm not vulnerable," Mattie said. "I haven't done anything."

"How shall I put this? I require a victim who everyone knows has a vital need for respectability."

"You mean a young unmarried lady."

Tennant cleared his throat. "Yes, and, well, you see, you're perfect because not only are you wealthy, but also because it's well-known that you wish to marry a nobleman of the highest rank. And therefore you must avoid even a hint of scandal."

"Oh." To hide her discomfort, Mattie began to walk across the bridge to the path beside the lake.

Tennant walked with her and watched her with concern. "I would never have mentioned so delicate a subject had it not been a matter of terrible import, Miss Bright."

"Guess it's not a secret," Mattie said faintly. "Plain talk is best."

Sighing, Tennant nodded. "That's another reason I'm talking to you. You're much more independent than most English debutantes, and God knows you're not afraid of adventure or concerned with appearing unladylike."

"You calling me unladylike?" He'd come too near her own estimation of herself, and Mattie had had enough honesty for one day.

"No, no. That is, you've got courage. Not that you'll be in any danger. You need only give the appearance of being engaged in some secret and scandalous behavior. I'll do the rest."

"All those poor people, dead."

"And there'll be more if I can't stop the bastard. Pardon my language, Miss Bright."

Mattie nodded; her thoughts elsewhere. "It's so cruel, to take advantage of a person's weakness like that and to make them suffer." She stopped walking and said, "I'll do it."

"Thank you, Miss Bright. I knew you'd agree, and I told Superintendent Balfour you would."

"You told him," Mattie repeated. She narrowed her eyes. "How long have you been planning to ask me to help?" When Tennant didn't reply, she looked at him, saw the mask of neutral pleasantry on his face and hissed, "You stinking rotten skunk. That's why you suddenly backtracked. You didn't care about being friends. You just wanted to get on my good side so I'd help you."

"Now, Miss Bright. I admit—"

"Ha!" Mattie swept away, turned, and glared at him. "You're a powerful good liar, my lord. And to think I was beginning to feel kindly toward you. I'd actually decided you weren't an uppity, slicked-up weasel."

"That will do, Miss Bright." Tennant stalked over to her. "You're right, I was deceitful in my approach, but that doesn't lessen the gravity of the case. Are you so small as to refuse to help simply to gratify some petty desire to avenge a slight?"

Mattie looked at her hands. "Never said I wouldn't help."

"I'm in your debt."

"Humph. I'm not doing this for you. I'm doing it to catch a polecat that's a sight nastier than you, if that's possible."

"I suggest we agree to refrain from insulting each other until our task is finished."

Shrugging, Mattie started to walk again. "I will if you will."

"Very well. Then we must make plans. You've got to have a guilty secret, Miss Bright, and the most obvious one is a clandestine attachment to someone unsuitable."

"You want me to write some letters that can be stolen like poor Juliet Warrender?"

"Not quite," Tennant said. "All you need is to have in your possession a number of indiscreet letters."

"You mean letters from a man. But I can't just suddenly acquire a bunch of letters. This fella knows his business, and he'll suspect if this correspondence isn't seen to develop. I'll have to get me a lover."

"No!"

Mattie gave him a long-suffering glance. "Not a real one, you simpleton. Everybody knows I'm considering Avery Richmond, so I'm going to have to pretend to lose interest. Then the whole city will start gossiping. If I act a little preoccupied and mope a little, rumors will whip around like cyclones in no time."

"You have a colorful way of putting it, Miss Bright. And for authenticity's sake, we must have a real lover. Someone to write letters to you."

"I could ask Avery."

"Barmy? Good God, no."

"I guess I could write them," she said.

"I shall write them."

Mattie gave him a skeptical look. "See here, my lord. We don't even like each other much."

"If you can act, so can I, Miss Bright."

"If you say so." Mattie headed for the bridge. "So what's his name?"

"Who?"

"My lover," she said. "You're going to have to keep up, if this is going to work, my lord."

"I do wish you'd stop calling me my lord. When I'm not forced to waste my time in Society I go by plain Mr. Tennant."

"Don't see why. You still act like a lord. Oh, don't get all huffy. What about a name for my fictional lover?"

"Michel. Michel François Phillipe Chevalier de Lorraine."

"A Frenchman."

"All young ladies are susceptible to sophisticated and dashing Frenchmen."

"They are, are they?"

"You met him on the Continent last year. He's young, penniless, married, and has two infant sons and a noble, long-suffering wife. Nevertheless, you conceived a violent attachment for young Michel, met him secretly and . . ."

"And?"

"Were indiscreet."

"You mean we became lovers," Mattie said without hesitation.

Tennant appeared rueful. "I forget how different your upbringing was from an English girl's."

"We can't all be born in castles, Mr. Tennant."

"No." He gave her a sideways glance. "Such an affair would ruin any young woman, and an unmarried one in search of a duke's son for a husband can't afford even a suspicion."

"I'm going to be desperate to hide it to keep my reputation."

"Exactly. So you must behave as thought you can't help yourself when Michel writes to you to renew your attachment."

"I'm torn between my ambitions and my desires."

"Let us hope you're believed. Now, what about your lady's maid? Will she succumb to a bribe, or should we provide you with another who's more susceptible?"

"Better find another. Mademoiselle Elise, whose real name is Tillie Nott, is an upright old stick."

"I'll provide a more pliable replacement. Send Tillie home to visit her mother or something."

They reached the motorcar and Tennant's horse.

"I'm going to walk home," Mattie said.

There was nothing that could induce her to climb on a horse with Cheyne Tennant. She watched him ride away in the direction of Hyde Park, then walked toward Lancaster House. Her stride quick, her thoughts racing, she passed St. James's Palace and Marlborough House, and wound her way over to Spencer House. With each step she scolded herself for falling prey to Tennant's pretense of goodwill. Things might have been different if she'd been sweet-natured and more like the other young women in Society. But what was the use of wondering? She was better off remembering that her chief attraction was her fortune. And Mr. Tennant didn't seem interested in that.

She was going to go home and have one of her mirror sessions. That's what was wrong. She hadn't been doing that. Otherwise the lessons of Samuel Pinchot would have been fresh in her mind, and she wouldn't have let secret hopes impinge upon her.

Of course, she hadn't realized she'd been harboring any expectations of Cheyne Tennant. They'd been vague, tentative, and uncertain, but they'd been there. No more. Cheyne Tennant was a skunk—a skunk with an honorable purpose, but a skunk nonetheless.

Once back at Spencer House, Mattie ran up the stone staircase, which was housed in a lofty well designed to imitate a Greek temple interior. Her low spirits lifted slightly, for she loved the plasterwork festive garlands threading between Ionic pilasters on the walls. Rather than risk running into Mama, she retreated to the Music Room. There, in front of a pier glass between the windows, she gave herself what she called her Samuel lecture. The only trouble was that this time it ended in tears.

Mattie slumped onto a Chippendale chair and roughly wiped the tears away. "Dang it. You stop that. No varmint like Tennant is going to get the best of you. Besides, you promised to help him. You aiming to blubber every time you seen him?"

Turning her thoughts to the part she must play to catch the blackmailer, Mattie was drumming her fingers on the arm of the Chippendale chair when

Mama came in with a vase brimming with pale pink roses.

"Oh, there you are, dear. I was wondering where you'd got to. It's almost time to receive callers, so you'd better get dressed." When Mattie didn't answer and continued to drum her fingers, Elsa Jane placed the vase on a table and raised her voice. "Mattie!"

Mattie jumped. "What, Mama?"

"What's got into you? Are you ill?"

"No, Mama."

"I noticed your room is full of newspapers from home again."

"I'm keeping up with the government corruption scandals in New York," Mattie said. "Governor Roosevelt is trying to clean house." She resumed her contemplation of the task before her.

Mrs. Bright plucked a rose from the vase and stuffed it into a more aesthetically pleasing position. "Hmmm. You haven't time to worry about politics. Your marquess is coming to call."

"He's not my marquess, and Mr. Roosevelt is a sight more interesting than Avery. That darned President McKinley is ignoring all the problems back home, you know. Doesn't do a thing about corrupt city governments, the giant gulf between rich folks and the poor or the way some of our friends treat their laborers in their factories." What if she began by confiding in Narcissa about this Chevalier de Lorraine? No, Narcissa didn't gossip about her.

"I'm not giving up my money just because other

people are poor, Mattie Bright. Now you go get dressed."

"What?" She would have to confide in someone with a bigger mouth.

"Honestly, Mattie, what's got into you? It can't be politics or poor folks that's got you so frazzled." Mrs. Bright suddenly became alert. "Is there some gentleman who's caught your eye? He's not a duke, is he?"

All at once Mattie woke from her pondering. "Who's not a duke?"

"This new young man you seem so taken with."

"What young man?"

Mrs. Bright came over to Mattie and shook a finger. "You listen to me, Mattie. Your father would be so disappointed that you haven't married a duke by now. You promised you would and you've had chances, but you've delayed and made excuses." Elsa Jane pulled a lace handkerchief from her sleeve and dabbed at her eyes. "When I think of how hard Papa worked to give us this wonderful life we've got, and how ungrateful you're acting . . ." There was a big sniff.

A boulder slammed into Mattie's heart. She'd forgotten about Papa for a moment. Then she heard Mama sniff with exaggerated hurt again, and something in her snapped. Wasn't she twisting herself into unnatural shapes so she could fit into Society? She'd acquired all the right graces; she spoke with the right accent, when she had to. Mama wouldn't be satisfied until she could refer to Mattie as "my daughter, Her Grace, the duchess."

Scowling, Mattie rose and brushed her skirts. "I'm not ungrateful."

"Then tell me, are you attached to someone else?"

Now was the time to start her pretense. Mattie assumed a guilty expression and turned from her mother.

"No, Mama. There's no one else. What makes you think there is?"

"Then you're going to make yourself agreeable to the marquess this afternoon?"

Mattie gave a dramatic sigh. "I suppose so."

Mrs. Bright watched her daughter closely, but Mattie felt it was too soon to plant more suspicions. She sighed again and wandered toward the door.

"You'll get dressed, then," Mrs. Bright called after her.

"Yes, Mama. I'm going to change." Mattie walked out of the room slowly, as if reluctant to do as she'd been asked.

Three days of this behavior were enough to drive Mrs. Bright into a frenzy. Avery Richmond was annoyed, and Narcissa Potter mystified. On the fourth day Mattie received her first letter from Chevalier by the morning post. The missive was handed to her at the breakfast table by Wynkin the butler. Mattie grabbed it and stuffed it in her pocket, causing her mother to eye her with curiosity. Then she shoveled her eggs into her mouth, mumbled an excuse, and rushed upstairs to read it.

She and Tennant had agreed that some of his letters should come by regular post. A real victim would trust the efficient British postal system for anonymity. Any real correspondence could be delivered by messenger.

In her room, Mattie settled on a chaise longue and opened the letter. She hoped Tennant had managed to be convincing in spite of his aversion to her, otherwise their whole plan would founder. It wasn't long, but it began well.

> *Ma Chère Mathilde,*
>
> *I can no longer remain silent, although I promised to do so last summer when we parted. Those nights we spent together haunt me. I am desolate without you, ma chère.*
>
> *How can I convince you of my love? Shall I tell you in my own language? Tu es ma femme de minuit. Ma belle dame sans merci avec qui je ne désire pas vivre. Tu es tres belle, et dans mon coeur éternellement. Je rêve au Mademoiselle Minuit seulement. Take pity on me, my lady midnight. Je t'implore. Allow me to see you again.*
>
> *I await your reply en douleur.*
> *Michel*

Tennant had enclosed something on a separate sheet. Mattie recognized it from *Romeo and Juliet*:

Oh, she doth teach the torches to burn bright!
It seems she hangs upon the cheek of night
Like a rich jewel in an Ethiop's ear—
Beauty too rich for use, for earth too dear!

Mattie folded the letter and put it back in the envelope. "I dream of my Lady Midnight. Humph. Wouldn'ta thought he could make up such things, him being an English lord and all." In Mattie's experience the English aristocracy were interested in horse racing and card playing, not poetry. And they were more ignorant of their artistic heritage than anyone. They sure didn't produce letters that contained bits of Shakespeare.

Her thoughts drifted back to the letter, and her expression softened as she murmured, "My Lady Midnight."

Wouldn't it have been lovely if he'd really meant the compliment? It would have been even lovelier if he'd meant it and wasn't a skunk.

10

❧

From the Music Room floated the exquisite strains of a Chopin sonata. A maid paused by the open doors, closed her eyes, and listened for a few moments before hurrying to her chores. Inside, the music seemed to float on light. Cheyne's fingers charmed the melody from the grand piano in front of the bow window that looked out on the garden. The semi-circular window, divided into five soaring French doors, allowed the outdoors into the room. It was his favorite in the house. When he was troubled Cheyne often came here and played while he allowed his mind to rest.

Peace was elusive this morning because he was worried about Miss Bright. Had she received the letter? What would she think of it? Composing a love letter to a lady he considered a provocative nuisance had been difficult. If he thought about her lovely neck and midnight hair, he became eloquent; if he remembered what a fool she'd made of him with her assorted tricks, he wanted to strangle her. What man could fall in love with a young woman who acted as if she were still on the prairie among the cowboys and cattle?

He finished the sonata and began an étude. His lip curled in bitter amusement. This piece had been composed by his father. That little discovery had brought some measure of tranquillity to his chaotic world. He'd been fourteen and furious at the duke for selling his favorite gelding. A fight had broken out during which His Grace had become apoplectic.

"You're a bully, a bloody ignorant bully!" Cheyne had shouted.

The duke roared, yanked him by the collar and backhanded his son. The blow sent Cheyne sprawling on his back. Before the boy could recover, Bracewell pounced on him.

"I curse the day you were born. I should have made your mother get rid of you, you bastard. God, I've wanted to say that for fourteen years. You're a bastard, do you hear? You're not my son, and I thank God for it!"

The words echoed in Cheyne's ears even now. Stunned, he'd gone to his mother for the truth. She admitted in her offhand way that there had been a brief liaison with a young French composer, Michel de Lorraine. He'd died of consumption a few years after Cheyne had been born.

The last notes of the étude died away, but Cheyne remained at the piano staring at the black-and-white keys. After he'd discovered the truth, the world had made sense. With time he'd stopped trying to earn the duke's love, or even his respect. And from this experience a gradual enlightenment unfolded—a man should earn his place in the world, depending on merit and not arbitrary inheritance. His real father's talent should have—would have—given him a place of honor among men. Ignorant bullies like the duke deserved none.

This novel viewpoint pitted him against his class. It was why he couldn't endure Society. The Americans had the right idea. Luxury, privilege, possessions should be earned. This attitude made the behavior of Miss Bright and her ilk incomprehensible. Why turn against the values that made one's wealth possible? Cheyne shook his head. He would have thought Miss Bright would have more sense, but perhaps she was as shallow as any aspirant to social position.

No, she couldn't be as vapid as it would appear, for she had been quite willing to help him catch the blackmailer. Cheyne shook his head. He didn't understand her, but understanding wasn't required. In any case, there was no comprehending a wealthy young lady, who was barely civilized, used rough language, drove motorcars and played hideous tricks on unsuspecting, innocent gentlemen. There was no comprehending a young woman who could wear a mannish driving costume and yet look like a princess.

Cheyne was smiling to himself when Mutton appeared beside him. "Dora Snape has come, gov'nor."

"Who?"

"Me niece, Dora Snape, what you asked me to send to be lady's maid to Miss Bright."

"Oh, yes. Send her in."

Cheyne got up to meet his visitor. A neat woman in a black suit and hat came in and curtsied. With her severe costume and tight bun, Dora Snape looked like a packaged patent medicine.

"I come as soon as I could get away, sir." Dora's speech was a bit more grammatical than her uncle's, but it would have to be if she was to be a lady's maid.

"Thank you, Miss Snape, and how are things going at Spencer House?"

"Very well, sir. Miss Bright is a pleasure to work for."

"Is she? That's a surprise." He stopped when Dora produced an envelope from her bag and held it out. "What's this?"

"It's from Miss Bright. The correspondence you said you was developing on account of the blackmailer."

Cheyne took the ivory envelope and tossed it on the piano bench. It bore no address, since this time Miss Bright had employed her maid to ferry the communications to and from her would-be lover. His instructions had been for her to stuff the envelope with blank sheets. There was no need for both of them to compose letters.

"Thank you, Miss Snape." Pulling another envelope from his inner coat pocket, Cheyne handed it to the maid. "Take this to your mistress, and send word to me the moment the blackmailer contacts you."

"Yes, sir." Dora hesitated.

"Was there something else?"

"Miss Bright said to tell you she thought she should write letters, too, to be authentic-like."

"Indeed?" Cheyne glanced apprehensively at the envelope on the piano bench. "Please tell her not to send any more. There's no need."

"I'll tell her, but she's made up her mind, and I don't think she'll pay no heed to me."

"Hmmm. Very well. Wait a moment."

He went to a small writing table and penned a note to Miss Bright. If she was taking initiatives on her own, she would endanger his plan and herself. She was headstrong, so he'd have to speak to her in person, which meant a clandestine meeting immediately. Might as well use the opportunity to make it appear that Miss Bright was meeting Chevalier.

He finished the note and sent Dora on her way. Then he opened Miss Bright's letter.

> *Michel,*
> *What heaven and hell to read your letter. You know what it cost me to give you up, and now I have it to do over again. Do you want me to end in madness? Please, leave me alone. I can't bear even to see your handwriting and know it is impossible to see your dear self.*
> *Forever,*
> *Mattie*

Cheyne stared at the bold strokes of the fountain pen. In her writing Miss Bright was less prone to those colorful frontier expressions and far more grammatical. But the essential Mattie came through, for the directness of the words jolted him. For he'd almost forgotten they were for a fictitious lover. Sparse, powerful, the language drew him in.

"Stop it, you fool. It's only a game."

He turned to the second page.

> *If ever thou shalt love,*
> *In the sweet pangs of it remember me;*
> *For such as I am all true lovers are,*
> *Unstaid and skittish in all motions else*
> *Save in the constant image of the creature*
> *That is beloved.*

Cheyne sat down on the piano bench slowly, his gaze fixed on the quotation. "For such as I am all true lovers are."

A breeze set sail to the pale green curtains, and Cheyne lifted his gaze past the windows to the garden. June had come, and with it the fullness of summer. Sunlit sprays of bluebells danced with delicate columbine. Miss Bright would like his garden, he was sure of it. She liked flowers, for she wore them often, nestling in her hair, at her waist or at her neck. And she always smelled as if she'd just stepped inside from a cool, breezy rose garden.

The wind riffled the pages of the letter in his hands and broke the spell of the garden. Cheyne blinked rapidly and swore. He started to crumple the sheets, but his hands froze. With deliberation he folded them, placed them in the envelope and slipped them in his coat pocket. He might need the letter. Yes, that's right. He might need to refer to it when he wrote another letter from Michel, which he'd do this evening. In the meantime, he would meet Miss Bright this afternoon and order her to follow his instructions in all things. She couldn't take action on her own. It was too dangerous, and the outcome unpredictable.

Leaving the Music Room, Cheyne went to his apartments and dressed to go out. All the while he felt vaguely disgruntled and irritated with Miss Bright. The fact that she'd earned the respect of Dora Snape without trying seemed a deliberate challenge to him. And the letter started to annoy him. He kept picturing her in some feminine bower writing it. How had she known what to write? She must have conducted a similar correspondence, perhaps in America.

By the time he hailed a hansom and jumped into it, Cheyne was in a carefully controlled temper. Miss Bright would have to resist any impulses to exercise her skills in the composition of love letters. From what he'd read, she needed little practice, and he could do without the distraction. At the thought of how easily he'd been swayed by her words his irritation grew. When he arrived in Parliament Square he dismissed the cab and stalked across the green to Westminster Abbey. Hardly glancing at the spires that pierced the sky, he entered through the great west doors and paused in the nave.

Before him soared the graceful Gothic fan vaulting that topped three tiers of arches—clerestory triforium and main nave. Ethereal, majestic, ancient, the beauty of Westminster always caught him off guard. Around him visitors moved through the shadows and paused before flagstones engraved with the names of notables buried under the floor. Here and there walked clergymen who tended the abbey and answered visitors' questions. Cheyne had chosen this meeting place because so many people came here; two more wouldn't be noticed, and no one in Society would bother to visit.

He wandered down the nave, glancing up as if examining the stonework, then down to the ribbed columns that upheld the roof. He turned left into the north aisle, brushing up against a stone image of some medieval church dignitary. It was begun on the site of a church established by Edward the Confessor in the eleventh century, and the English had been building Westminster and refining it ever since. It was stuffed with monuments. Its aisles, side chambers, transepts, and chapels overflowed with relics accumulated over eight centuries.

The caretakers had to stack effigies, screens, and stonework in every corner to make room, so that one was likely to encounter the head of a medieval knight resting atop a reclining Baroque statue, on top of which might lay a medieval screen. Walking past the choir, Cheyne moved in shadow across the north transept.

The longer he remained here, the more weighed

down with history he felt. This was the place where every sovereign except Edward V had been crowned. Henry VII, the founder of the Tudor dynasty, lay here with his wife, Elizabeth of York, as well as many Plantagenet kings and countless noble families like the Percys. But what caught at Cheyne's heart was the little tomb of Geoffrey Chaucer. In his opinion Chaucer and George Frideric Handel deserved their places in the abbey far more than did some of the nobles whose ornate monuments crowded the old cathedral.

He'd reached the stairs behind the chapel of Edward the Confessor and entered the Henry VII chapel, turned right again and slipped into the north aisle. Here rested the joint tomb of bloody Mary and her sister, the great Elizabeth. There were no visitors in this area at the moment, and the chapel was quiet. Cheyne walked to the corner of the tomb and glanced around the chapel for Miss Bright. She wasn't here.

His steps echoing in the empty space, he walked to the other side of the tomb and surveyed its veined white marble surmounted by black columns. He studied the hawk-nosed effigy of Elizabeth I in the silence of this stone cavern. The sculptor had reproduced the queen's masklike features and ornate costume so faithfully, Cheyne expected her to open her eyes and rise from the catafalque.

The woman beneath this effigy had been dead since 1603. Almost everyone in the cathedral had been dead for centuries. His gaze drifted down the queen's figure to the foot of the tomb, and something rose from the grave. Cheyne gasped, then cursed as Miss Bright placed her hands on the effigy and got to her feet.

"Dang. There's a lot of dead people in here."

"Damn it, Miss Bright, what were you doing down there?"

"Reading the inscription."

"It's in Latin."

"I know, but I like to read it anyway."

Looking over his shoulder to make sure they were alone, Cheyne offered his arm. Miss Bright stared at it, then took it, barely touching his coat sleeve.

He rolled his eyes. "Miss Bright, we've got to appear like any other couple visiting a historic monument. I have no evil intentions."

She looked up at him, her dark eyes snapping with ire. "I know that. I'm not stupid."

"Merely ignorant," Cheyne snapped.

He regretted his impulsive words at once, for Miss Bright freed her hand, whirled around and sneered at him. "Listen to the college man. I declare, Mr. Tennant, you musta had a powerful lot of book larnin' in that big school o' yorn. Bet you cud read that there Latin like greased lightnin'."

"Shhh! Will you please stop playing the country bumpkin? It doesn't suit you."

"I thought you said I was a savage colonial."

"I find that there are degrees of savagery."

"You throwing me a bone of approval, Mr. Tennant? How generous."

Cheyne raised his gaze and prayed for patience. "I regret my poor choice of words, Miss Bright. You're obviously educated, more so than many English girls."

"Dang right."

Cheyne bowed and offered his arm again. She took it as several visitors came in. The whispering of the newcomers faded as he guided her across the chapel to the south aisle. They reached the small effigy of Henry VII's mother and were alone again. Miss Bright dropped his arm, went to the opposite side and faced him over the stone image. Raising a brow, she folded her arms and said nothing.

Another flash of irritation made Cheyne grit his teeth. It was disconcerting to feel so infuriated with a young woman whose appearance was so arresting. She wore her pearl-gray suit as if it were a simple maid's uniform, yet the style suited her. Severe pleats crossed her shoulders and fell down the front of the gown. The open jacket revealed a pale pink blouse with pearl buttons, and it was trimmed with delicate embroidery. A jaunty hat with pearl-gray ostrich feathers perched atop her upswept hair. The clothes, the colors and the matching parasol combined to create the impression of a princess out for a stroll. The stark contrast between her obsidian hair and the pearl gray captured the attention. Cheyne was distracted trying to decide if the color of her blouse was the same as her lips.

"Well?" Miss Bright tapped her foot on the flagstones. "What did you want to see me about?"

"Oh, er, yes. It's about your letter. There's no

need to send me any. The blackmailer will ask the maid for the ones you'll keep in your room, not the ones you supposedly sent to me."

"You don't know that."

It was Cheyne's turn to raise an eyebrow. "My dear Miss Bright, I'm the private inquiry agent, not you. I assure you that the criminal will bribe your maid and not bother with me."

"You don't know how closely we're going to be watched. You don't know when he's going to waylay Dora or contact her or what. He might stop her on her way to deliver a letter. I would. Less risk of being spotted. If he looks at the letter from me and finds blank sheets, we're ruined."

"None of the servants in the previous cases were waylaid."

"Doesn't mean they won't be."

His manner stiff, Cheyne said, "Miss Bright, I don't want you to write any more disguised and colorable letters."

"Disguised and colorable?"

"That was how bloody Mary described Elizabeth's letters to her protesting her devotion."

Dropping her parasol on the effigy, Miss Bright said, "Now, you see here, Mr. Tennant, I'm going to write the blamed letters because that's what a girl in love would do. And you've got to answer them."

Cheyne threw up his hands and walked away from her. "This is a trap, Miss Bright, not a romance."

When there was no reply, he turned. She was glaring at him, her cheeks crimson. Her voice was low, but in the lofty space of the aisle it shot into him like electricity.

"That does it. I've had enough of your nasty temper and rattlesnake tongue. I may have to put up with a passel of money-hungry suitors for Papa's sake, but I don't have to put up with the likes of you."

He'd done it again—lost his temper and antagonized her. He had to find some way of reconciling his feelings toward her.

Clearing his throat, he swiftly approached the tomb and inclined his head. "I apologize, Miss Bright. I was snappish, and it was uncalled for. Please forgive me."

"You wouldn't have to apologize all the time if you'd keep your manners."

"I seldom have trouble keeping my manners, as you put it." They regarded each other quietly. Then he said, "Why for your father's sake?"

She looked at him in confusion.

"You said you had to endure your money-hungry suitors for your father's sake."

"Oh." Miss Bright looked down at her parasol and touched one of its pearl-gray ruffles. "I promised Papa I'd make something of myself by marrying well. Papa set a powerful store by gentility, and he figured that a noble family was the most genteel of all. But he—he died, you see."

"Yes?" he asked gently. When she didn't answer, he said, "Come, Miss Bright. We're to be partners in a dangerous game. Perhaps we should know more about each other."

She shot a look at him. "You first."

"What do you mean?"

"If we're telling secrets, you go first."

"Ah, I see." He shrugged. "Very well. If you must know, my own father is a perfectly appalling blighter. The word *art* is a curse word to him. He uses books for firewood, and he has the sensitivity of a fence post."

"Oh."

"So you can see why I'm not enamored of Society and the idea of lineage."

"You like art and books, and he doesn't. He must think you're a . . ."

"Indeed." Cheyne smiled. "My military career annoyed him tremendously."

Miss Bright smiled back at him.

"So," he said. "Why did you make such a promise to your father?"

Picking up her parasol, Miss Bright twirled it. "Papa wore himself out making us rich. Wore himself into the grave, I think. The doctors said it was his heart. And when he was dying, he begged me to make him proud by bringing a title into the family. See, back home we weren't accepted. The society folks thought we were uncivilized like you do. Mrs. Astor called Papa crude and boorish, even though she'd never met him. Nearly broke his heart." She put a hand on the tomb and leaned toward him. "You see, Papa loved all the fine things people have made in the world, like great art, and music, and beautiful houses. He wanted to share his love, and he thought Society people were the ones to do it with."

"Unfortunate."

"Yes, I know." Miss Bright straightened. "He never realized what they were really like. He never wanted to give up his dream."

Cheyne walked around the tomb and stopped in front of Miss Bright. "And when he knew he was dying, he asked you to carry on making his dream real."

"I guess you could say that." She sighed. "Anyway, I promised, and I've never broken a promise to Papa. Not going to start now. And of course there's Mama. Ma*ma*."

"Who has a more practical view of the benefits of a good marriage."

Miss Bright chuckled, causing Cheyne to feel gratified that he'd lifted her spirits. She'd seemed so sad when she spoke of her father.

"Pardon me, Miss Bright, but don't you think it's unwise to make so crucial a choice based on the wish of someone who's gone?"

"And on what would you base that choice, Mr. Tennant?"

"On the merits of the gentleman in question."

"Kind of like choosing a good horse?"

It was Cheyne's turn to flush. "It's better than choosing a man for an accident of birth. A more shallow and vapid manner of reasoning I've never encountered."

Miss Bright stabbed the tip of her parasol into the flagstones. "That's enough. You keep your sour opinions to yourself, 'cause you got no call to set yourself up as my judge, Mr. Saintly Tennant. Just you write those letters, and I'll write mine. The sooner we catch this blackmailer, the sooner I'll be rid of you."

"I agree," Cheyne said. He gave her a mocking bow and offered his arm.

Miss Bright snorted, turned in a whirl of pearl-colored skirts and vanished through an archway.

11

She had lost the will to marry.

It was the first week of August, and Mattie sat at the secretary desk in her bedroom with the antique French gilt box that held Cheyne Tennant's letters. She opened the box and placed his latest missive on top of the pile, then opened the cabinet in front of her and placed it inside. Dora was bringing her dress for this evening's dinner party. The electric lights flickered, then settled down. It was the third time this week, and Mama was threatening to resort to candles.

She sighed and took up her pen, then put it down. During the almost two months she'd been engaged in this plot to catch the blackmailer she'd received seven letters, each of which served to make her feel worse than the one before. Reading them had made her realize what was missing from her life and from her relationships with her suitors.

Violent passion, a grand love that swept away any milder affection—these she never felt when she was with Avery Richmond. The only man who evoked passion in her was Cheyne Tennant.

Mattie's hand reached for the cabinet, hesitated, and then opened it. She took out the newest letter and read it again.

Ma Chère,

You make my life complete, and without you there is nothing. I meant what I said when we last met. I cannot imagine the rest of my life without you. C'est vrai. When I think of you, my world brightens. But the longer we are apart, the more bleak the days become until the sun no longer burns through the clouds of misery in my soul.

To see you with your obsidian hair and jet-black eyes is to see a midnight sun. The fire of your lips keeps me warm, your gentleness quiets the storm of suffering within me. In your presence I am complete. When you left me I hated you, but you have made me understand, et tout comprendre c'est tout pardonner.

À bientôt, my love,
Michel

Mattie sighed and put the letter back in the box. She'd never imagined that Mr. High and Mighty Cheyne Tennant could write like that. Each time she received one of the envelopes, she had to prepare herself to read them. She'd tell herself he didn't mean what he wrote, he was just pretending, he didn't feel the emotions he described. It did no good. She would read his words and long to inspire them, to have someone say them to her, to feel as passionate as the imaginary lovers they had created.

What was even harder was having to respond, to match the emotions and the appeal of those letters. She should have done as Mr. Tennant asked and not written responses. She would have saved herself a lot of misery.

Hardest of all was separating Cheyne Tennant from the letters he wrote. She knew he was pretending, but against her will she felt the appeal of the man who could write the way he did. What would it be like to be loved by such a man?

Yes, she'd lost the will to marry. On top of that her efforts to reform her character seemed futile. Every time she behaved well, Tennant would destroy all her good intentions either by making her mad or by sending her one of his magical letters.

There was a knock at her door. Mattie shut the cabinet and rose as Dora entered holding a dinner gown draped over her arms.

"Phew. This thing's heavy, miss."

"Hmmm." Mattie looked at the dress glumly.

Dora spread the gown on the bed, and they stood surveying it. Mama was giving her last dinner party of the season, a small one. Mattie was certain her mother intended it as an opportunity for the Marquess of Stainfield to propose. Wearing this particular dinner gown had been a special request of Mama's. The dress had four skirts—teal-blue *peau de soie* under accordion-pleated chiffon under plain chiffon and then a lace overskirt.

"That, Dora, is what's called a décolleté dress, which means it practically doesn't have a neck. And the weight of all those skirts makes it hard to keep it from slipping down, if you know what I mean."

"Yes, miss."

Mattie glanced at the maid. "No sign of the blackmailer today?"

"No, miss."

"Something better happen soon. The Season's almost over, and Parliament adjourns next week."

"Now, miss, you know what Mr. Tennant said. It'll take a bit of time for the blackmailer to get wind of the affair, and time for him to plan his move."

"I know," Mattie said. She slipped off her dressing gown. "Help me climb into this rig, and then you can have your night off. You've been working straight since you came. One night isn't going to hurt, and Mama's maid can see to my hair."

"Thank you, miss."

An hour later Mattie helped her mother receive their guests in the hall of Spencer House. Mama had invited the Countess of Ixworth and Mr. Cheyne Tennant, the Honorable Lancelot Gordon, Dr. Elland Capgrave, Narcissa Potter, Sir William and Lady Julia Stellaford and, of course, Avery.

Sir William and Lady Julia were the first to arrive. Sir William was a hearty young man of solid build with eyes that belonged to a humorist on a music-hall stage, and his *joie de vivre* found its match in his wife's ability to look at the world through a lens of merriment. He'd brought his new Kodak camera box with the intention of commemorating Mrs. Bright's last dinner party.

"Shall I have to sit very still?" Mrs. Bright asked.

Sir William grinned and held up the camera box. "No, dear lady. I push a button, and it's over."

"Sir William has photographs of Egypt and Persia, Mama," Mattie said.

As Mrs. Bright chatted with the Stellafords and Avery, Mattie turned to see Cheyne Tennant enter with his friend Lancelot Gordon. Tennant greeted her coolly and went to introduce Gordon to Narcissa Potter. Soon everyone had arrived and assembled in the Painted Room upstairs. Mattie spent most of the time talking to Rose Marie and Dr. Capgrave in order to avoid Avery. He was growing more attentive, and she suspected he'd soon make an offer of marriage.

"You were very kind to have invited me," the countess said.

"Nonsense," Mattie said. "You're one of the few ladies in Society who can put two sentences together and make sense. You and I are going to have a long talk about women's suffrage here in England."

"I shall be delighted, my dear."

"Of course, I'm sure we'll scandalize your friends with such talk," Mattie said.

Rose Marie nodded. "Yes, but the greatest obstacle before us is the fact that women don't have money."

"I do."

"But you're an exception." Rose Marie put her hand on Mattie's arm and drew her aside. "Ask some of your married friends. Most of them hardly see ten pounds cash in a month. They have accounts with merchants, and their husbands pay the bills. There lies the source of a husband's power and a wife's dependency."

Rose Marie's body was stiff with repressed indignation. "The great Society hostesses who refuse to call on me don't know the value of tuppence, much less a pound."

Mattie caught a glimpse of deep unhappiness in the countess's eyes and turned the conversation in another direction. She couldn't imagine what it would feel like to be rejected publicly year after year. Rose Marie Seton had given countless balls, contributed a fortune to Society's favorite charities, all to no good. Her low birth counted more than her good character. Rich Americans escaped this ostracism in spite of their origins, mostly due to their vast fortunes and the patronage of the Prince of Wales. Mattie wouldn't have blamed Rose Marie if the woman had resented her for the ease with which she'd been accepted in the highest circles.

While Mattie was contemplating the unfairness of life, Lancelot Gordon sought out the countess, and she was joined by Dr. Capgrave.

"Are you as contemptuous of Society as you were a few months ago, Miss Bright?" Dr. Capgrave asked her.

Mattie had been watching Tennant, who was part

of the group around Narcissa, but dragged her attention back to the doctor. "I'm not contemptuous."

Capgrave only smiled. He was from an old county family the lineage of which predated that of the royal family, and Mattie remembered Mama saying that he came to London more for the theater, the opera, and the paintings he could buy than for the delights of the Season. Tennant had told her Dr. Capgrave's lack of a title or position was deceptive. His friend had a unique ability to bring men of power together and convince them to work together. His opinions influenced ministers, royal judges, banking magnates, and generals. Leonine and auburn-haired, he appeared younger than his forty-five years and looked at the world through a heavy-lidded gaze.

"He's a remarkable young man," Capgrave said.

"Who?"

"Cheyne," Capgrave said with a look of amusement. "I noticed that you've been staring at him."

"I don't think so," Mattie said, hoping her face wasn't pink.

"You needn't protest. You wouldn't be the first young lady to lose her heart to him. But I wouldn't take too long to recover. Cheyne has never lost his in return, and I encourage him not to."

Mattie gave Capgrave her full attention. "Why not?"

"How shall I put it? Let me just say that Cheyne has demons to fight, and in any case I have plans for him."

"Oh?"

"I've been trying to get him to stand for Parliament. He'd make an excellent M.P."

"That doesn't sound like something Mr. Tennant would want to do."

"Cheyne doesn't know what he wants. Not completely. In time, I shall guide him to the right choice."

"Really? I didn't know you had that kind of power." Capgrave laughed gently, and goose bumps raised on Mattie's arms at the sound.

"Power, Miss Bright, especially the power to mold and influence strong minds, is the ultimate gratification."

Mattie stared at Capgrave, round-eyed.

"I meant to ask you if you would speak to Cheyne about his future, as he seems to value your opinion."

"I think you're mistaken. Mr. Tennant has only just learned to tolerate me."

"Nonsense. He has spoken of you with admiration several times." Capgrave glanced at the subject of their conversation, his gaze resting on Tennant with lazy speculation. "You might say he's softened toward you."

"You are talking about Mr. Tennant? There's nothing soft about him."

Capgrave's gaze remained on Tennant, who was deep in conversation with Lancelot Gordon. "I disagree, Miss Bright. While it's true that he was a ruthless military officer, he was also a gentle and affectionate child." He turned to give her a slight smile. "And I assure you he speaks of you with regard. He called you valiant."

"Dang."

"I beg your pardon?"

"Oh, nothing. I'm most gratified, Dr. Capgrave."

Mattie marveled at Capgrave's remarks as the company went down to dinner. They were proceeding two by two down the staircase when the lights flickered and went out.

"Wait, everyone," Mattie said. "They come back on quickly."

They waited, but nothing happened, and confusion resulted when Mrs. Bright tried to go back upstairs, nearly sending Sir William toppling over the banister. People separated and went in different directions, and it took a while for the servants to bring candles. A few more minutes passed while the guests found the dining room from wherever they'd wandered. Eventually the electricity burst to life, and the dinner progressed with an animated discussion of the perils of the new form of power.

"It's just that the steam turbine needs work," Mattie said.

Mama sniffed. "I don't approve of newfangled inventions. Ladies, shall we have coffee in the drawing room?"

Mattie followed their guests until Mama stopped her. "Dear, would you fetch my shawl? I think I left it in the Painted Room."

Hurrying upstairs, Mattie was searching the Painted

Room when she heard the door shut. She turned to find the Marquess of Stainfield standing with his back to it. Avery had slicked back his hair to reveal his aristocratic bone structure. His legs were long in proportion to the rest of his body, and he reminded Mattie of a regal greyhound.

"What are you doing, my lord?"

"Please, call me Avery."

"I don't think so."

"Your mother was kind enough to arrange this moment with you, my dear." Stainfield rushed to her and grabbed her hand. "Dearest, sweetest Matilda, you can't be unaware of the regard in which I hold you. Over these past months I've come to cherish you. Your beauty is divine, and your—"

"Stop, my lord." Mattie disentangled her hand and stepped back. "You don't want to say these things."

"Yes, I do." Swooping at her, Stainfield captured her hand again and kissed it. "Please allow me to say how much I adore you."

"No."

Stainfield blinked. "No?"

"No, you can't say how much you adore me. Not now."

Mattie pried her hand free and retreated to put a sofa between her and Stainfield. She was alarmed by her unexpected revulsion for this man whom she'd taken so much care to encourage. When he touched her, all she could think of was how soft and clammy his hands were. He spoke words of ardor, but there was something missing. He wasn't acting like Cheyne

Tennant had at the Lutterworth ball. When Cheyne had held her, he'd been driven by an urge so desperate that it had communicated itself without his saying a word. Stainfield needed too many words.

Stainfield had been staring at her in disbelief. He rushed around the sofa, and Mattie backed away until she hit the fireplace mantel. Her pursuer snatched her hand again and kissed it.

"Dear Matilda, I can't wait."

Trying to pull her hand free, Mattie said, "Yes, you can."

Stainfield pressed her hand to his heart, then started kissing it.

"When, then, my dearest?"

"Next year."

Stainfield stopped kissing her hand. "That will be too late!"

"Too late for what?" asked Mattie as she twisted her hand in his grip.

"Oh, er, nothing. Forget what I said."

He moved closer, and Mattie's vision filled with his lips. She gasped and shoved him, but he still clung to her hand. Darting sideways, she yanked on it.

"Let go, dang it."

A low voice interrupted Stainfield's refusal. "I should do as the lady requests, Barmy, or I shall pull both your arms off, then stuff them down your throat."

Mattie stopped struggling to stare at Cheyne Tennant. He was on the threshold, one hand at his side clenched in a tight fist, the other behind his back.

His gaze was fixed on Stainfield with the intensity of a cobra eyeing a rat. Stainfield dropped her hand.

"See here, Tennant. This is none of your affair."

"That's where you're wrong." Tennant strolled over to the marquess. "You've refused the request of a lady. No gentleman would stand by and witness it. Go down to the drawing room, Barmy."

Stainfield straightened his coat. "I shan't. You go."

Tennant sighed. Then his hand lashed out to grab Stainfield's arm, which he twisted behind his back. Mattie gawked at the two as Tennant ushered his captive out the door and shut it. He returned to her, the corners of his mouth turned down, his brow furrowed.

"Are you all right?"

Mattie recovered herself. "Oh. Yes, yes."

Tennant moved nearer, and Mattie's eyes widened when he reached for her. She took a step away, but his hand reached for a curl that had come undone from its pin in her struggle with Stainfield. She held her breath while his fingers stroked the curl. Drawing close, he drew the curl up and plucked a pin from her hair to fasten it in place. All she could feel was a strange pulsing energy that enveloped her. Tennant lowered his hands and stepped back, leaving her bereft and disappointed. She nearly jumped when he took her hand. She stared at it, amazed at the way it vanished inside his. He turned her arm over and scowled at the red marks on it.

"If he's marked you, I'll whip him from here to Kensington Palace."

She lifted her gaze to his, and the room faded. His eyes narrowed, then widened, and his breathing grew more rapid. Somehow he was closer than he'd been. Mattie held herself still as he leaned down, slowly, as if his mind were fighting his body. She wanted to scream. After what seemed hours, Mattie felt his lips brush hers with the slightest of pressures, like the sweep of a feather against her skin. His breath entered her mouth. Then he stopped. Sucking in that hypnotic breath, he pulled back and dropped her hand. Avoiding her eyes, he turned from her.

"I should . . . Damn."

"Why did you—"

Tennant's hand sliced the air. "Don't ask the question, Miss Bright. Let's just say I was dazzled by the midnight sun."

Before she could say anything, he was gone. Mattie stared at the closed door for a long time. She finally snapped out of her daze.

"The shawl. I came up here for the shawl. Yes, got to fetch the shawl."

It wasn't in the Painted Room. Distracted, Mattie retrieved one from her mother's room. On her way back she noticed that the door to her own room was slightly ajar.

"The letters," she muttered.

In her bedroom nothing seemed amiss. She went to the secretary and noticed that the chair in front of it was at an angle. She opened the cabinet, took out the gilt box and lifted the lid. The letters were gone.

Desolation rushed over her. All her beautiful let-

ters, gone. She felt a sense of loss so great she nearly
started crying. The strength of her grief startled
Mattie. Cheyne's letters were gone. She hadn't realized how much they meant to her until now, and
there was nothing to replace them. He would never
repeat the things he'd written to her. Never speak of
love as he had written about it in those letters.

What was she thinking? She didn't want Cheyne
Tennant to say such things to her. *Forget about
love, Mattie Bright. Love and Cheyne Tennant—you're
being ridiculous.*

She had more important matters to think about.
The blackmailer had been in her room, for God's sake.

Fear shuddered through her. Someone had stolen
the letters between the time she left her room to
greet her guests and now. That meant that the blackmailer or an ally of his was in the house. Dora was
gone, and the rest of the servants were busy downstairs under the eye of Wynkin.

"Land sakes," Mattie said to herself. "It's one of
the guests."

She controlled her agitation, replaced the letter
box, and went downstairs with the shawl. The rest of
the evening passed uneventfully, with Mattie studying each visitor with secret wonder. Someone in the
drawing room was a blackmailer.

Tennant. She had to tell him. There wasn't an opportunity until people began to leave, but as he
waited for Wynkin to bring his coat, she passed by
him and whispered, "The letters are gone. Come
back tonight at one."

He moved away to allow Wynkin to help him with his coat. In moments he was bowing over her hand.

"Good evening, Miss Bright. A clear sky with a veil of stars. One always wonders what mysteries are abroad on such a night."

12

❧❧❧

Still wearing his evening clothes Cheyne threw his
coat over his shoulders and slipped out of his house.
His hand was on the latch of the wrought-iron gate
surrounding the service yard when a bulky form
emerged from the darkness.

"Going, are you?"

"Blast it, Mutton, don't creep up on me like that."
Cheyne went through the gate and shut it before Mutton could follow. "I told you earlier, you're
not going."

"He's shown his face, so to speak. He'll be wary."

"The blackmailer won't return to Spencer House
tonight. I'm going to speak with Miss Bright and
find out what happened. I don't need you."

"Right."

"Go to bed," Cheyne said.

"Right."

Shaking his head, Cheyne set off for Spencer

House. He took a cab to Green Park and walked across the grass.

It had begun. The rat had taken the bait, and he should feel elated. Cheyne paused beside a plane tree, fighting the rage that had exploded in him when he had encountered Barmy Richmond pawing Miss Bright. The gentlemen had been passing around the port after dinner when Barmy excused himself. Cheyne noticed a peculiarly avid expression on his face. Intrigued, he'd followed his old school friend, saw him speak to Mrs. Bright and then go upstairs. Curiosity took him the rest of the way, but he almost left when he saw Barmy join Miss Bright in the Painted Room. He struggled with his conscience, but not long. It had been easy to open the door in order to see what Barmy was about.

Cheyne hadn't expected to react the way he had. Seeing Barmy clutching Mattie Bright had aroused something in him he'd thought he'd left behind in South Africa. There he'd seen so much blood. His closest friend had been killed by a hidden rifleman, a shot in the back. The rage he'd felt against poor Barmy had been almost as great. Something primitive stirred in his gut, uncoiled and crouched, ready to spring. Only the most rigid discipline overcame the urge to strangle, rend, and crush. The violence of his feelings frightened him.

He had wanted to tear Mattie Bright from Barmy's grasp and snarl a warning at him. Deep within himself he acknowledged that he'd wanted Barmy to challenge him so that he could unleash the beast imprisoned within the civilized and gentle-manly veneer.

"Get hold of yourself, old man," Cheyne muttered to himself.

He knew what was wrong. He'd fallen victim to Miss Bright's eloquent pen. He still remembered her last letter. She'd written of her loneliness and how different love was from ideals and fairy tales.

"Shall I tell you what I've learned?" she'd written. "Love isn't all grand feeling and starry skies. It is finding a companionable soul with whom you can sing in harmony, not the same tune but a complementary one. Love is liking and admiring, yet seeing truth about someone with unclouded, unfearing eyes, and accepting that truth."

Cheyne leaned against the plane tree. "Unclouded, unfearing eyes. She's certainly got those."

If she knew him, knew everything, would she still look at him with those unclouded, fearless black eyes? Could she accept the truth when the truth bore the stain of illegitimacy?

Pushing away from the tree, Cheyne squared his shoulders and walked on. There was no use wondering. He was never going to confide in a young lady whose mission was to marry for a title. Also, Mattie Bright was haunted by the ghost of her father, and too stubborn to admit it. Marcus Bright must have been a single-minded fanatic about success and earning his bit of tin. From what Cheyne had learned, the old man had worshiped Mattie as she'd worshiped him. Cheyne sometimes envied her, but at other times, he was grateful not to have been burdened with a father who mistook his needs for the wishes of his child.

He came to a fork in the path and hesitated. To his right stretched the route that would take him near the grounds of Buckingham Palace, to the left, Spencer House. He could sense the rage he'd felt at Barmy Richmond. It lay like a white-hot coal under a bed of ashes, ready to ignite an inferno. Before he saw Mattie he had to extinguish it.

"Think of something pleasant," he muttered to himself.

Immediately one of Mattie's letters came to mind. In it she described how she felt about her supposed lover. "Do you know how I came to fall in love with you? Through your goodness. Not a fashionable trait these days, I'll allow. I saw how you cared for those in trouble, how you care for lesser creatures—your horse, a stray dog. My love, your soul is more beautiful than your visage. Great beauty indeed."

Cheyne sighed and wondered if there was anyone on the earth worthy of such admiration, and he reflected that he was glad the blackmailer hadn't been in a position to steal Mattie's letters from him. Then it occurred to him that the criminal would see the letters he wrote to her. All at once a feeling of violation overcame him. An evil stranger had read what he wrote to Mattie Bright. Damn him!

Standing on the path, staring into the darkness, Cheyne struggled with a rage that almost dwarfed what he'd felt toward Avery Richmond. Then he shook his head and laughed. He was being ridiculous. No one knew he'd written those letters. They were a ruse to trap a criminal, and nothing more. He must be more tired than he thought to allow himself to be carried away by such misplaced sentiments. With another sharp laugh he took the left fork in the path.

Cheyne approached a line of shrubs contained by the low iron fence that surrounded the grounds of Spencer House. As he neared the gate, Mattie Bright emerged from the shelter of a tall bush and let him in.

"Everyone's asleep," she whispered.

She led him to an arbor beside a pool in the center of which stood a tiered fountain. Water sprayed from the mouths of stone dolphins and cascaded down the tiers.

Sitting on a bench beneath the arbor, Miss Bright beckoned to him to join her. "In case someone gets restless and looks out a window." She nodded over her shoulder at the house. "You can't see in here, and the water will cover our voices."

"You're very good at clandestine meetings, Miss Bright."

"Thank you. I've been thinking that you should call me Mattie since we're working together."

"Then you must call me Cheyne."

He could just make out her features in the pale moonlight, especially the gentle curve of her face below her eyes. It was odd how he noticed such fine details about her. He never noticed those things about the ladies with whom he was intimately acquainted. He studied her face and the long slope of her neck while she told him of the disappearance of the letters.

"So Dora didn't take them—she wasn't here," she concluded. "And Wynkin keeps a hawk eye on the rest. They had to have vanished during the time the lights were out, and I'm sure it was one of the guests who took them."

"Damn." Cheyne thought for a moment. "Damn. I expected him to make his approach as he's done before. He would have, if not for the infernal electricity. That's what comes of relying on new inventions. The turn of the century will bring more plagues like this."

"Don't blame electricity. He's been doing just fine without it, since most houses around here aren't on it."

"You're right. It's just that these are people I know well, and none of them could be a blackmailer."

"Look, I've been thinking about what happened, and all of them had the opportunity to go upstairs after the lights went out. It would have taken time in the dark, but it could be done. It was done."

"Lance was with me."

"Not the whole time."

"True," Cheyne said.

"Remember, everyone was on the stairs when the lights failed. The Stellafords, Avery, you, and Gordon came from upstairs when the candles were lit.

Mama, Narcissa, and the countess went downstairs, as was Dr. Capgrave. They were in the stairwell when Wynkin brought the candles, but any one of them could have gone up unnoticed while we waited. I remember talking to Narcissa and Mama once or twice, but not to the others."

They lapsed into silence. The fountain sprayed and dripped its watery song while they thought.

"Narcissa isn't the blackmailer," Mattie said. "She's rich, and there's no spite in her."

"There's no spite in Lance Gordon or Dr. Capgrave, either."

Mattie leaned back so that she could look up at him. "You sure about that? He told me that he likes power—power over people."

"Elland spends his time working for the good of the kingdom, not tearing people apart."

"If you say so."

"I do."

"Well, it's not Mama, Ma*ma*."

"Of course not." Cheyne couldn't help smiling at the way she kept correcting her pronunciation. "But it could be Sir William Stellaford. He's got a lot of curiosity, and who knows what his financial situation is?"

"I thought everyone knew everybody's financial situation in Society."

"Not completely. You can go along on promises and evasions for years."

Mattie turned her gaze to the fountain. "Is that what Avery's doing?"

"Avery needs a load of tin. Everyone knows that. He's got several enormous houses that gobble money for things like dry rot and drainage and roof repairs. His estates aren't producing enough income anymore. There's an agricultural depression here, you know, and it's American wheat that's done it. Too much of it, too cheap."

"What about Lady Julia?"

"Julia Stellaford has no malice in her, either. She makes me laugh."

Mattie grinned. "Me, too. What about our friend the countess?"

"Rose is unhappy at her exclusion from the most exalted dinner tables, but she has many friends, and she needs no money."

Mattie rose and paced back and forth in front of him. She walked with a distinctive wide-legged gait and swung her arms in a way no finishing school would allow to go uncorrected. Cheyne was glad that her preoccupation had made her forget to walk in the approved ladylike manner.

His smile turned to a frown as he recalled the implications of what had happened tonight. One of the people at the dinner was the blackmailer, or was cooperating with the blackmailer. Could it be a lady? He'd always thought the ruthlessness of the crime belonged to a man. But he didn't want to think it could be Capgrave or Gordon.

Lance was too busy falling in and out of love. He spun in a toplike manner around a central point of goofiness that seemed incompatible with crime. Elland Capgrave's passion for molding events and people might qualify him, but the man had been his only confidant after Cheyne had separated himself from the duke and duchess. If Elland had wanted to blackmail someone, surely he would have tried the proud Duke of Bracewell.

"Balfour will investigate their financial situations," he said. "And I'll make inquires."

Mattie paused before him. "Me, too."

"No."

"Don't snap at me like a bullwhip, Cheyne Tennant."

"It's too dangerous, Mattie. Someone ruthless enough to drive people to their deaths won't hesitate to do you harm should he suspect you've become a threat."

"I'll be careful, and subtle."

Cheyne stood abruptly. "This isn't one of your pranks. You'll do nothing."

"You can't order me around, Cheyne. I can find out more than you from the ladies."

The image of the dead Juliet Warrender swam into his ken, and fear shot through him. "I forbid you to interfere."

"You can have all the conniption fits you want. I know what I'm doing."

Visions of Mattie's body floating in the fountain, crushed beneath carriage wheels, crumpled at the foot of a staircase flooded his mind. Cheyne grabbed her shoulders and gave her a little shake before drawing her close.

"Do you know what can happen? I've seen it, Mattie."

She rammed her fists against his chest. "Let go, dang it!"

"Not until you promise to do nothing."

She tried to wrench free, but he pulled her against him. Once she was trapped in his arms, he realized he'd designed a small torture for himself, but she wouldn't listen to reason. Before he could say anything further, she tried to stomp on his foot, caught his instep and he hopped backward. His legs hit the stone bench, and he dropped onto it with Mattie on his lap. In acute discomfort that had nothing to do with his foot, Cheyne set his jaw.

"Bloody hell, woman, stop squirming like that!"

"Don't you cuss at me, you mangy skunk. Let go."

Desperate to stop her from moving her hips against him, Cheyne tightened his grip on her. She gasped as air rushed from her lungs, but she filled them again and shouted at him this time.

"What in blazes do you think you're doing?"

Furious and frustrated, Cheyne suddenly loosened his arms. Mattie cried out and fell backward. He grabbed her, drawing her back against him before she could fall. She landed on his chest with a small "Oof" and glared at him. He could barely see her expression. Her eyes narrowed, and she opened her mouth as if to shout at him again.

This time he stopped her. It seemed the right thing to do at the time. After all, someone might hear her. Cheyne quickly took her mouth with his, stabbing with his tongue and muffling whatever she'd been about to say. He sank into a world of soft, hot sensation, only to be ripped from it when she tore her lips free.

Mattie leaned her head back and glared at him. "You had no call to take such a liberty."

"Mattie, my midnight sun," he said with a voice roughened by the hunger that drove him. "Will you please be quiet for once?"

"No, you can't try to bully me like a range rider after a maverick and expect—"

Cheyne couldn't help but smile. He had no idea what she was talking about. Still smiling, he kissed the tip of her nose. At last she went silent, her mouth slightly open in astonishment. Cheyne's gaze fastened on her lips. Fire washed through his body, then swept down his arms to make his hands close convulsively over her arms. He pulled her to him slowly. His lips were nearing hers when he glimpsed the fluttering of her lashes, the look of confusion in her eyes. What was he doing?

"Blast." He turned on the bench, pushed her off his lap beside him and stood. "Blast, blast, blast."

"What's wrong?"

Rubbing the back of his neck, Cheyne charged over to the fountain and back, then to an apple tree and back.

"Forgive me, Miss Bright. I've behaved terribly. Not the thing, taking advantage of a lady simply because one is—most unchivalrous."

"Yes," she said quietly.

"It won't happen again."

"Oh."

"I give you my word."

"That's nice."

Cheyne came a little closer at the distant tone in her voice. "I'm not like Barmy, if that's what you're thinking. I've no need of your tin, and I'm not after it."

Now he was close enough to see her astonishment.

"That's the last thing I'd think."

There was a strained silence. Then Mattie cleared her throat.

"I wanted to thank you for your help this evening. Avery wouldn't listen to me."

"He's of the opinion that any woman to whom he pays court is the most fortunate in the country." It suddenly occurred to him why he'd been so furious at Barmy. "I assumed you'd accepted his proposal and he was carried away with his excitement."

"Nah, I told him to ask me next Season, and he didn't take to the idea of waiting. From what he said, I reckon he can't wait that long."

"Next Season? I've never heard of a young lady putting off the son of a duke for almost a year." Cheyne felt a burst of elation. "Good God, you've seen reason, haven't you? You realized your father's request was unreasonable, absurd even."

Mattie planted her hands on her hips. "My pa wasn't unreasonable, and he certainly wasn't absurd."

"That's not what I meant."

"Heavens to Betsy, no. You meant Papa was selfish and silly. You don't know anything about my pa, and I've had enough of your judgmental attitude."

"Really, Mattie," Cheyne said. "You react to a small criticism as if it were a public condemnation. You know as well as I do that you're incapable of marrying merely for the purposes of gaining an exalted but empty title. You're an American romantic, my dear Mattie, and the moment your husband began to misbehave, you'd take a shotgun to him."

"There you go again, calling me ill-bred."

Cheyne drew nearer to see her lips press together and a hiss escape them.

"You're peeved because I'm right."

"I'm peeved because you're a rude, uppity son of a gun."

Cheyne grinned. "You've lost your courage, haven't you? Can't face marrying a blighter like Barmy, or some ancient old buster with gout and yellow teeth just because everyone calls him Your Grace."

"Now, you see here, Mr. Highfalutin Tennant, I'll marry a titled gentleman when I'm ready, and not before. I haven't gone sour on the idea, I'm—I'm just not in a hurry. I got things to do. I'm going to work to get women the vote and get them into colleges and universities, and I got modern inventions I want to take a look at for investment purposes. I'm busy, dang it."

"What a cheery prospect," Cheyne said with a mocking laugh. "You ensconced in some ancestral country seat trying to convince His Grace and the whole family that your role isn't that of a breeder of future dukes, but investor and civic agitator."

"That's exactly what'll happen."

Cheyne's smile vanished. He stalked close to her and hissed, "Silly fool. Once they've got you and your millions, they'll stash you in the country to breed regardless of your wishes. And once you've produced a couple of sons, your dear husband will ignore you for the next three or four decades."

Mattie didn't answer at once. She bit her bottom lip and rocked on her heels. Finally she tossed her head. "The man I marry won't ignore me."

"If you say so."

"You tried, and look what's happened to you."

She turned her back and marched into the house before he could reply. Standing beside the fountain, he watched the door shut behind her. He looked around the dark and deserted garden.

"Dang."

13

Mattie was so furious with Cheyne that she almost forgot to act the part of a distraught young lady. She was too busy doing something that was certain to annoy Tennant; she decided to question Lance. She convinced Narcissa that the Honorable Lancelot Gordon needed to be taken in hand.

"Someone has to, Narcissa, before he decides to fall in love with a professional thief or one of those depraved Pinchbeck sisters."

Thus the day after the letters vanished she had Mama invite Gordon to tea. Mama was having her own set of friends over, but Mattie and Narcissa cornered their victim on a settee in the Palm Room.

Gordon turned his head from Mattie to Narcissa and beamed at them. "I say, Miss Bright. Awfully kind of your dear mother to invite me to tea."

"We've never gotten to talk, what with all the parties and balls and such," Mattie replied.

"It's wonderful timing," he said, "because there's a secret I've been dying to share."

Narcissa batted her lashes and said in a breathless voice, "Oh, tell us."

With an air of imparting state secrets, Gordon complied. "I've fallen in love."

Mattie and Narcissa exchanged meaningful glances.

"With a perfect angel. Lady Jane Rothburg."

Mattie nearly choked on her tea. "Jane Rothburg. The Jane Rothburg who has twelve children and is such a great friend of your mother's?"

"That's her. She's amazing, delightful, so calm and unflappable."

"She's calm because she doesn't have enough energy to be excited," Narcissa said.

"I shall change all that," Lancelot said with a wave of his teacup.

Narcissa rolled her eyes, but Mattie gave her a warning look and said, "We're happy for you, Mr. Gordon."

"Thank you. It's nice to be congratulated instead of tolerated the way Tennant does. He said perhaps I could live in her nursery along with the children."

"That wasn't kind," Mattie said.

"I know, and Tennant's usually an amiable chap. He's been distracted lately. This morning he was in an evil temper. I think he's got trouble with a lady. Oops. Shouldn't have said that."

"Nonsense," Narcissa cooed.

Mattie asked, "Does he have lots of problems with ladies?"

"Rather the other way around. They have trouble with him. Usually there's one who's trying to catch his attention or entice an offer from him. Several years ago there was this enchanting French princess. I thought she'd go the distance, but Cheyne danced out of her reach at the last moment. Then there was that business with Lady Drake."

"Oh?" Narcissa smiled and handed him a cake plate.

Lancelot glanced around at the others in the room, then lowered his voice. "It was the talk of London two years ago. My dears, she suddenly announced she was leaving her husband for him. Said it aloud in front of a dining room full of people. Cheyne wasn't there. In fact, he'd gone to the Continent on business, but the woman was mad for him and wouldn't listen to reason. He came home to find her waiting for him. He won't say what happened, but after an hour with him she packed herself off to Italy to some villa in the country. She's still there."

"How sad," Mattie said. "He must have said something terrible to her to make her abandon her family and country."

"I don't think so." Gordon stabbed a piece of cake and ate it. "Tennant's not like that. He has the devil of a temper sometimes, and a vicious tongue when annoyed, but he wouldn't hurt someone who's so obviously distressed. He's as kind as my dear Lady Jane."

Narcissa excused herself, and Mattie suspected she'd lost patience with the irrepressible Lance. Mattie poured Gordon more tea. She'd proceeded to pry some information from him without being too obvious. His income was substantial, but not in league with most of his wealthy friends, and Gordon had been upstairs "wandering in the dark" at the time the letters were stolen. He'd bumped into Elland Capgrave and the countess at different times in his attempts to find his way around. Still, Mattie had trouble believing that anyone so open and guileless could be a blackmailer. However, her having talked to him should annoy Cheyne Tennant.

Mattie scowled at the thought of him. He'd kissed her and then regretted it. The skunk. His lips had been so hot, just like the heat of his body, and he'd stirred her senses in the most amazing way. She didn't understand the man. One minute he was kissing her, the next he was treating her like some brainless doll who couldn't be trusted to make inquiries about suspects.

"I say, Miss Bright, is something wrong?"

"Hmmm? No."

"You were frowning."

Mattie smiled at him. "You were saying you thought Cheyne Tennant was a good chap."

"Yes, especially considering."

Nodding encouragement, Mattie waited for Gordon to continue. He chewed his lip for a moment.

"It's really no secret, I suppose." Lance set his cake plate on the table in front of them, turned to Mattie and said, "The duke is a simple man. Not what one might call a thinking man. Ever since I can remember he's sneered at Cheyne because he was so different from his other sons, Harry and Eustace. Cheyne is the youngest, and he's gifted. He'd have been invited to attend either Oxford or Cambridge even if he hadn't been the son of a duke. But his intelligence only annoyed Bracewell."

"Why?"

"I think because he doesn't understand Cheyne, and what he doesn't understand, he dislikes. Cheyne once told me his father could remember—how did he put it—infinite equine trivialities such as the names of the Derby winners since the seventies and recite in excruciating detail the events of every hunt he ever attended, but he can't abide the arts. Hates music in particular. Well, you know Cheyne."

"Not that well."

"He can hunt, shoot, ride with the best, but music, paintings, sculpture and such are as necessary to him as food. And he's the only one in his family like that."

Lance waved his hand. "The duchess appreciates art, but only as a setting for herself. The others would rather watch a boxing match than go to a museum. Once when Cheyne was home from university he brought a small painting, the first he'd purchased with his own money. I think it was a Constable. The duke tossed it in the fireplace while Cheyne was dressing for dinner."

Mattie scowled at him. "You mean that man destroyed a painting?"

"Not the first, I understand. I was there when he did it. When Cheyne came downstairs, he saw the charred frame and turned the color of the ashes in the fireplace. He never said a word."

"I think I would have come after the old coot with a poker. I wish he was here so I could do it right now."

Lance smiled at her. "Cheyne could have used your defense when we were growing up. The duke is a harsh man."

"How harsh?"

"Cheyne doesn't talk about that, but I've seen him come out of his father's study bleeding."

"I take it back," Mattie said quietly. "Bracewell should be shot."

"Oh, don't worry about old Cheyne. No one hits him now. Wouldn't dare."

"I'm sure."

Mattie subsided, her feelings about Cheyne Tennant in an uproar. The man who seemed so dignified, so assured and unflappable, had earned his self-possession in a hard school. Her heart ached for him. Dang. Every time she thought she was too angry with him to feel anything softer, something happened to change her mind. She hated having all these conflicting emotions about him.

Narcissa appeared, smiling brilliantly. "My dear Lancelot. May I persuade you to view Mrs. Bright's lovely garden?"

They rose to accompany her, but as they crossed

the threshold Narcissa said, "Oh, Mattie, your Mama asks that you join her. Mrs. Arbuthnot has a new French gown that's simply deevie."

Mattie went back inside, stood behind a drape, and watched the two stroll around the garden. She frowned when Narcissa placed her hand on Lancelot's arm and gazed up at him in admiration. Narcissa was engaged. True, she showed little anxiety at the absence of her fiancé, but she liked the earl's son.

Narcissa had never said she loved him, but Mattie had assumed her content with her most suitable match. Perhaps Narcissa was trying to rescue Lance from his latest debacle by attaching his interest to herself. If this was so, Mattie was going to have to warn her. Once attached, Lance could be most trying. For a few weeks anyway.

After tea Mattie had the luxury of an entire evening without engagements. Mama's appetite for Society had at last begun to wane. She was exhausted from the frantic pace, the late nights, and the plotting to catch a titled husband for her daughter. Mattie dressed for dinner and considered herself lucky that they only expected Narcissa and an elderly friend of Mama's. She was exhausted too and desperately wanted a little peace. In the hall, Wynkin appeared with the evening post. At the bottom of a stack of letters for Mattie lay a plain envelope with no return address.

Mattie's heart jumped in her chest. She hadn't expected it so soon. Clutching her mail, she rushed back upstairs and locked her bedroom door. She opened the envelope, and one of Cheyne's letters to her dropped out. She cried out and snatched it up.

It was one of her favorites, and having it in her hands again brightened her spirits. In it he'd called her "my fearless midnight sun." He said she had warm summer in her eyes and described a walk in the country they'd taken—in his imagination, of course. "I remember the brightness of the day, almost as bright as your dear face. Several white and curious clouds followed us, longing to decipher the secret to our happiness. You stopped to chide them for their intrusion."

Her finger traced the bold strokes of Cheyne's pen. Why couldn't he behave like the lover he created in his letters? Closing her eyes, she imagined walking beneath a bright sky with Cheyne Tennant, imagined him speaking the words in his letters. She looked at the letter again. He'd called her his midnight sun. Her fingers brushed the ink again. Then her hand stilled, and she stared at the paper without seeing the words.

"Mattie Bright, it's true. You've fallen in love with his letters." She jumped up from the bed, and another sheet caught her eye. The blackmailer's note. She'd forgotten it. How could she do that?

The note had been folded over the letter and read, "The others are safe. If you want them back unpublished, it will cost you ten thousand pounds."

Her hand began to shake. "Thursday night at two o'clock in the morning. Use large bills to make a small bundle. Wrap the money in a plain brown paper and leave it by the south end of the footbridge in St. James's Park."

Mattie snatched the envelope to look at the postmark, but it was from a central London station through which tens of thousands of letters flowed each evening.

"Thursday," she muttered. "That's the night of the Countess of Trillford's costume ball."

It was a grand affair, one of the highlights of the Season, at which the Prince and Princess of Wales would make an appearance. The prince loved dressing up, and he planned to go as Louis XIV, while the princess would dress as Marie Antoinette. Rose Marie was going as Napoleon's empress, Josephine. Mattie couldn't remember what Lance had decided to wear, but Narcissa planned to go as Eleanor of Aquitaine. Mattie would have to attend and wear her Mary, Queen of Scots, costume before sneaking out to leave the money in St. James's Park.

A shiver of excitement rushed through her. They were close. She would deliver the money, and Cheyne would pounce on the blackmailer. She wouldn't want to be him when Cheyne got hold of him.

The hunt would be over soon. Over. Then there would be no more magical letters. No more secret plotting with Cheyne Tennant, no meetings in the dark garden. No more arguments, and she had come to almost delight in pitting herself against him.

No more chances that he might kiss her again. Suddenly the world grew dim and featureless, and her body filled with a strange craving that increased with each breath drawn. Soon there would be no encounters in which he might touch her and feed this craving. Mattie shook her head, drew in a deep breath, and blew it out slowly.

It was true. All the excitement in her life would be gone when her reason for seeing Cheyne vanished. She would be left to pursue her original aim of marrying well. She would still have her interests in politics and inventions, but somehow they weren't enough anymore.

Until now she hadn't realized how vibrant her days had become with Cheyne Tennant in them. She liked working with him; she even liked fighting with him, which was fortunate, since he was such a skunk. Did he feel the same? He seemed to like kissing her, but that didn't mean he felt the same way she did. He wanted her; she knew this. But was that all?

"How am I going to know?" she asked herself. "He wrote the letters to catch the blackmailer. They're not really to me. I have to remember that. He doesn't really think of me as his midnight sun. That's just a ruse, nothing more."

She repeated the thought over and over. The letters weren't really for her. She wouldn't fool herself again. Cheyne Tennant was attracted to her as he had been to many women, but he'd been in love with none of them. Lancelot Gordon had assured her of this. She wasn't going to throw herself at his feet like that foolish woman who banished herself to Italy.

Besides, she could look in a mirror and see the truth—that she was passable, but hardly irresistible. Cheyne was drawn to her because they'd been thrown together by circumstances. Once those circumstances changed, he would forget about her. He wasn't responsible for her falling in love with his pen.

Swallowing hard, Mattie folded the letter and went to her secretary, where she found one of the envelopes from her store of personal stationery. Placing the letter in it, she glanced around the bedroom looking for a hiding place no one could discover. She didn't want the blackmailer stealing it again. None appeared at first glance, so she slipped it inside her dress against her corset. Then she sat down and penned a note to Cheyne, summoned Dora, and sent her to deliver it.

They must meet in the garden again tonight to make a plan for the delivery of the blackmail money. Mattie groaned and rested her head in her hands. Seeing Cheyne now would be difficult. She was going to be awkward and she just knew she was going to reveal her foolish feelings somehow. He would be embarrassed by them and feel sorry for her. Like he'd felt sorry for Lady Drake.

Mattie straightened and set her jaw. She'd just have to pretend indifference. No doubt he would say something to annoy her. If she could get mad at him and stay mad, she wouldn't do anything that might expose her feelings. He must never suspect. Of all the nightmares in the world, enduring Cheyne Tennant's pity would be the most dreadful.

There was a knock, and the door handle rattled. "Mattie? It's time to go down to dinner."

Mattie opened the door for her mother.

"Are you feeling all right?"

"Yes, of course."

"You don't look well, my dear. You're pale, and there are blue smudges under your eyes."

"I'm fine." Mattie tried to smile but failed.

Mama didn't look convinced, but Mattie didn't have the heart to try. As they walked downstairs together, Mama forgot Mattie's appearance and brightened.

"I've been most peeved at you about the Marquess of Stainfield, Mattie, but since Lord Geoffrey has been coming around, I realized what you're up to."

"Lord Geoffrey?"

"The Duke of Bracewell's son. You know."

Mattie stopped three steps from the bottom of the stairs to stare at her mother. "You mean Cheyne. What about him?"

"You're so secretive sometimes, Mattie. It's annoying. But I've discovered your secret." Mama tapped Mattie with her fan.

Mattie's heart flip-flopped in her chest. "I don't have any secret."

"Yes, you do. You're angling for Lord Geoffrey— Lord Cheyne. He's the son of the duke, and you're thinking he'd do if Avery doesn't make an offer. And I must say, it's wise of you. I don't understand why

Avery hasn't proposed. I've given him several oppor-
tunities. Why, the night the electricity went out I
sent him up to you while you were getting my shawl,
and nothing happened." Mama eyed her. "Nothing
did happen?"

"No, nothing." Mattie rushed on, "Mama, I'm
not angling for Lord Cheyne."

"Nonsense, my dear. It's a good plan. If you can't
have the oldest son of a duke, another will do in
a pinch."

"But I'm not—he's not . . ." Mattie sighed.

"I shall invite him to our country house party."

"No!" Mattie shut her mouth as the word echoed
in the stairwell.

"Now, Mattie, don't be difficult. I know it will be
a challenge to manage Avery and Lord Cheyne at the
same time, but you can do it. I'll help you." Mama
continued downstairs, chattering as she went. "There
will be plenty of other people there, so it won't look
like I invited Lord Cheyne especially. You'll see. It
will all work out, and by the end of the house party,
you'll be engaged to one of them."

Mattie remained on the stairs gawking at her
mother in horror. Mama's mind was made up. Cheyne
would be invited.

Forcing her feet to move, Mattie followed her
mother. Her only hope now was that Cheyne would
refuse the invitation. If they caught the blackmailer,
there would be no reason for him to come. Wasn't
that right? And they would catch him. So there was

nothing to worry about. She wasn't going to have to spend day after day in the country in the company of Cheyne Tennant.

Now all she had to do was catch that danged blackmailer.

14

❧❧❧

Wearing a black lightweight coat, top hat, and evening clothes, Cheyne strolled along the path beside the lake at St. James's Park a few minutes after midnight. He carried a walking stick with a gold handle and did his best to imitate a gentleman of leisure on his way to one of the many balls that were being held at the close of the Season. Other men dressed in the same fashion crossed through the park on their way to various social engagements. The coming fall suffused the air with sweet-smelling crispness, and the moon illuminated the lake with silver light. He passed the line of bushes where Balfour and his men lurked. The dense vegetation along the lake provided concealment, but the footbridge was exposed, and the blackmailer would see anyone who approached it.

Balfour had been diligent about inquiring into the suspects' financial affairs. As Cheyne had predicted, nothing had turned up to incriminate anyone.

However, the superintendent's men were still working and might uncover something. The demand for
money had come before they'd completed their
investigations.

Cheyne swung his stick as he walked, went by the
footbridge and rounded a bend. Stepping off the
path, he entered a grove of willows whose trailing
branches skimmed the surface of the lake.

"Nothin' stirring here, gov'nor," Mutton said.

"We've half an hour yet," Cheyne replied. "You're
sure Dora will be on time?"

"She'll be here. And so will your Miss Bright,
mark my words."

Cheyne stabbed the turf with his stick. "I told
you she's not coming. We had a most serious discussion about it when she told me about the blackmailer's demands. I impressed upon her the danger
of her coming and ordered her to remain at the
Trillford ball."

"Right."

"Don't use that skeptical tone with me," Cheyne
said. "It's annoying."

Cheyne turned his back on Mutton and walked to
the bank to frown at the moon-streaked water. He
was irritated with Mutton, who he was sure followed him on his late-night excursions to Spencer
House. But the real cause of his vexation was Mattie
Bright. She'd summoned him, revealed the blackmail letter and had assumed she would place the
money in the appointed spot herself. When he told
her he'd arranged for Dora to disguise herself and

perform that function, Mattie had protested. The resulting argument had been fierce. How could she think of exposing herself to that kind of danger? The idea of Mattie coming near such a ruthless criminal frightened him and made him want to lock her in her room to keep her safe. She had argued with him in that blunt, stubborn way of hers until he'd been tempted to shake her. Only the knowledge of what might result from touching her had stopped him.

He'd won that argument, though. He told her that Dora was going to be there, so if she tried to come, there would be two Mattie Brights, which would ruin everything. Mattie had fumed and called him an ornery skunk, but she'd acquiesced to his decision.

"Pssst."

Cheyne turned to find Mutton beckoning to him. He joined the valet beside the trunk of a willow. From this hiding place, they had a good view of the south end of the footbridge. The paths on both sides of the lake had grown more crowded, and Cheyne had to admire the blackmailer's choice of time and place. The park bordered the grounds of the Royal Palace and lay within easy walking distance of Mayfair. Lancaster House, Clarence House, and Marlborough House were close, as was Spencer House. When fashionable London was abroad, the park filled with pedestrians. On this particular night, Cheyne knew of at least five costume balls and half a dozen more functions, all being held to mark the Season's end.

Mutton nudged him and pointed to a group of luxuriously dressed people that had crossed the Mall from the direction of Carlton House. They laughed and danced their way onto the footbridge while nearly a dozen more spilled onto it from the opposite direction. The two groups met in the middle of the bridge, merged, laughing and teasing, and parted again. Cheyne peered through the darkness and could just make out a lone figure that had trailed behind the first group.

It was Dora dressed in a copy of Mattie's costume for the Trillford ball. He'd seen Mattie dressed and ready to leave earlier this evening. She had chosen to go as Mary, Queen of Scots, and wore a wine-colored gown with a square neck, stiff bodice and farthingale. The jeweled caul she wore on her head like a cap sparkled in the midst of waves of black hair. Luckily they'd been able to put the maid in a hooded cloak, because Dora's first attempts to resemble Mattie had been disastrous. Cheyne had ended up buying a wig of black hair and high-heeled boots to make Dora tall enough. No artistry of padding or painting could give Dora Mattie's curves or her tulip lips.

Cheyne gripped his walking stick hard as Dora walked onto the footbridge holding the parcel by the twine wrapped around it. She moved slowly as she approached the south end. Cheyne held his breath as she stooped, set the package down by the last post in the balustrade and straightened. She glanced around as if uncertain, then clutched her cloak about her and hastened down the path. She passed Cheyne and Mutton without glancing at them and disappeared around a turn in the path. As she left, a man approached going in the other direction. Tipping his hat, he passed Dora and neared the bridge. Mutton stirred, but Cheyne held him back. The man walked past the bridge without stopping.

Two men walking side by side crossed the bridge without seeming to notice the parcel, and Cheyne's grip on the walking stick tightened. Voices carried across the water, and they turned to see a large party in Elizabethan costume begin a dancing parade toward the footbridge. He saw several William Shakespeares, Queen Elizabeths, and Sir Walter Raleighs. Several couples in evening dress followed them, while another group costumed in medieval garb hurried down the path on the other side of the lake.

The crowds met at the end of the bridge near the parcel of money. Cheyne craned his neck, but there were too many people around for him to be able to keep the parcel in sight. Cursing, he left the shelter of the willow and hurried toward the bridge. Beyond it he saw Balfour and his men coming. Cheyne reached the south end first, but the package was gone. A harlequin jostled him, apologized, and ran to catch up with several people in Elizabethan dress.

Balfour ran up to him. "Did you see who got it?"

"No, damn it."

They surveyed the retreating partygoers. The two groups had dispersed in different directions. None of them appeared to be holding the package. Suddenly

Cheyne heard a low whistle. A figure in gentleman's evening dress emerged from the shadow of a tree and pointed at a retreating group as he went after them. Cheyne narrowed his eyes and studied the man's wide-legged gate. It was Mattie.

There was no time to be furious or shocked. He pointed to the group of costumed revelers Mattie had indicated.

"We'll follow them."

Balfour was already running toward his men, who had split up to keep track of the various groups. Threading his way through several groups of pedestrians, Cheyne hurried after Mattie and caught up with her as she approached the Mall with its heavy carriage traffic. Cheyne grabbed her arm but didn't slow as they crossed the street in front of a town coach. He said nothing to her, and she didn't speak, either.

The three of them chased after the group in costume as it swept past St. James's Palace. At Pall Mall several of them parted from the main group and headed in the direction of the Reform Club.

Cheyne stopped in the shelter of a doorway but kept a tight grip on Mattie's arm. "Mutton, you go with them. We'll stay with the main group."

Once the valet was gone, he dragged Mattie close to him. "Wait till this is over, Mattie Bright."

Undisturbed, she shrugged out of his grasp and pointed at a glittering costume of Elizabeth I. "You got no call to threaten me, Cheyne Tennant." She looked down the street. "They're getting too far ahead."

She pushed him aside and rushed after their quarry.

"Blast," he muttered. He sprang into a quick walk that wouldn't attract attention. Mattie and the party-goers were headed for Berkeley Square.

He increased his pace as they approached the Georgian home of the Countess of Trillford. Carriages and cabs filled the street, and Mattie seemed not to notice them in her haste to keep up with their quarry. When the Elizabethan costume disappeared into the house, Mattie dashed across the busy street. At the same time a hansom careened around a corner. Cheyne sprang off the curb, hurtled into Mattie and shoved her out of the cab's path. They hit the pavement on the other side of the street, and Mattie's top hat flew off. Cheyne rolled off her, snatched the hat, and stuffed it back on her head in one swift movement. Several bystanders arrived, expressing concern. He thanked them, and they left. Furious with Mattie for making his heart leap up his throat, he yanked her to her feet.

"Damn it, Mattie. They almost saw you without that bloody hat, and then you'd be ruined."

"You can yell at me later," she said and she hurried into the house.

He chased after her, caught her in the hall, and they searched the ball together. The crush of people made their task difficult. The only advantage was that no one seemed to notice that Mattie kept her hat on. With so many odd outfits being displayed, a mere hat provoked no curiosity. Cheyne and Mattie threaded in and out of the hundreds of people around the ballroom floor. They even pried into the retiring rooms. Finally they ended up in the garden. Cheyne led the way to shelter behind a statue of Apollo.

Slapping his walking stick against his leg, he said, "I counted seven Queen Elizabeths, half a dozen Sir Walter Raleighs, five Henry VIIIs, and three William Shakespeares."

"I saw two Mary, Queen of Scots, two King Arthurs, two Guineveres, and six Sir Lancelots, including Lancelot Gordon."

Cheyne gave a sigh of exasperation. "Lance would never blackmail anyone. And don't try to distract me. You lied to me. You said you'd stay at the ball." His gaze swept over her, noting the tight fit of her waistcoat and the novel sight of a woman's legs in trousers. He dragged his eyes up to her face and asked, "What possessed you to dress as a man?"

"I never said I'd stay at the ball. You ordered me to stay at the ball. I said you were probably right, and I should stay at the ball, but I never said I would."

"Sophistry—" Cheyne began.

"We don't have time to argue. Let's round up everyone in Elizabethan or medieval costumes and search them."

"No. He's already gotten rid of the money. We'd warn the blackmailer and destroy any chance of trapping him. We'll have to wait and try again."

"But he's here, I know it."

"No, you don't. He could be somewhere else entirely. Mutton or Balfour could be chasing him right now. So we'll do nothing. That is, I'll return to the ball and you'll go home before you begin to attract attention in that absurd disguise."

"It's not absurd. It's convenient. I don't know why women wear dresses at all when trousers are so comfortable. When I was younger in Texas, I used to wear trousers when I rode. Much safer in the brush."

Damn her. Now he had an image in his head of Mattie dressed in cowboy's jeans and a man's shirt. In an instant the jeans vanished, leaving a picture of her in nothing but the shirt. A jolt of arousal caught him off guard.

He hadn't meant to snap, but he was suffering. "I suppose you carried a rifle, too."

"No." She sneered at him. "It was a Colt revolver. Papa gave it to me."

Hell. Now the image contained Mattie in nothing but a shirt brandishing a revolver. He was sure he made some kind of strangled noise because Mattie's eyes widened, but he was past caring.

His hands closed over the lapels of her evening coat. Pulling her closer, he bent, avoiding the black silk hat, and whispered in her ear, "You really should be more careful in your language, my little savage."

His lips brushed her cheek and found her mouth. Wrapping his arms around her, he dove between her lips to lose himself. Soft, urgent pressure from her lips drove him harder, compelled his response and sent him to the edge of a precipice. His hands slipped under her evening coat, tore aside the waistcoat and found her hips. He felt her arms encircle him. He hardly noticed his own clothing loosen because his hands had dropped to her buttocks. It was an involuntary impulse that made him squeeze. At the pressure Mattie gasped and drew back to look at him in surprise. Breathing hard, Cheyne looked at her for a moment before pushing her against the base of the statue. His hips worked against hers while their mouths joined.

From a great distance he heard waltz music, but what jolted him out of his frenzy was the feel of her small hand on his bare skin. Mattie had opened his shirt and was rubbing her palms over his ribs. Sucking in his breath, Cheyne managed to thrust himself back from her. She pulled at him, but he held her at arm's length.

"No!"

Her hat had disappeared, and her hair was in wild tangles around her face. "No?" She sounded distant, distraught, as if the word were foreign.

Desperate, Cheyne shoved her away and stumbled to a bench opposite the statue.

"What do you mean, no?" she asked harshly.

"It's impossible, you little fool."

Didn't she know yet what he was? He couldn't ruin her. He wouldn't. And bastards like him didn't deserve a woman like her. He pressed his hands against the cold stone of the bench and fought to speak, to say anything that would keep her from closing the distance between them. If she touched him . . .

"Why did you stop? Is it—"

"Shut up!" Cheyne closed his eyes and fought to control his body. When he opened them, she was beside him and reaching out to touch him. He sprang from the bench, putting it between them. "Keep away from me, damn you. God deliver me from all ignorant colonials."

He started down a path that would take him around the house to the street but stopped and turned to see her gawking at him, her lips slightly apart and swollen from his treatment of them.

"Fix your hair, damn you. Put that cursed hat on and go home. I'll send Mutton to escort you."

"I don't need him."

He felt a muscle twitch in his jaw. "My dear Miss Bright. I think you've just proved you need half a dozen escorts, and possibly a chastity belt for added insurance."

Turning his back on her, Cheyne walked rapidly around the house and into the street. Ravening, almost uncontrollable, his body fought him with each step. His hand shook, and he wanted to howl. He had to get off the streets. Luckily he wouldn't see Balfour until tomorrow at Scotland Yard. Had the detective's search been more fruitful than Cheyne's, he'd have sent word.

He reached the corner, his body still in torment, and didn't see Mutton until the valet appeared at his side. He ordered him to escort Mattie home. Then

Cheyne began to walk. Removing his overcoat and evening jacket, he loosened his tie and allowed the cold night air to bathe his skin. He didn't feel the cold until he reached his own house, but by the time he was in his room, he was shivering. Dropping his coats on the floor, he sat on the bed and rested his head in his hands.

"You're mad," he announced to the bedroom. "Lusting after a little barbarian in trousers. Master yourself, old man, or she'll turn you into a blithering imbecile."

Cheyne jumped up and began to pace. He would control himself. It was one thing to dally with women who understood the rules of Society. It was another to satisfy one's ephemeral desires with an impetuous and innocent young lady, no matter how dashing or brave. He, the fruit of a jaded liaison and corrupt circle, had no business trampling upon Mattie's ideals. And that's what he'd do if he seduced her. Despite her misguided attempts to participate in the marriage market, Mattie Bright had ideals of marriage and love that wouldn't be squelched by her parents' ambitions.

Mattie believed in true love and sacred marriage vows. That belief shone in her soft black eyes. Should she learn just how vile his origins were, she would turn from him in disgust. He'd seen her disgust at the behavior of so many of his friends and acquaintances. Her nose twitched upon hearing gossip about infidelity, and her perfect fingers drummed on tables and chair arms at hints of the dark pleasures in which gentlemen indulged.

No. He might want to satiate his lust for the maddening and incomparable Mattie Bright. But doing so was unthinkable. Cheyne picked up his discarded clothing, tossed it over his shoulder and pushed open the door to his room. He might abandon Society's more absurd conventions, but that didn't mean he was lost to all honor. He might have been born a bastard; he wasn't going to act like one to Mattie.

15

The Panhard–Levassor furrowed through the morning mist in the Kent countryside. Mattie was on her way to the railroad station to collect Narcissa Potter, and she was miserable. She'd been miserable for over a month, ever since that night she and Cheyne had tried to catch the blackmailer and ended up kissing at the Trillford ball.

The motorcar clattered over a rut filled with mud, but for once she failed to curse the lack of good roads for horseless vehicles. Hauling on the wheel, she skirted another watery hole and blinked back tears. Once she had thought nothing could hurt like being used by Samuel Pinchot. After Cheyne's rejection, a scalping by Comanches seemed like a cotillion.

He'd shown her the red-gold world of passion, given her the gift of the wonders of physical love, and then ripped it from her, tore himself from her as if he couldn't bear the fact that she had inspired his offering. He was ashamed to want her. It had been so clear in his manner, in his words.

Mattie prided herself on looking at the world without useless fuzzy-mindedness and rosy clouds to obscure her vision. Until desire grabbed her and twisted her in knots. Certainly she knew that men looked at the world differently. She wouldn't have been surprised to find that Cheyne Tennant could want a woman without loving her. What had caught her unprepared was that he wanted her. He evidently had conceived a weakness for her, and just as obvious was his disgust at not being able to overcome it.

She didn't understand why he found her irresistible. No one else had. And when he touched her he swept her into a cyclone. It was as if he breathed desire into her with each kiss. Each time his hands had touched her skin, she grew more and more agitated. Then his hips had pressed against hers and suddenly she felt the same animal compulsion she'd witnessed in the past on the ranch.

At that moment comprehension burst upon her. This was desire—limitless, obsessive, undeniable. And if she didn't pursue it, she might never find it again. Even now she could call up its power by envisioning Cheyne, his sapphire eyes glittering like the sunlit sky after a rain at sunset.

She'd taken a chance; she'd allowed herself to respond to him, and he'd betrayed her trust. Long hours of tears, remorse, and speculation had yielded the answer to Cheyne's vicious conduct. He found her unworthy of him and his superlative lineage. Like so many men, he blamed her for inspiring desire in him, as if she were responsible for his feelings.

Tears obscured the road again, and Mattie stopped the motorcar while she wiped her eyes with a gloved hand. To be shoved away as if she disgusted him had been mortifying. She had wanted to die, and even now she burned with shame.

Sniffing, Mattie stopped the Panhard, found her handkerchief and wiped her nose and eyes. Broad green lawns stretched into the distance on either side of the private drive. She glanced back at the trees that screened her view of Chèremere, Cheyne's castle. The man owned a blamed castle, for God's sake. Bought it from some fool who'd rather live on the Continent.

"Dang, dang, dang."

No matter her aversion to him, she'd been forced to come here, and now she was a guest of the last man in England she ever wanted to see again. Because, whatever her personal feelings, she couldn't refuse to go along with Superintendent Balfour's continued attempts to trap the blackmailer. They wanted to draw all the suspects together in one place, with her there to tempt the criminal into making more demands. With fewer people around in the country, their chances of isolating the real blackmailer were far better. She would have preferred to play the hostess at the country house Mama had rented for the fall, but Cheyne invited Mama without consulting her, and Mama had been only too pleased to accept. If Mattie had refused to cooperate, she'd have had to explain why, and that she couldn't do.

Thus Mattie and her mother had come to Cheyne's country house along with everyone who had been present the night her letters had vanished. Avery, Dr. Capgrave, the honorable Lancelot Gordon, Narcissa, and the Stellafords. Rose Marie Seton would arrive this afternoon. Everyone seemed to be having a good time, especially Mama. She was ecstatic at the chance to lure Stainfield into a proposal and at the same time keep Tennant in reserve.

A wave of guilt burst over her. She hadn't yet told Mama of her plans, but as soon as they caught the blackmailer, Mattie was going home. Stainfield could find himself another rich bride. She wasn't going to stay a moment longer than necessary in the same country with Cheyne Tennant, much less the same house.

She had another reason for leaving as well, one just as painful. Agonizing reflection had revealed something to Mattie: in her quest to marry well, she'd been trying to make up for all the things Papa had missed. While he was alive he'd always worked to provide for others and hardly ever thought about his own enjoyment. Then he'd died before he could really experience the beautiful life he'd earned. Without realizing it, Mattie had been trying to recompense Papa for what he'd missed by working so hard and then dying so soon. But she could never make up for the past. It was wrong to try to live according to what Papa might have wished. When she'd understood this at last, she finally admitted to herself that her father's dying request had been misguided. He wouldn't have wanted her to be unhappy. Marrying Avery Richmond would make her unhappy, and staying in England with Cheyne Tennant around would make her miserable. So she wasn't going to stay.

With renewed determination, Mattie put the motorcar in gear and drove to the station, where she collected Narcissa and her luggage. In the motorcar it took only a quarter of an hour to reach the Chèremere lands. Climbing a tree-covered hill, Mattie slowed to a halt and pulled the brake to give Narcissa the same view she'd had upon first seeing the castle.

"Oh, Mattie," Narcissa breathed.

Before them lay an emerald valley sprayed with golden gorse and dark green woods. The mist lay over everything in silver clouds that were fast burning away in the sunlight. The shimmering veil was thickest on the lake where it kissed the ramparts of Chèremere, whose revetment walls rose sheer and white out of the water. The castle had been built on two flat islands connected by stone bridge corridors. The massive arches of the bridges thrust from the water to support turrets that were repeated throughout the outer walls.

A fortified barbican guarded the bridge to the gatehouse and had once protected Chèremere from invaders, but now it nestled among aged trees. Giant oaks shaded the buildings inside the bailey, while a green expanse of lawn held back the mighty drum towers of the revetment wall. The main castle guarded access to the next island, upon which rose the Gloriette, the medieval keep pierced by loopholes and leaded glass windows that had been added during the Renaissance.

The whole castle was constructed of cream-and-white stone and floated in the blue glass lake like a white rose on a pond. No longer a fortress, it remained an idyllic treasure amid the woods and fields of the valley.

"Yes," Mattie said with a frown. "When we saw it the first time, I thought I'd never seen anything so pretty in all my born days."

"One might be tempted to try to attach Mr. Tennant's interest if Chèremere comes with him."

"The problem is that he comes with it."

"I thought he'd rehabilitated himself in your estimation."

"Oh. Um, yes. He's all right."

"Back in London your opinion of him seemed a bit higher than that."

Mattie's hands worked on the steering wheel and she managed a pained smile. "Mama sets great store by him."

"By his lineage, you mean."

Nodding, Mattie released the brake and drove down the hill toward the barbican.

As they approached the castle Narcissa said, "I

called on the Countess of Ixworth before I left. She'll be down on the evening train."

"Hmmm." Mattie was looking around the grounds, fearing that Cheyne might have gotten up early.

"Don't you want to know what we talked about?"

Was that him walking around the ruins of the Norman tower next to the barbican? "What? Oh, sure." No, it was a gardener.

"She said Mr. Tennant bought this place with money he earned himself."

Mattie snorted. "He might have earned it himself, but who gave him that fancy education and helped him into the cavalry? It's not like he started with nothing, like Papa did."

"That's not his fault, Mattie. I've heard that he scandalized Society by supporting the extension of the vote."

"To women?"

"Well, no."

"Ha!"

"I don't know of many men who support votes for women."

"Afraid they'll lose their privileges and have to answer for their miserable treatment of us. Lying, uppity skunks."

"Mattie, what's got into you?"

Pulling the car up to the entrance to the great hall, Mattie shut off the engine and stepped down from it as a footman opened the door. "Nothing's got into me. I'm just tired of English Society with its petrified conventions and hypocrisy."

Narcissa got out and joined her. She swept an arm around, indicating the crenellated rooftops and turrets. "You can't be tired of this."

"I don't have a place like this," Mattie said as she trudged up the steps and into the great hall. "I have to live in a musty old Jacobean place with smoke-darkened paneling and smelly drains because Mama says it's picturesque. If I owned this place I'd never go to London, except maybe to see plays and such."

"And never go to balls? How dreadfully boring."

"I've had enough balls to last seven lifetimes," Mattie grumbled.

"If you're going to snipe the whole time we're here, I'm leaving."

They bickered like the old friends they were until they reached Narcissa's bedroom. Mattie left Narcissa there to oversee the unpacking of her trunks and rest after her journey. Having ordered an early breakfast tray in her room to avoid seeing Cheyne, she had no need to join the rest of the party at the morning meal. Soon the men would go out shooting, but until then she needed a place to hide. One of the drum towers would do.

Mattie crossed the bailey, shoved open a door leading to the western towers and mounted the stone stairs. Placing her hand on one wall, she climbed the dark staircase as it wound its way to the roof. Once on top, she hoisted herself onto the ledge between two stone crenellations and gazed out at the lake. Beyond the water lay a wood from which emerged a herd of deer. Black swans floated below her, joined by ringed teal and shelducks. In a field in the distance cattle grazed, and through it ran a meandering stream bordered by willows and birch. Mattie breathed in the scents from the garden that lay just beyond the barbican. Hydrangea, rhododendron, and azaleas bloomed there.

The peace of Chèremere soothed the ache in her heart. The brilliant colors of the garden lifted her spirits a bit. But nothing could assuage her frustration. Cheyne and Balfour had been unable to make anything of the blackmailer's note. The paper could be purchased all over London, and the ink was common as well. None of the suspects could be eliminated by tracing their movements at Spencer House the night the letters were stolen. Everyone had some time for which they couldn't account. No one seemed especially in need of money. Of course, a successful blackmailer wouldn't need money.

She'd tried to sound out the Stellafords, about whom she knew the least. Sir William was from an old county family. He and his wife Julia had five children—three sons and two daughters. All of them were still in the schoolroom, but the Stellafords delighted in travel and managed to go on several trips a year to places like Australia and Egypt. Sir William seemed to have no trouble affording a large family, five carriages, two country estates and a London town house as well as his adventures. Everyone liked him, and Julia had more women friends than any other lady in Society. The great hostesses of Society fought for Sir William's presence at their dinners, especially when the Prince of Wales was coming, for His Royal Highness was known to delight in Stellaford's humor. With Sir William present they could be assured that the prince wouldn't grow bored, and boring the Prince of Wales was social death.

Mattie sighed and jumped down from her perch. Her investigations so far had been unfruitful. In his high-handed manner, Cheyne had ordered her not to try questioning people herself, but she was desperate to end the search for the blackmailer and get away from him. Defying his orders and making him furious was simply an additional pleasure.

She felt her way back down the dark stairs and came out of the tower into brilliant sunlight, blinking at the sudden change, and stumbled into someone.

"Mattie," Cheyne said. "I've been looking for you. Where have you been? Oh, never mind. I want to talk to you."

Still blinking, Mattie backed up and forced herself to look at him. He was standing with his arms folded, an irritated expression marring those perfect features. He looked like a medieval lord about to chide some neglectful varlet. Mattie's chin came up, and she opened her mouth to spit a defiant reply at him, but he turned, offering his arm.

"You're supposed to be my guest. We'll pretend I'm showing you the garden."

"Why aren't you off shooting?"

"I don't like slaughtering hoards of birds in order

to amuse idle amateurs. I sent the men off with my gamekeeper, and he'll limit the ammunition so that the flocks aren't decimated."

"We don't need to talk."

Uttering an exasperated sound, Cheyne grabbed her hand and placed it on his arm. "Someone could be watching us from the windows."

Mattie glanced at the tall rectangles set in stone across the front of the hall. Each glittered with diamond-shaped panes. Mattie pressed her lips together and began to walk. She said nothing as they went through the gatehouse, across the bridge, and out through the barbican. The castle drive bordered a smaller lake on the left, and to the right lay the garden surrounded by a stone wall. Cheyne opened an iron gate for her, and she stepped inside. Not waiting for him, she marched down one of the neat gravel paths that meandered through a riot of flowers and bushes.

Cheyne caught up, pulled her around to face him and said, "You've been interfering again."

"I don't know what you're talking about."

"You've been prying, asking the Stellafords and Lance all sorts of questions. If the blackmailer hears of your little endeavors, he'll suspect something. You're going to ruin everything."

"I will not. I've been subtle."

"You haven't been subtle, you've been as obvious as a puppy sniffing after a fresh cut of beef. From now on you'll play the part of the distraught young lady. Whatever happened to the swooning and tears?

You were supposed to faint and generally waste away from worry."

Mattie rolled her eyes. "I decided that was stupid. Anyone who knows me knows I don't swoon and blubber."

"No, you shout and berate." Cheyne shook his head, walked down the path and returned. "You're going to have to cooperate, Miss Bright. This may be our only chance to trap the criminal. Do you want someone else to die?"

"I am cooperating, dang it. I'm not the one who changes his tune at the blink of an eye."

Cheyne frowned. "What do you mean?"

Her mouth was dry and her nerves stripped. Damn her loose tongue. She hadn't meant to make such a revealing remark.

"Oh, nothing."

He was eyeing her now and seemed to notice her rigid stance for the first time. Despite her efforts to remain calm, Mattie reddened under his stare. He looked away.

"Ah, yes." He walked over to a bed of blue hydrangeas and contemplated them. "Forgive me, Miss Bright. My conduct at our last meeting was ungentlemanly. It won't happen again. However, I suggest that you refrain from wearing trousers in the future. It's most unladylike, and it—"

"Land sakes!" Mattie exclaimed.

He stared at her. "Now what's wrong?"

"Do you always blame women for the way you act?" It was her turn to fold her arms and glare.

"You're the one who dressed like a man," Cheyne snapped.

"I don't care." Mattie marched up to him and planted a finger on his chest. "No matter what anybody says, Mr. Cheyne Tennant, you and every other man in this world are responsible for your emotions and your behavior. No one else is to blame if you can't learn what any three-year-old learns— that you just don't act on every feeling you get." She stood on tiptoe so she could meet his gaze on an equal level. "I am not responsible for what you feel and how you act. You feelings are your own danged responsibility."

Mattie swept around him and strode over to a small glade. She stopped by a swing that had been strung from the largest tree and gave the wooden seat a violent push. She was still fuming when Cheyne joined her, caught the swing and brought it to a standstill between them.

Watching her, he began to speak quietly. "You're right."

"What did you say?"

"I said you're right, Mattie."

She hadn't expected him to agree with her, so she said nothing and continued to gawk at him.

"I beg your pardon, Miss Bright."

"You do?"

"Yes. I must admit the truth when it's placed before me in so eloquent a manner." He stopped and ran a hand through hair the color of ripe wheat. "I've never been unable—that is, I'm not accustomed to being . . . Oh, hell. I shall do my best not to forget myself again."

"Seems to me all you have to do is remember I'm an ignorant colonial."

There was a long silence.

"I've been a bloody bastard."

"I'm not arguing with you," Mattie said coldly. She didn't trust him; wouldn't. No matter how many lovely apologies floated from those talented lips.

"Aren't you going to curse at me and call me a— what was the term?—a skunk?"

"No."

"Why not?"

"Never you mind why not. From now on you keep your personal comments to yourself. I'm here to help Superintendent Balfour catch this blackmailer, and the sooner we do that, the sooner I can get out of here and go home."

"You're going back to New York?"

"Yup."

"What?"

"Yes, Mr. Tennant. I'm going back to New York. I got things to do, and I've gone sour on the idea of catching a titled husband. It seems to me I don't need any husband at all. So I'll thank you to hurry up and catch this varmint who's causing all the trouble and do it quick."

Cheyne was still looking at her as if she'd sprouted horns and a tail.

"What about your promise to your father?"

"Papa will understand. It's Mama who won't, but

I'll handle Mama. All I ask is that you and I behave with civility to each other until this is over."

"I think I can promise you that, Miss Bright."

"Good."

"As long as you promise not to wear trousers again."

16

The reason the Queen's Gallery had white plaster walls was to keep the room true to its medieval origin. Cheyne hadn't intended for it to serve as a studio for Sir William Stellaford to photograph Mattie Bright. That was what had happened, however, and Cheyne didn't like it.

After dinner he and his guests had come to the gallery for coffee, wine, and conversation, but Sir William had produced his box camera and was taking pictures of Mattie. He'd led his subject to one of the arched windows that overlooked the lake. She stood beside it, one arm draped on the sill. His other guests were playing cards or had gathered around the piano to listen to the Countess of Ixworth's playing. Cheyne prowled the gallery while he strove not to appear to be watching the photography session.

He walked to the fireplace and traced the pattern carved into the mantelpiece. It was a castle, the heraldic device of Castile. On the other side the spandrels bore the pomegranates of Aragon. Together these belonged to the badge of Catherine of Aragon, Henry VIII's first queen. Cheyne stared hard at the castle surmounted by a crown and listened to Sir William.

"That's lovely, my dear. Just allow your arm to drape naturally along the sill. Turn your head to the side. Excellent. You see, this angle displays your lovely neck to perfection."

Cheyne's head whipped around. Sir William was standing much too close to Mattie, and his fingertips touched her chin, showing her the correct angle at which to hold her head. Cheyne took an involuntary step toward the two, but Sir William left Mattie to pick up his box camera and fiddle with it. Swinging away from the fireplace, Cheyne stalked over to the group around the piano.

Mattie remained still, her dark hair a vivid contrast to the white plaster wall. Her gown, a deceptively simple one made costly by the thousands of tiny pearls sewn onto the silk, clung to her figure and swept to the floor. Sir William had swirled the train around her feet.

"Perfection," the photographer cooed as he took the picture.

"I believe this is your favorite," Rose Marie said to him. She began Mozart's *Eine Kleine Nachtmusik*.

Cheyne nodded and smiled at her absently. Out of the corner of his eye he glimpsed Sir William draw-

ing Mattie's arm down from the sill and gently placing her hands in front of her. He grasped her shoulders to straighten them, and Cheyne shoved himself
away from the piano and strode in their direction.
At the last moment he regained sense and changed
his course to flop down in a medieval chair carved in
the shape of a bowed X. His fingers drummed on
the arm while Sir William took another picture. He
shifted position in the chair as the photographer
again approached his subject.

"Now, Miss Bright, let's try a classic pose." Sir
William took Mattie's elbow and turned her to the
side. "Place this arm at your back. Good."

Cheyne leaned forward as Sir William's voice began to purr.

"Now, my dear, stand very straight. Lift your
chin. Imagine a wire is pulling the top of your head
to the ceiling. Shoulders back, like this."

Cheyne watched as Mattie drew herself up. He
scowled as her chest was thrust forward. Shooting
out of the chair, he was halfway to her when the
Marquess of Stainfield passed him and reached her
first. Cheyne glanced at Sir William, stepped in front
of Mattie before he could take a picture and gave the
man a look that would have been found at the sack-
ing of Rome.

Sir William gawked at him, then flushed and
turned away to fuss with the box camera. Cheyne
dragged his enraged stare away from the man, only
to find Stainfield escorting Mattie past him.

"You must see the chapel. It has Flemish tapestries and panels from the early fourteenth century."

Cheyne watched the two sail out of the gallery, his suspicions alerted. Old Barmy was interested in antiquities, but only his own. As far as Cheyne knew, he'd never set foot in the chapel. Glancing around to make sure his guests were occupied, he slipped out of the room, took the bridge corridor across to the main castle and reached the chapel as the doors shut. He opened them again in time to see Barmy walk down the central aisle with Mattie. He stopped halfway down and turned to her.

"We could be walking down the aisle to our wedding ceremony, my dear. Look at you, so lovely in your virginal white gown."

Mattie disengaged her arm from Stainfield's. "You promised you weren't going to bring up the subject of marriage."

"I'm sorry. Don't be angry, my dear. I've brought something to show you."

"Here?"

"I left it here before dinner. It seemed a good place."

Stainfield led Mattie to the front pew. He produced a locked box, which he handed to her. Opening it with a key from his coat pocket, he took it from Mattie, held it in front of her and lifted the lid. Inside, on black velvet, rested a crown glittering with diamonds, rubies, and emeralds.

"My duchess will have the right to wear this."

Cheyne winced and released his stranglehold on the door. Ignoring the ache in his fingers, he saw with dismay Mattie's awed expression. Stainfield took the crown in both hands, raised it high above Mattie's head and lowered it slowly to rest on her head. He stood back to survey her.

"You're the image of regal dignity, my dear. Look." He turned Mattie so that she could see her reflection in the glass of one of the windows.

Dread clamped down on Cheyne as he watched her look at herself with astonishment. The crown might have been made for her, and Cheyne began to hate Stainfield for showing Mattie this lovely image of herself. He had no crown to give her, no peer's robes with which to drape those lovely shoulders. Light from the wall sconces bathed her in a gentle glow and set the gems dancing. Most women would have been obscured by the grandeur of the crown. With her elegant neck, royal posture and flashing eyes, Mattie Bright matched the richness with her own.

Then she broke the spell by reaching up and grabbing the crown as if it were a straw hat and handing it back to Stainfield. "Thanks, but I don't think so."

Stainfield blinked, then cried, "Are you mad?"

"I'm sure most folks would think so." Mattie patted her hair. "But the truth is, in order to wear that crown I'd have to go to places and spend time doing things I'd sooner avoid."

"Any woman in England would—"

"Good," Mattie said. "You'll have lots of choices."
Stainfield shook his head in a stunned manner.

Mattie patted him on the arm and spoke gently.
"You wouldn't be happy with me, my lord. I like
driving motorcars by myself, and I won't give up
managing my money. I support causes that would
make you choke, and I hate frittering my time away
at balls and horse races and such."

"All that would change. When a woman
marries—"

"No." Mattie tapped the crown with her finger.
"For me, this is playacting. This crown, titles, divine
right of kings, all of it belongs to the old way of doing things." She walked away from Stainfield and
turned in a circle, her arms thrown wide. "We're on
the verge of the twentieth century, my lord. Soon
we'll travel by flying machines. We have Mr. Edison's moving pictures. We've got motorcars and telephones and electric lights. And the people who
made them possible don't have titles and crowns.
The future belongs to ordinary people with extraordinary brains in their heads." Mattie glanced at the
chapel's Gothic windows. "It's nice to live in a beautiful castle, my lord, as long as you realize it's just a
big stone house."

Cheyne found himself smiling.

"You can't mean that," Stainfield said.

"I do. The future will be made as it always has
been, by those with the courage and intelligence to
change things." She glanced around the chapel.
"Like Mr. Tennant."

Cheyne poked his head farther over the threshold to hear better.

"Tennant? Courageous? Ha."

"Yes," Mattie replied. "To be born into this mummified aristocracy, to be born to privilege and wealth, and then break out of it, that takes courage. Something inside him is different. He was able to recognize how static Society is, how utterly lacking in creativity and intelligence." Mattie walked over to Stainfield, put her finger-tips on his arm and leaned toward him. "And he did something about it before he was swallowed whole."

Now Cheyne was grinning.

"It's Tennant!" Stainfield exclaimed.

Mattie flushed and lowered her hand. "What are you talking about?"

"I've seen the way he looks at you." Stainfield shoved the crown back in its box. "Everyone has re-marked upon it. Even Lance has noticed, and I must say you've done nothing to discourage him."

Turning quickly in a whirl of skirts, Mattie marched toward the window. "You're imagining things."

Muttering his agreement, Cheyne scowled at Stainfield.

"Not likely," Stainfield said as he locked the box and slipped the key in his pocket. "As I said, I've seen the way he looks at you. Cheyne Tennant has never looked at a woman like that, even when he was at university. He can't keep himself from staring. It's almost as obvious as the fact that you're afraid to look at him."

"I am not!"

"Then why are you shouting? If you were indifferent or merely friendly toward him, my remarks wouldn't fluster you into screeching at me or make you turn the color of a ripe apple."

Suddenly Cheyne was enchantingly happy. The world seemed a miraculous place. He was so happy he almost forgot to duck when Mattie babbled a denial at Stainfield and turned to leave. He darted away from the chapel and around a corner. Spinning around, he adjusted his evening coat and walked back the way he'd come. Mattie ran into him because she was watching the closed doors of the chapel. He caught her before they collided, and she gave a little cry.

"Steady, Miss Bright."

Mattie scooted out of his grasp, her face crimson and her hands shaking. "Oh, I didn't see you there."

"I was just coming to see where you'd got to. You've been gone with old Barmy for quite a while, and your mother is pleased."

"She won't be for long."

"Oh?"

Mattie's gaze avoided his, and her hands were clasped in a strangling grip. When she didn't elaborate, he went on.

"Unless you want to set people talking, you'd better come back to the Queen's Gallery."

"I don't feel—"

"But before we return, I'd like to ask you to meet me after everyone has retired. About one o'clock should do. There are one or two matters we haven't discussed yet."

"I don't think—"

"It's not required." Cheyne grabbed her arm and guided her back across the bridge corridor before she had a chance to recover her composure. As they entered the Queen's Gallery he whispered, "In the Banqueting Hall. Everyone's rooms are in the main castle, so the Gloriette will be deserted."

He propelled her into the room to meet the excited and questioning looks of her mother. He spent the rest of the evening attending to the needs of his other guests. One part of his mind concentrated on perceiving any hint that could lead him to the identity of the blackmailer. The other part whirled with confused feelings about what he'd just heard from Mattie. The hours before bedtime passed uneventfully. Once everyone had retired, he lay on his bed in his evening clothes and waited for the appointed meeting time.

She had refused a man with a dukedom to offer her. Oh, she'd said she was going home, but he'd seen many young ladies scoff at exalted titles until actually offered one. Not Mattie. Mattie Bright was an original. A woman with a sterling soul and the courage to stand by her beliefs and go against her mother, her promise to her dead father, Society, everyone. He hadn't treated her well, but she'd praised him to Stainfield as a man of principle. She admired him for the very qualities most people deplored.

The admiration women accorded him had always been of a different nature. Aristocratic women trapped in loveless marriages seemed to find him the perfect diversion. He remembered the first time a young married lady had chosen him for the purpose. He'd been quite innocent, barely fifteen. Lady Ursula Race had been visiting his mother, and one day she followed him when he went riding. Catching up with him in the wood that surrounded the Bracewell estate, she pretended that her saddle needed adjusting and asked him to help her. What issued from that chivalrous act made him blush for weeks.

Once he had begun attending balls and country house parties, life seemed filled with feminine bounty. Ambassadors' wives, ladies married to peers and ministers. He sailed from one to the other, liking many, wanting most, loving none of them. But the eligible girls—they weren't for him, because he was a younger son. No title, no prospects of ever getting one, no estates. But by then he'd been poisoned by the uselessness of existence in Society and knew he had to leave or perish on a diet of sterility and posturing.

He'd made a mistake once. He'd fallen in love with the daughter of an earl. At twenty-three it was easy to do. Her name had been Violet. She had red-gold hair, loved puppies and kittens, and laughed at him when he became too serious. She brought humor into his life, and he adored her. But her parents whisked her off to the Riviera and arranged a more profitable match with an old buffer who possessed a title and lots of tin.

Cheyne had tried to see her before she married, but she wouldn't agree. In the end her fear of being expelled from the best parties and drawing rooms outweighed her affection for him. He had stood in the street in the rain watching her bedroom window the night before her wedding, unable to believe she'd go through with the ceremony. Soaked and shivering, he'd watched her get into the family coach wearing her wedding gown and drive out of his life.

The pain of losing Violet remained with him for years, and he'd always wondered if her parents had discovered the secret of his birth. Had Violet abandoned him because he was illegitimate? After that he stayed with married ladies who knew what they wanted. It wasn't his fault if their husbands left them alone while they pursued other women.

He heard a clock strike the quarter hour and began to feel agitated. He found himself dreading the thought of Mattie knowing about his real father. Would she still admire him? As he left his rooms and slipped down dark corridors, he chided himself. He was only going to talk to Mattie, just talk in a comfortable manner. A chasm had opened between them after the Trillford ball, and he needed to close it. He'd been thrown off balance by her sudden appearance in those cursed trousers. It wouldn't happen again. All he wanted to do was talk, restore their relationship. Ask her if what she'd said to Stainfield was the truth. No, he couldn't do that. What would he say? *I say, Mattie, do you really admire me?* How ridiculous.

He entered the Banqueting Hall at one o'clock and was lighting a lamp when Mattie came in. She hadn't changed, either, and the pearls on her dress gleamed a soft ivory that nearly matched her skin. She walked stiffly to one of the Italian Savonarola armchairs and sat with a rustle of silk against silk.

He was thinking that her hair was darker than the Banqueting Hall's ebony floorboards and must have missed something, because she bent toward him and said, "Did you hear me?"

"I beg your pardon?"

"What did you want to talk to me about? Has something happened?"

He loved the little parallel furrows of skin that appeared between her brows when she was confused or angry. She'd removed the choker of pearls she'd worn to dinner. Her neck was bare, every perfect inch of it. And he found it impossible not to follow the long slope of it down to her bosom. The gentle curve was barely revealed by the neck of her gown. His hands clenched. He wanted to peel the silk and pearls away from those curves.

"Are you hard of hearing, my lord?"

"What? Oh. No." Hell. He'd been lying to himself all night. He wasn't interested in talking to her. Especially not now; in fact, he couldn't. He began to walk toward her, slowly. "Miss Bright. Mattie. I was wrong."

She eyed him suspiciously as he drew near. "Wrong about what?"

"It makes no difference."

He was five feet away when she jumped to her feet and moved away from the chair. He changed his path and kept coming. He was three feet from her when she sidled behind the Italian chair.

"What makes no difference? Stop stalking me like a mountain lion after a calf."

Cheyne smiled. "What makes no difference?" He stopped, leaned over the chair and whispered, "The trousers."

Now she was staring at him in confused alarm. "What do you mean?"

Holding her gaze with his, Cheyne quickly laid his hands on her forearms to prevent her from stepping out of reach. She started when he touched her and pulled back.

"I mean, sweet Mattie, that you drive me insane whether you're wearing trousers or not."

She gave a little cry and tried to get away. He laughed softly and pulled her. She stumbled, and as she fell against him, he wrapped his arms around her with the chair still between them.

"Let go, dang it!"

He felt her chest heave. Her breast rose and fell against the pearls at the neck of her gown, and he had to fight to drag his gaze from the sight. He lifted his eyes to her lips. They were tight and pale. He wanted them loose and red from kissing. His mouth was almost on hers when she hissed at him, "Trousers. Is that all you think about?"

He leaned back and met her angry look. "No. I think about your hair and wonder how something so dark can shine like that. I think about your eyes and how they seem to catch fire from your hair. I think about your lips and what they feel like beneath mine."

Her mouth dropped open. "I—you think all that?"

He nodded and touched her cheek with his. "I assure you."

"Seems—" She cleared her throat as he brushed his lips across her forehead. "Seems like you think about me a powerful lot."

His fingers toyed with a lock of hair that had escaped its pins. "I think about you constantly." He breathed into her ear, and she shivered.

"I didn't know. I thought . . ." Her voice trailed away as his lips slid from her ear to her neck.

"Don't think, my midnight sun. I'm not."

He kissed his way from her neck back to her mouth and captured her lips. Submerging into a dark whirlpool, he was dragged to the surface when she tore her lips from his and stared into his eyes.

"You don't even like me."

He grinned at her. "How could I not like a young lady who thinks I'm courageous and intelligent?"

"You were eavesdropping!"

"Old Barmy was wrong. Your blush isn't apple-red, it's the most delightful shade of scarlet."

With an enraged and rueful cry, Mattie squirmed out of his grasp and bolted for the door. He caught up with her as she opened it, pushed it closed and trapped her against it. She whipped around and he dodged a jab she had intended for his stomach.

"Will you calm down?"

"Spying on me. Listening to private conversations. Sneaking and skulking and sniggering at me."

Cheyne grabbed her wrists and gave her a little shake as his own temper flared. "I wasn't sniggering, damn it. I was honored to have gained your admiration."

She stopped fighting him and stared. "Honored?"

He looked away. "Yes." He still hadn't told her the truth about his birth, but nothing seemed to matter now except her regard and her touch on his body. He couldn't lose either. Suddenly he knew the devastation would be irreparable. "Yes," he repeated softly.

"You were honored," she whispered.

"Yes."

Mattie said nothing, and he grew more and more reluctant to look at her. He almost laughed at himself. He was afraid of what she thought. He, Cheyne Tennant, who could have a dozen women with a mere nod of his head. After long moments of silence, he felt her move. She stepped closer to him and gave him a shy smile.

"You could kiss me again, if you wanted to."

He felt a spasm of relief combined with the pain of holding himself in check. "Bloody hell, Mattie. If I kiss you again, I'm not going to stop."

"I know."

This time he raised his eyes to hers and didn't look away.

17

Mattie knew she was in some kind of dreamlike fog. Cheyne Tennant had caused it with his sudden reversal in conduct. He'd been as distant and wary as she had until this evening. Her mind couldn't keep up with the impulses her body was sending faster than the pistons churned in her motorcar. First he pounced on her. Then, when he'd stirred her senses and her alarm, he'd burst out with that admission. He was honored by her regard. He'd said it with such humble shyness that she'd lost all wariness.

They were staring at each other now, in that suspended moment after she'd as much as admitted she wanted to be here in the Banqueting Hall with him. Her mistrust and anger had vanished, and with them her defenses.

Cheyne took her hand and kissed it, and then stared into her eyes as though searching for something he needed desperately. "Mattie, are you certain?"

"I—I'd rather spend this time with you than spend my life with some fool with a fancy title and the sense of a drunk armadillo."

She started when he threw back his head and laughed.

"Mattie, Mattie, Mattie, my little colonial savage. There's no one like you."

"You got no call to—"

His lips silenced her protest. Mattie pressed her hands against his chest, still irritated at being called a savage, but the irritation faded at the feel of his body. Her hands kneaded the flesh over his ribs, then slipped around to feel the muscles over his back. He breathed into her ear, sending violent stabs of sensation through her. It seemed as if his lips were everywhere—her mouth, her cheeks, her neck, her breasts. Then her gown seemed to melt from her body, trickling down her legs to pool at her feet. She followed it, dragging Cheyne down with her onto the black floor and piles of silk.

She heard someone cry out, and realized it was her voice that burst into the silence when his tongue touched her nipple. Vaguely she wondered where the rest of her clothing had gone, but the thought dribbled away under an onslaught of kisses that pressed a wet path down her stomach. She fought her way through his clothing to find hot skin and working muscles. Digging her fingers into his biceps, she almost cried out again as the kisses became impossibly intimate. Soon she had no breath and gasped, only to find his mouth on hers again.

At the same time she felt him nudging her. She opened in answer to his plea, and felt pain. She jumped, but he held her against him until she moved again. Then he joined her in a hot race, holding himself back, guiding her, encouraging her with rapid, hard kisses that matched their rhythm until Mattie felt her body explode.

As she shivered and clawed at him Cheyne threw his head back and groaned. Mattie grabbed him and pulled him deep inside her while she shoved with her hips, desperate to relieve herself of this madness. Finally they collapsed, she to the floor and he on top of her.

Mattie didn't know how long they lay there, but after a time she began to feel thousands of tiny pearls pressing into her flesh. Cheyne lifted his head. His gaze was unfocused for a moment. Then he shook his head and looked at her. He gave her a slow, pleased and lazy smile. When he kissed her nose, she giggled, and he moved off of her.

"I can't move," she said.

"I've never felt this drained." He winced and pulled her corset from beneath his hips.

Mattie took it and tried to sit up. "Ouch. Danged pearls."

Cheyne stood and offered his hand, but she remained on the floor looking at him.

"What's wrong?" he asked.

She surveyed the long legs, the bulge of thigh muscles and wide shoulders that had blocked her vision during those moments of madness, and smiled. "Nothing's wrong. Not a blamed thing."

"Are you trying to make me blush, Miss Bright?"

They grinned at each other. Teasing and laughing, they began to search for their clothing. Cheyne had his trousers on, and Mattie was trying to fasten the buttons of her stained gown when what sounded like a cattle stampede echoed outside the Banqueting Hall. Holding his shirt, Cheyne quickly stepped in front of her as the doors flew open to admit Mutton, Lady Julia Stellaford, and two footmen. Mattie huddled behind Cheyne, clutching her gown, mortified. The men halted in confusion when they saw the room occupied, but Julia rushed to Cheyne.

"Have you seen my husband? He came this way."

Scowling, Cheyne said, "I beg your pardon. Please leave—"

"I fear for his life!" Lady Julia cried. "He found a note in our room tonight, and just now he got up, took his shotgun and ran out."

Mutton and the others had turned their backs. Mattie held her dress together and tried to make sense of what Lady Julia was saying. She heard Cheyne's tone change to one of concern.

"Mutton, you search the cellars and the dungeon. Niven and Panby can take the upper rooms."

Before he could finish, an explosion sounded nearby. Without a word, everyone rushed out. Cheyne kissed Mattie, told her to stay where she was and ran after them. Her embarrassment forgotten, Mattie fastened the top buttons of her gown, stepped into her slippers and raced out of the Banqueting Hall.

She found Cheyne, Mutton, and Niven on the floor above, clustered around a small closet. Cheyne was kneeling beside Sir William Stellaford, whose boots lay over the threshold. As Mattie ran up to them, Cheyne rose and grabbed her.

"No, Mattie."

"Is he all right?"

"He's dead," Cheyne said as he guided her away. "No, you're not going to have your way in this."

She almost protested, but when she saw Cheyne's remote and chilly expression, she allowed him to escort her to the stone bridge corridor.

"He's dead."

Cheyne stopped at the entrance to the corridor. "Yes. Panby took Lady Julia to her room. He'll find Capgrave and have him see to her." He looked at her in the light from a gas lamp mounted on the wall outside. "You're trembling. Are you all right?"

Mattie hugged herself. She couldn't seem to keep warm. "I'm fine. I've seen dead men before. A fella was thrown from his horse at the ranch one time and broke his neck."

Warm arms surrounded her, and she lay against Cheyne's chest with her eyes squeezed shut. She opened them because she kept seeing Sir William's boots.

"I must go, Mattie. Promise me you'll stay in your room until I can sort this out. I'll send for you."

"I can help."

"No, you can't. Not this time."

"Why?"

He held her at arm's length. "They saw us to-gether, Mattie."

"How can you worry about that when Sir William just shot himself?"

She heard the strain and horror in her voice and bit her lip. Cheyne pressed her hands together and held them to his lips.

"I have to worry, as you call it. Your reputation and my honor demand it."

"What are you saying?"

Footsteps and voices came from the main castle. Cheyne glanced down the corridor. "This isn't the time, Mattie. Do as I say."

He gave her a little shove, and because she was shivering and trembling at the same time, she did as he ordered. It was his house, and his responsibility lay with the dead man. He didn't need her arguing with him. She could do that later. Mattie hurried back to her room. On her way she met several servants, who stared at her as they hurried toward the Gloriette.

Narcissa had the room next to hers, and she was hovering outside her door when Mattie arrived. "What's happened? Where have you been? Goodness, what's happened to your hair, and your dress?"

Mattie shook her head and went into her room, but Narcissa followed. "Mattie, what's happened?"

"Sir William shot himself in a closet in the Gloriette."

Narcissa sat down on the bed while Mattie began

to unfasten the buttons on her gown. The dress fell off her shoulders.

"Mattie, what happened to you?"

Narcissa rushed to her and picked up the dress. She walked around Mattie. "Your back is red." Narcissa's hand went to her mouth, and she sucked in her breath. *"Mattie."*

"Go back to bed."

Her mother's voice came at the same time as a knock on the door. "Mattie, dear, are you all right? There's such a commotion."

Narcissa rushed to the door and assured Mrs. Bright that she and Mattie were fine.

"You girls stay here. I'm going to find out what's going on."

Mattie sighed; she didn't want to see Mama right now. She found the water pitcher and basin and began a quick sponge bath while Narcissa rummaged in an armoire for a nightgown. She was slipping the gown on when she heard cloth ripping. Poking her head through the neck of the nightgown, Mattie emerged to see her friend tearing her soiled petticoat. The pearl-studded gown had been folded into a bundle.

"What are you doing?"

"I'm going to burn this petticoat. Stir the fire."

"Oh, Narcissa."

Narcissa tore the garment into two pieces. "The dinner gown, too."

Mattie swooped down and grabbed the gown. "Oh, no, you don't. I'm keeping it."

"Whatever for?"

"Never you mind what for." Mattie stuffed the gown into the bottom of the armoire and shut the door. "You can burn the petticoat if you like."

Narcissa dropped a section of the undergarment on the coals and turned to her. "Well?"

Walking calmly to the bed, Mattie got under the covers. "Well, what?"

Her friend scampered across the room and got into bed beside her.

"What happened? Is Sir William really dead?"

Mattie rubbed her forehead. "Yes. I think he killed himself."

"But why?"

"I don't know."

"He was such a jolly kind of fellow."

Mattie nodded, unable to reveal anything. "It's terrible." Any words seemed banal and inadequate for the horror of an unnecessary death.

"Who was it?" Narcissa asked.

When Mattie looked at her in confusion, she made a sound of irritation and poked Mattie's arm. "Who were you with?"

"No one."

Narcissa gave her a skeptical look. "Did no one undress you and stain your underclothing?"

"Shush, Narcissa."

"It was the marquess."

Mattie slid farther underneath the covers and drew them over her head. Narcissa yanked them down.

"I knew it. It was Mr. Tennant."

Popping up, Mattie scowled at her. "How did you know?" She could have bitten her tongue when Narcissa grinned.

"Ha! I knew it, I knew it. You thought you were so secretive and clever. Nobody fights like that with a man unless she's in love."

"Well, you could have let me in on the secret."

"You wouldn't have believed me."

Narcissa scooted closer and lowered her voice. "Tell me, Mattie. What was it like?"

"It was wonderful," Mattie said with a tremulous smile that faded as she remembered Sir William. "It was incomparable, until Lady Julia and Mutton and the others found us."

After a short silence, Narcissa slipped her arm around Mattie. "Oh, dear." They sat side by side for a while. Then Narcissa sighed. "Not the most respectable way to announce an engagement, but I suppose it can't be helped. . . . What? What's wrong?"

Mattie pulled the covers up to her chin. "We— we didn't talk about an engagement."

"Of course not, not after Sir William—but you must, after this horrible business is over."

"I'm terrible, sinful." Mattie lay down and turned on her side. "I didn't think of marriage. All I thought about was him. And now poor Sir William has killed himself, and all I think about is Cheyne Tennant."

"We didn't know the man well, Mattie. Of course it's a tragedy. I'm horrified, but neither of us can change what's done."

"Poor Lady Julia," Mattie whispered.

"Yes. But Dr. Capgrave and your mother will take care of her," Narcissa said. "You should rest. Mr. Tennant will manage everything, and he'll talk to your mother about marriage, too. You'll see."

Turning on her back, Mattie stared up at the ceiling. "He never said anything about marriage." She blushed. "I don't think he meant to make an offer."

"That doesn't matter."

"Why not?"

Narcissa got off the bed and began arranging the covers around Mattie. "Because you've been seen in a most compromising situation. Mr. Tennant is an English gentleman, and he knows what has to be done. He'll arrange for everyone's silence." She smoothed the covers. "And he'll make the offer his honor demands. Any other action is unthinkable for someone like him."

Mattie sat up quickly. "He said something like that. He said he had to worry because my reputation and his honor demanded it."

"There. You see? Everything will be fine." Narcissa sat on the bed again.

Shaking her head, Mattie said, "I'm not sure."

"Why not?"

"He didn't say anything about marriage before we . . . He didn't make an offer before."

"But he will now."

Mattie turned to stare at her friend. "That's just it. He'll make an offer now. Like he said, his honor demands it. How am I ever going to know what he'd have done if we hadn't been discovered?"

"Oh."

"If he asks for my hand out of duty . . ." Mattie turned to Narcissa and blinked back tears. "I couldn't marry a man who only wanted my money. How can I marry a man who only wants to save my reputation?"

"You don't know that's his only reason."

Mattie shook her head. "I don't know anything. I won't until I talk to him. But it will have to wait."

"Yes," Narcissa said. "Poor Sir William. I wonder why he did it."

Mattie didn't answer. She was certain the blackmailer had struck again. The criminal was here at Chèremere. Sir William had been a victim all along, and this last demand had driven him to kill himself rather than face ruin.

Mattie's heart flip-flopped. How much longer was this nightmare going to last? How many more people had to die? Her own problems seemed paltry in comparison to what was happening to the victims.

The blackmailer! Cheyne had to see to it that none of those who saw them in the Banqueting Hall spoke of it. Otherwise their trap would be ruined.

And she couldn't accept an offer of marriage to Cheyne Tennant even if he made one. She was supposed to be lovesick for eloquent Michel. Of course, she was supposed to be anxious to marry a titled gentleman as well. The whole premise behind her vulnerability to blackmail was that she wanted a title in spite of her attachment to Michel. No, she couldn't suddenly abandon her quest for a duke. The ruse must remain in place until the blackmailer was caught. Any other course risked arousing suspicion.

She wouldn't have rejected Stainfield so definitely had he not forced her to make a decision. Luckily she knew him well enough to know he wouldn't tell anyone she'd refused him. Stainfield was too proud. He'd say nothing until forced to, and then he'd say he lost interest in her. The last thing he'd admit was that some little no-account American had tossed him aside.

Mattie squeezed her eyes shut and listened to Narcissa's steady breathing. Her friend had fallen asleep. Covering her face with her hands, Mattie wished she could do the same. She was confused and anxious, and she longed to throw herself into Cheyne's arms. She wished she'd never become involved in this trap for the blackmailer.

Mattie's thoughts chased each other around and around until, as the first gray light of dawn peeped through the curtains, she dozed. She dreamed of ebony floors, Cheyne's taut, strong body and his sapphire eyes. But she woke remembering Sir William's boots sticking out of that closet.

18

❧❧

Chèremere's Tudor kitchens huddled against the bulk of the main castle, a red brick labyrinth bristling with chimneys. Cheyne walked into the narrow alley called Fish Court and paused to rub his temples. Sir William Stellaford had killed himself in the early morning hours, and it was now dusk. Cheyne had spent most of the time since then dealing with the consequences of the tragedy. There had been the coroner to summon, and the local constable, and Lady Julia to be comforted. This last became impossible once the constable discovered Sir William's collection of photographs.

Who would have thought jolly old Sir William had a taste for taking pictures of women without their clothes? No wonder the blackmailer had nearly ruined him. Balfour had called to say he'd discovered a secret bank account from which Stellaford had paid his tormentor. Although his other accounts appeared untouched, the Stellaford reserves had been depleted, leaving Lady Julia with a questionable future. Luckily she had relatives anxious to assist her. Cheyne had seen her to the train that would take her to them. Elland Capgrave had gone as her escort and would return to London afterward. Sir William's body would be released by the coroner tomorrow and be shipped to his wife.

Leaning against a brick wall, Cheyne contemplated a pair of windows across the court. On the second floor, they were fitted with aged glass cut into diamond panes. He closed his eyes and sighed. Sir William's death weighed heavily on him. If he'd been attending to his job instead of lusting after Mattie, he might have stopped the blackmailer by now. As it was, he'd failed to prevent another death, and he'd ruined Mattie's reputation, too. Oh, he'd spoken to everyone who'd seen them. Silence was assured, for now. But nothing could prevent rumors from spreading. Word would get about, as it always did.

Now that Lady Julia was gone, he had to think about Mattie. Indeed, all the time he'd been speaking to the authorities and dealing with the necessary business of death, her words kept haunting him. He remembered clearly how she'd told him his feelings were his responsibility, as were any actions he took because of them. What a sharp little mind she had.

He'd allowed his emotions to rule; now he must accept the responsibility for his conduct. Succinct and pointed, those words failed miserably to capture what had happened and how he felt. Certainly she'd driven him to distraction for want of her. But he couldn't lie to himself anymore. He'd wanted other women, many quite beautiful. None had kept him whipped into a state of frustration by haunting his thoughts. Too late he'd realized how powerful his attraction to this obstinate and untamed young lady had become.

In truth, he hadn't wanted to admit what he felt. And he hadn't, even when she'd given him the gift of her love. Being with Mattie had wiped all thought from his heated mind. She had been like a cleansing flame, burning away old hurts, his armor of cynicism, his distrust. He could even point to the moment the flames had begun their purification; it had been when he gave her the chance to say no. *I'd rather spend this time with you than spend my life with some fool with a fancy title and the sense of a drunk armadillo.* If he lived another century he'd never find a woman who could make him feel so blessed and make him laugh at the same time. No other woman had given him her love and her care at the same time. To find that he'd inspired such a gesture was humbling.

After their joining, his body felt as renewed as his spirit, and he liked to think he would have had the courage to tell her. Any chance of it had been ruined by the interruption and Sir William's death.

Confound it. How could he have been so reckless? Seducing her in the Banqueting Hall, of all places. If word got out, she'd be disgraced, unmarriageable even in America. The thought of Mattie Bright the object of scorn and ostracism aroused his rage. Of course, it wouldn't happen. He'd see to that. Before another night passed he would ask Mattie to marry him.

Cheyne continued on his way. He'd come here because Mutton had informed him Mattie was touring the old buildings. When he purchased the castle he'd left the kitchens as they were and modernized the ones in the main castle. Lately he'd restored many of the rooms—the larders, boiling house, confectory, and pastry office. Chèremere had been a seat of great families since Saxon times, and wealthy barons under the Tudors had expanded on the medieval kitchens. Few such structures had survived, and he felt it his duty to see to it that his did.

She wasn't in the buttery, pantry, or any of the smaller cellars. Cheyne looked in the great wine cellar to no avail, then went into the court in front of the great kitchen. There he heard a door slam.

"Dang."

There was only one person in Chèremere who used that word. Cheyne hurried across the court and into the oldest of the Tudor kitchens. Mattie was standing beside a roasting fireplace, a twelve-foot cavern blackened with countless fires. The top of the fireplace arch was higher than her head, and she had bent over an iron pot suspended inside it.

"Mattie."

She gasped and turned, knocking the pot. Grabbing it, she held it still, then walked to the timber plank table where earthenware jars and jugs had been displayed. She picked up a ladle sitting in a stew pot and examined it. Cheyne joined her, but she still didn't look at him.

"Lady Julia has gone?" she asked.

"Yes." Standing this close, he could smell the lemon-scented soap she used, and he could see delicate blue veins just beneath the skin on her hands.

"We should have caught the blackmailer before he drove poor Sir William to his death. What did he have to hide?"

The question penetrated the lemon-scented fog into which he'd descended. "He had a taste for photographs of a particularly scandalous sort."

"What do you mean?" She turned to look at him, her reserve forgotten.

"He liked to photograph ladies—women."

"That's hardly scandalous."

"It is when they haven't any clothes on."

Her eyes widened. "Land sakes."

"Indeed."

"Why would he want to do that?"

Cheyne was growing more and more uncomfortable. He wouldn't have mentioned the photographs at all, but he'd learned how difficult it was to keep Mattie in the dark.

Mattie seemed to be thinking hard. "If he wanted to see women without their clothes, there are plenty who would oblige."

"Mattie!"

She glanced at him and rolled her eyes. "You're

scandalized that I know such things. Lots of women do, you know. We're not all sheltered princesses protected from every bit of unpleasantness."

"Mattie, I don't want to talk about photographs or Sir William. I want to talk about what happened between us."

She gave a great sigh, squared her shoulders, and nodded. Cheyne smiled, thinking she expected him to try to wiggle out of any commitment. He took her hand and kissed it.

"Last night you made the sun shine at midnight."

She looked down at her shoes as she slipped her hand out of his. "You were powerful amazing yourself."

"Now, Mattie, it's a little late to be shy." He took her hand back. "Look at me, my sweet. God, what startling eyes you have."

"Cheyne, I—"

"Will you marry me, Mattie?"

"No."

He didn't recognize the word at first, so unexpected was the refusal.

"No?" All at once he felt a jolt of fear. Had she discovered the truth of his birth? She was kind and loving, but that didn't mean she'd want to marry a bastard. He swallowed hard. "Why not?"

Mattie tugged her hand from his grasp and burst into speech. "I can't marry you just because we got carried away. It wouldn't be right. I know you're trying to do the honorable thing, but . . ." She turned her back for a moment, then faced him. He could see damp places on her cheeks where she'd wiped tears. "You don't have to do it," she said in a shaking voice.

"I don't have to," he repeated, stunned. She didn't know the truth after all.

Mattie picked up the topmost of a stack of wooden bowls and set it on the table. He should tell her about his real father right now. While he was trying to find the words with which to explain, he watched her hands. They were unsteady and she almost knocked the bowls to the floor.

"I'd be a hypocrite if I didn't try to live up to the same standards I apply to other folks," she said in an unsteady voice. "You didn't make me do anything I didn't want to do. I won't force you to do something you don't want to do."

He couldn't bear to see her so miserable. "Hell."

"Don't you cuss at me, Cheyne Tennant."

His own fears forgotten, Cheyne grabbed her by the shoulders and pulled her close. "Do you really think I'd allow you to force me into anything?"

"Your honor would require an offer. Danged English pride."

He laughed and kissed the tip of her nose. "Yes, but I also happen to be so in love with you I walk into walls and fall over furniture."

Her face was close to his, so he saw enlightenment burst over her. The tulip lips formed an O, and her lashes fluttered, but it was his turn to frown and step back.

"Have I made a mistake?" he asked. "I thought you returned my regard, but perhaps I've been presumptuous. I never thought— Mattie, I assumed you'd never have allowed me to . . ." A chasm opened before him, and he couldn't go on.

As he stood there in fearful misery, Mattie came to him, placed her fingertips on his cheek and whispered, "No mistake."

He closed his eyes in relief. He kissed the palm of the hand that touched him. Then he strode to the door, pulled it closed and slipped a bar across it. He did the same to another door and came back to Mattie.

"This time I'm not taking any chances on being interrupted."

They took greater care this time, each wanting to savor the experience. Cheyne had intended to go slowly, but Mattie would have none of it, and her wishes ruled. They ended up on the plank table and sent the wooden bowls clattering to the floor.

Later when they began to dress, it was dark. Cheyne hunted around until he found a lantern and lit it. He watched Mattie button her blouse and stuff it in the waistband of her skirt. He knew he was smiling like a fool, but he didn't care. She picked up her belt and buckled it in place. Her fingers fidgeted with it.

"Cheyne, we can't get married. I'm supposed to be hunting for a titled husband and in love with Michel."

"We'll wait to announce our engagement until after we've caught the blackmailer."

She looked up, her face alight with pleasure. "You mean you still want to marry me?"

"Damn it, Mattie, your distrust of my intentions is becoming insulting."

"I'm sorry. It's just that there was this fella who asked me to marry him once and then took it back." She scowled at the bowls scattered on the floor. "His name was Samuel."

Cheyne lifted Mattie, sat her on the table and kissed her. "Samuel was a pillock, as Mutton would say. I'm going to find this hell-cursed blackmailer and then I'm going to marry you."

"Oh, I meant to talk to you about that."

"What?"

"Now that Sir William's death has called attention to this little gathering, the blackmailer isn't going to risk revealing himself here. I think we should go back to London for the little Season. He's lost one of his victims and might be in need of some quick money. I bet I get another demand if I go back to Spencer House."

This time he wasn't going to allow her to risk herself. "I don't think you should go back. It's too dangerous, especially with your habit of turning up in the wrong places. I'll go to London and you stay here."

"That's silly, and it will look suspicious if I stay here."

"All right, go to that place your mother rented. As long as you stay away from London."

Mattie jumped off the table. "I'm coming with you."

"No, you're not."

"Now, you see here. Just because I said I'd marry you doesn't mean you can tell me what to do."

"It certainly does."

They confronted each other. Mattie folded her arms over her chest, glaring at him. Cheyne lifted his chin and stared down at her.

"I'm going to be your husband."

"Right."

He relaxed. "I'm glad you understand."

"And I'm going to London."

"Matilda Bright, you're not going anywhere if I have to lock you in this kitchen to make you stay."

"You will not."

She knew him too well, but his lip curled as an idea occurred to him. "Promise you'll keep away, or I'll tell your mother what you intend, and she'll stop you."

"You won't do that."

He walked to her and stuck his face close to hers. "I will, with pleasure."

"Danged ornery skunk. Uppity highfalutin polecat. I have a mind to . . ."

"What were you going to say?"

"Nothin'."

Cheyne lifted the bars off the doors. Shoving his way outside, he waited for Mattie to stomp after him. She sailed past him into the passageway. He caught up with her and matched her stride.

"I can see we're going to have to have a serious discussion about marriage," he said.

"We certainly are," she snapped.

"About who's the master."

"Yes," she said.

"And obedience."

"Anything else?"

"I'll think about it," he said.

She rounded on him. "You do that. And while you're at it, you think about this. Not that long ago we fought a civil war in my country over freeing slaves. I'm not about to become one myself."

With that she marched down the Fish Court and out of sight.

19

In the end Mattie won the argument about returning to London because there was no quick way to smoke out the blackmailer without her presence. She hadn't looked forward to a battle with Cheyne over who would be boss in their marriage, but the journey to London postponed the confrontation. In a few weeks Mattie had reestablished her social routine at Spencer House.

She passed Christmas in a state of agitation and wonder—agitation because no word had come from the blackmailer, and wonder that she could love a man as autocratic and stubborn as Cheyne Tennant. Just when she thought she'd scream from the suspense, another demand arrived that set a date for delivery of a payment for New Year's Eve day. Once the suspense over the blackmail demand had lifted, Mattie had more time in which to stew over her personal predicament.

She didn't understand quite how it had happened, falling in love with someone she'd once considered a mangy varmint. But there it was, an unchangeable fact. That encounter in the Tudor kitchens had been a revelation. She'd prepared herself to be noble, to set him free so that he didn't have to sacrifice himself for a moment's weakness. How was she to have known he didn't consider marrying her a sacrifice? He'd made love to many women without marrying them.

It had taken a while for her to believe what he said. After all, Samuel had been eloquent. Then he'd spoken of her letters. It had been after they'd made love, and Cheyne had spent a few minutes staring at her with a rather dazed expression.

"It's my own fault," he said at last.

"What's your fault."

"My falling in love with you. If I hadn't asked you to help me catch the blackmailer, I'd have never read those exquisite letters of yours."

Mattie put her hand on his arm and whispered, "You too?"

They exchanged bemused looks.

"Your letters revealed such beauty of spirit," Cheyne said, "such a loving soul."

Blushing, Mattie lowered her gaze. "I fell in love with your letters too."

He lifted her chin with his fingertips and she met his eyes. "All those beautiful words had to come from a man with a soul to match. But I figured you'd loved someone else and put all those feelings in the letters. For someone else, not me."

Cheyne took her hand and kissed it. From another man the gesture might have been awkward, but he accomplished it as if grace were woven into his soul, which it was.

"Those feelings were for you, my midnight sun, and no one else."

Sometimes the dreams you never knew you had came true. Mattie sighed as she remembered their time together in those ancient kitchens. She'd never expected to crave making love to Cheyne so much that not seeing him caused her physical pain. She ached without his presence, yet they had to remain apart in London and carry on as usual.

So now she sat in the Palm Room in Spencer House thinking about the new demand from the blackmailer while her friends and suspects in the blackmail case talked around her. She'd already shown the note to Cheyne. Mattie was instructed to leave another installment of money in Westminster Abbey at three o'clock in the afternoon on New Year's Eve day. That was tomorrow. She was to prepare a parcel as before and leave it on Chaucer's tomb in Poet's Corner in the south transept.

As she was thinking, the butler announced Cheyne, who came in, bowed to her mother and joined Mattie, the Countess of Ixworth, and Lancelot Gordon. Mattie poured tea for him while Lance regaled them with a story about his latest true love.

"She is perfection," Lance said. "And she sings."

Cheyne took the cup and saucer from Mattie, gave

her a look that would have melted the china, and spoke to his friend. "She sings? I fear to ask where."

"She sings in a music hall."

"Oh, dear," said the countess with a dismayed glance at Mattie.

"Lance," Cheyne said with an indulgent look, "you can't be serious."

"Of course I can. She does bird imitations, too. You should hear her do a robin. You won't be able to tell the difference from a real one."

"Does she do other imitations?" Mattie asked.

"Dogs and cats," Lance said.

Mattie sighed. "Sir William would have liked that."

"He was always ready for a good piece of entertainment," Lance said. "And my sweet Hattie is a jolly sort."

"I suppose we'll always wonder why the poor man became so desperate that he killed himself," said the countess.

"Yes," Cheyne said with a glance at Mattie.

She forestalled more speculation. "Ah, here's Dr. Capgrave."

Elland Capgrave joined them, taking a seat next to Mattie. "Is everyone looking forward to the Rutherfords' New Year's ball? I'm going as Richard Lionheart."

"I'm tired of dressing up," Lance said. "I shall go as myself."

"Certainly better than having to wear a stomacher and farthingale," the countess said.

"I hate panniers," Mattie said as she poured

herself another cup of tea. "Last year I went to a costume ball as Marie Antoinette and nearly set myself on fire because my gown stuck out so far it touched the flames in the fireplace."

Capgrave eyed a finger sandwich and said thoughtfully, "I think it would be most amusing to dress as a woman. Queen Anne, perhaps, or a nun."

"Why?" Cheyne asked. "Haven't you done it at school for plays? I did, and I hated it. All those petticoats dragging at one. Taking tiny steps. Managing a fan. And corsets. Horrible."

Mattie grinned at Cheyne as he gave a mock shudder. "I feel the same way, but once women get the vote and begin working more in business, things like corsets will vanish."

Everyone turned to stare at her. She flushed, but continued. "It's true. Women are going to vote and become doctors and scientists. They already have, and someday soon they'll realize doctors and scientists can't afford to be hindered by whalebone."

No one took her seriously except Cheyne, and the topic changed to the impending New Year. The world was frantic with excitement at the dawn of the new century. Everyone in England and America seemed to have an opinion about the future. Some predicted disaster, the end of the world, Armageddon. Others looked forward to a new era filled with advancements, inventions, and increasingly wise and enlightened human conduct.

"I have no idea what the new century will bring,"

said Lance. "I'm only certain that tonight I'll be at the Prince of Wale's grand ball. I understand he's brought in a Chinese firm to do the fireworks."

Mattie saw the frozen expression on Rose Marie's face and changed the subject. The countess had been omitted from the royal guest list again. Elland Capgrave seemed more interested in the German emperor's blustering excesses than the dawn of a new century. Cheyne agreed with him that the Kaiser needed watching.

"The Prince of Wales is his uncle and deals well with him," Cheyne said. "but he was raised to think himself almost a god. I'm worried about what will happen once Wilhelm no longer fears his grandmother's disapproval. Once Her Majesty is gone, there's no telling what Germany might try."

Speculation continued for a while before Mattie's visitors began leaving. Before Cheyne left, Mattie tried to speak to him alone. They'd had another quarrel about her leaving the money for the blackmailer, and she was worried he'd try to stop her. Luckily he seemed resigned to her presence.

She'd given Dora permission to visit her family in Chelsea, so next day she dressed without help for her outing to Westminster Abbey. Her black velvet suit was perfect, for the weather had turned cold and rainy. She was pulling on black kid gloves when she stepped outside Spencer House expecting to see her motorcar waiting. Instead a carriage stood before the steps and a groom saluted her.

"Afternoon, Miss. Mr. Tennant sent his carriage for you."

"Oh." She glanced over her shoulder to make sure no one was watching, especially her mother. The footman opened the carriage door, and Mattie climbed in. Mutton was sitting inside and tipped his hat.

"Good afternoon, Miss Bright. The gov'nor sent me to look after you."

"Very well, Mutton, but you can't come inside the cathedral with me. Three o'clock is the busy time for visitors, and I don't want the blackmailer to see you with me."

"Yes, miss."

The carriage rolled into Piccadilly, dodging omnibuses and cabs. Not five minutes passed before Mattie leaned to stick her head out the window, then sat back down and glared at the valet.

"Mutton, where are we going?"

"Hyde Park, miss, for a nice drive."

"What in blazes does Mr. Tennant think he's doing?

"Protecting 'is future wife, Miss."

"Now, you listen to me, Mutton. You tell the coachman to drive us to Westminster right now."

Looking like a well-dressed bear in his thick wool coat and bowler hat, Mutton said, "No, miss. The gov'nor would have me hide if I was to do that."

"Then I'll get a cab." Mattie put her hand on the door handle.

"Please don't do that, miss. I don't want to have to stop you."

She looked at Mutton's unhappy but resolute expression and dropped her hand. "Dang it, Mutton." Fuming, she drummed her fingers on the leather seat. "He was planning this all along. He sat in the Palm Room blabbering about tea and costume balls when all the time he meant to send me on this blamed useless ride in the park." She crossed her arms and glared out the window. "Smiling and nodding and saying as how he hadn't liked women's clothes. So amusing. Even the countess laughed. Dang, dang, dang."

Mattie slumped against the squabs, her brow furrowed. If she'd known what he was planning, she would have thrown petticoats, fans, corsets, stomachers, and farthingales at him. She lapsed into silence for a moment, and then she sat up to stare into the distance.

"Wait a minute."

"Sorry, miss, but we got to keep driving around the park for an hour."

"No, no." She snapped her fingers. "The costumes!"

"Steady, miss. You're getting the vapors and chattering nonsense."

"Hogwash."

"Pardon?"

Mattie scooted forward and put her hand on Mutton's thick arm. "I know who the blackmailer is."

Mutton stared at her. "Who, miss?"

Lifting her hand, she waved her forefinger at him. "No, Mutton. I'm not telling you unless you take me to the abbey."

"Can't do that, miss."

"If you don't, and your master fails to catch the blackmailer because he was looking for the wrong person, it will be your fault." Mutton raised an eyebrow, but said nothing. Mattie turned her head and looked at him sideways. "He might be taken unawares." Still nothing. "If he's surprised, he might make a mistake and get hurt." Mutton stirred and gave her an unhappy look, so Mattie lowered her voice to a whisper. "He might even get killed."

Mutton chewed his lip, but made no move to stop the carriage.

"Listen," Mattie said. "The blackmailer revealed something to me in a conversation. It was a mistake, and I don't think he knows he made it. We can catch him off guard and end this before someone else dies!"

Giving her a hard stare, Mutton moved closer to the carriage window. "You certain?"

"I'm certain."

It took twenty minutes to reach Parliament Square. By then the rain had ceased. Mattie ordered the carriage stopped, and before it rolled to a halt she jumped out, with Mutton close behind her. They stepped onto the pavement as Big Ben tolled the quarter hour. She searched the crowds of pedestrians for Cheyne, who was to have stationed himself on the green and follow her into the abbey.

"There he is, miss." Mutton pointed to a tall figure lounging on the grass opposite the small but exquisite sixteenth-century church of St. Margaret's that lay between them and the cathedral. He was holding the brown paper parcel.

Mattie sailed over to him when he wasn't looking, snatched the parcel from his hand and said, "Good afternoon."

"Hell, Mattie, what are you doing here? Give that back."

"What will Mutton think of you, cursing in the presence of a lady?"

"He'll think me well justified, if he knows what's good for him. He's in enough trouble."

Mattie ignored him and looked around the green. "Where's Dora? It's obvious she isn't really visiting her family. She has to be around here somewhere posing as me."

"She'll be here in two minutes," Cheyne said as he consulted a pocket watch.

"You'd better send her away."

Cheyne put a hand on her arm. "You're not going into the cathedral."

Mattie slipped out of reach. "I am, or I won't tell you who the blackmailer is."

"What?" Cheyne glared at her.

"Tell him, Mutton."

"She's figured it out, gov'nor. Did it while we was driving in the park. That's how she made me bring her here."

Something feral and primitive stirred in Cheyne's

eyes as understanding dawned on him. "No. You're not going in there. Especially if you know who he is. If he finds out you know, he'll kill you."

Mattie had anticipated his reaction and moved farther away from him. As he started toward her, she dove into a knot of pedestrians on the walk that led to the cathedral. She heard him calling to her, but she reached the west entrance to the abbey and plunged inside. Merging with the crowds filing into the nave, she became part of the rush to visit Westminster before evening services began. This was why the blackmailer had chosen the afternoon.

Turning right and skirting one of the enormous fluted columns that supported the graceful fan vaulting, she walked down the south aisle. She passed the choir, turned right and her gaze skimmed over the rose window in the wall of the transept. She glanced at the dorter staircase that had once been used by monks to reach the choir, then surveyed Poet's Corner. The place was dedicated to artists, and set against the walls were statues of Shakespeare and George Friederic Handel, busts of Ben Jonson, Robert Southey, and, recently, Henry Wadsworth Longfellow.

Mattie gripped the parcel and walked to a niche in which rested a humble stone rectangle. Dark and small, it contained the remains of Geoffrey Chaucer. She looked over her shoulder and saw a couple engrossed in trying to decipher a Latin inscription.

There was no one else in the transept at the moment, so she placed the parcel in a dark space between the tomb and the niche. She looked around again, but saw no one. She waited until more people wandered into the transept, then walked back down the south aisle. As she went, she looked around for someone she knew, to no avail.

Not daring to linger, she left the abbey and went back to Parliament Square. As she set foot on the green, someone latched on to her arm.

"Cheyne Tennant, you startled me."

"Serves you right." He held her arm tightly and guided her across the Green. "We're going for a walk."

"What about the blackmailer?"

"Balfour has men all over the abbey. He's quite capable of doing his job without us."

Mattie found herself marched away from the square, across the street and under the shadow of Big Ben. By the time they reached the clock tower, Mattie was out of breath and angry. Cheyne finally let go of her, but he gave her a frigid look that told her she'd be wise to remain where she was. Clasping his hands behind his back, he gazed at the palatial building that housed England's Parliament.

"Tudor Perpendicular," he said.

"What?"

Cheyne nodded at Parliament. "The style, it's Tudor Perpendicular. After the fire, Barry designed it. It's a warren of eleven hundred rooms, one hundred staircases, two miles of corridor, and, of course, old

Ben in the clock tower." He turned on her. "And if you don't tell me what you've discovered, I'll drag you to the top of Big Ben and dangle you over the edge until you talk."

Mattie wasn't listening carefully to his words because she'd seen the fear in his eyes. "You won't do that."

Uttering a sound of supreme frustration, Cheyne threw up his hands, "Mattie, what am I to do with you?"

"Calm down. I'm going to tell you. I was thinking about how rotten you were, having me abducted, and I got to thinking about our conversation yesterday in the Palm Room. Everybody was talking about costumes and corsets and such, and I remembered—" Mattie broke off as she saw three large and rough-looking men get out of a carriage and come toward them. "Cheyne."

She got no further. The strangers surrounded them quickly. One pulled a revolver from his coat pocket, stuck it in Cheyne's side, and took hold of his arm.

"Quiet, now, laddie. You come with us, you and the lady."

Cheyne stared at her, a warning clear in his eyes. Mattie looked at the two men, who had positioned themselves so that she was between them. One had a scraggly beard stained with tobacco and the other had protruding eyes that gave him an insectlike appearance. When they grabbed her arms, she dug in

her heels without thinking, but the man with the revolver clucked at her.

"Now, now, missy." He pulled Cheyne closer and
jabbed him with the gun. "Behave yerself or I'll
shoot the lad here full o' holes."

"Mattie, do as they say or they'll hurt you," Cheyne
said calmly.

"That's right, you be a good girl," the leader said.

Allowing her captors to take her to the carriage,
she waited while one got in. The other boosted her
inside and climbed in after her. Then Cheyne was ordered to get in, but when he mounted the step, the
leader reversed his gun and hit his captive on the head.
Mattie cried out as Cheyne collapsed on the floor and
was dragged inside.

"You good-for-nothin' saloon slags, keep your
hands off him!"

She fought to reach Cheyne, but one man grabbed
her while the other shoved a cloth in her face. She
gasped, breathing in a sickly odor that made her gag.
She hit a chest and a face, but her blows seemed to
land on carpenter's putty. Then everything receded
into blackness.

❧

Mattie surfaced from oblivion slowly. Voices floated
around her, disembodied and hollow, but she couldn't
distinguish words because of the nausea that clawed
at her belly. Sinking into darkness again, she climbed

back to consciousness without any idea of how long she'd been insensible.

This time the nausea wasn't as bad, and she could make out other sensations. She was lying on a flat surface with the side of her face pressed against something rough. The voices were still floating around her. As her body began to return to something like normality, Mattie risked opening her eyes.

She was in a dimly lit room bare of furniture except for a rough wool carpet. A few feet away from her Cheyne lay on his back, one leg bent with the other over it. She couldn't see the wound caused by the ruffian's blow because his face was turned toward her. The leader of their abductors was standing over Cheyne, and behind him were his fellow criminals.

A door opened, and she heard the rapid tap of heels on the bare floor. As the newcomer gained the carpet, the tapping grew muffled. Giving their leader uneasy glances, the two assistant criminals scuffled out of the room. Mattie half closed her eyes so that she appeared to still be unconscious. She waited for the newcomer to move into her range of vision. She wasn't surprised to see Rose Marie Seton, but the countess evidently had been surprised to see her. She was staring at the ruffian leader with a mixture of amazement, exasperation, and fury.

"Correct me if I'm mistaken, Gamp. This afternoon when I saw them at the abbey, did I not tell you to get rid of them discreetly? Perhaps my choice

of words was above you. Discreet means without at-
tracting attention; it does not mean bring them to
my house and toss them in my lap!"

Gamp scratched his head, impervious to his em-
ployer's sarcasm.

"Weren't no choice, m'lady. The coppers was
thick as worms on a corpse, stopping carriages an all.
They was looking for 'em. We barely got out o' there
by heading west. If we'd of tried for the docks, they'd
have got us for sure."

"You're an idiot. You could have taken them anywhere but here."

Gamp shrugged. "You hired us to do a simple job.
You didn't say anything about Scotland Yard crawl-
ing all over the place. We had to get off the streets,
and you was close."

The countess narrowed her eyes, but seemed to
think better of arguing with her employee. "It's
done and can't be helped. Keep them here until
dark, then take them to the docks. Don't kill them
here. I don't want them traced to me."

Scratching his chin, Gamp nodded. "Don't you
worry. They'll just be two more floaters fished out o'
the river."

Rose Marie glanced at Cheyne's prone form, her
upper lip curling. "I knew I was followed after I
picked up her first payment, but I never suspected
the police had recruited her and Tennant."

"Lucky you hired me to watch who came to the
abbey, then," Gamp said.

The countess gave him an irate glance. "The whole point to this excursion was to get rid of who-ever was trying to trap me, not risk exposing me by dragging them here."

"Don't get yer knickers twisted, m'lady. Me and the boys'll take care of everything soon as it's dark and the streets are full of traffic for the New Year's celebrations."

"You'd better."

Rose Marie stalked out, and Gamp followed. After the door shut, Mattie heard the click of a key turning a lock. She waited a moment as their footsteps re-ceded. Rising slowly, she crawled to Cheyne, touched his cheek and whispered his name. No response. She turned his head and felt a lump on the back of it as large as a hen's egg. Tears gathered in her eyes, and she lifted him so that his head rested in her lap. Tap-ping his cheek gently with the palm of her hand, she whispered again.

"Cheyne! Cheyne, wake up."

He didn't move. His eyelids were tinged with blue, and he seemed to be in some deep oblivion. She'd heard of people receiving blows to the head and never regaining consciousness. Mattie went cold and hugged him to her.

What was she going to do? What if he didn't wake up before Gamp came to take them away? Mattie looked around the bare room. There was a narrow window sealed with a wooden shutter, and the ceiling slanted. They must be in an attic room. Maybe they could climb out. She didn't know if the window was blocked; she didn't know how long they had.

All she knew for certain was that she wasn't leaving without Cheyne. Her fingers stroked soft blond hair. She held one of his elegant, strong hands, knowing she'd rather risk death than leave him behind.

20

❧❀❧

She should have figured it out sooner. Rose Marie was supposed to have worn the costume of the Empress Josephine to the Trillford ball. Why, then, would she have complained about stomachers and farthingales? Because she'd changed at some point, disguising herself as Queen Elizabeth I to pick up the blackmail money in St. James's Park. A sixteenth-century lady would wear a farthingale, not one who lived two centuries later.

Mattie shifted Cheyne so that his head rested on one of her legs, and watched his steady breathing. The light that had penetrated the shutter was gone, and it was New Year's Eve. It must be close to ten o'clock, and she could hear muffled street noises. She had explored the room, but the only other way out was through the locked door. She could hear voices down the hall. Gamp had left his assistants on guard, so there was no way out except through the window. It shouldn't be too hard to break the shutters, but she couldn't drag Cheyne with her. She strained to hear any approaching footsteps, and as she did, Cheyne stirred.

"Wake up," she whispered, patting his face. "Cheyne, we've got to get out of here. Try, honey. Try to wake up."

He moaned, then winced and opened his eyes. "Mattie?"

"It's me, honey. Wake up now. We're in trouble."

All she got was a groan, but he tried to sit up, only to collapse in her arms.

"Wait a bit and try again." Mattie glanced at the door, expecting Gamp at any moment. "Cheyne, honey, they're going to come for us any minute. They plan to take us to the river and . . ." Her courage failed. She didn't want to put their intended fate into words.

"Floaters," Cheyne mumbled as he tried to turn his head.

"Yes. So try to sit up."

She braced him, slowly helping him raise the level of his head. He got halfway up before dizziness knocked him down again.

"It's no use," he said when the vertigo had passed. "Go without me."

"What in blazes do you think you're saying? They'll kill you."

"And you."

He winced as he tried to pull her close. She kissed his hand.

"I won't leave you."

Cheyne caught the neck of her jacket and dragged her down to face him. "Listen to me, Mattie. I'm going to be dizzy for at least another half hour. Too dizzy to travel. You've got to escape."

"No, I'm not leaving—"

"Bloody hell, Mattie, if you don't go for help, they'll kill us both. This way I'll have a chance, but only if you do as I say, for once in your life."

Cheyne sucked in a breath and went white from the effort of speaking. Mattie bit her lip and stared at him with a terrible helpless feeling in the pit of her stomach. He was right. If she didn't get help, he would be killed anyway. She had to leave him if she was going to save him.

"I'll go."

He opened his eyes and gave her a painful smile. "I knew you would. Kiss me first."

She lowered her mouth to his, gently. His lips were cool, but they warmed beneath hers. Tearing herself from him, Mattie went to the window. She didn't even know if she could get it open. It was nailed shut. She tried shoving on the panels of the shutter, but she couldn't get enough force behind her.

"You'll have to use your feet," Cheyne said faintly. "Come help me stand."

"You can't."

"I can for a short time. I'll hold you, and you kick. Do it quickly, because I'm going to fall."

Mattie helped him stand, turned her back to him and allowed him to lift her. She hopped up, kicked the shutters hard, and they popped open. At the same time, Cheyne fell with her on top of him.

"Are you all right?"

He covered his eyes with his forearm, not answering at first. Mattie hovered over him and wrung her hands until he sighed.

"I'm fine." He lowered his arm and gave her a look of mingled love and urgency. "Go, Mattie."

She bent down and kissed him again. Before her resolve wavered, she jumped on the windowsill and stuck her head outside. It was dark, but light came from lamps mounted on the walls of the house. The roof slanted down at a steep slope to join a flatter one below. They were in an attic room at the rear of the house. She could see the service area, but no light came from the windows of the kitchen.

"Mattie, you have to go. *Now.*"

Giving Cheyne a last, torn look, Mattie lowered herself out the window and slid down the roof. She almost dropped off the edge, but caught a gutter in time. She hung over the next roof and dropped gently, thanking God for the size of aristocratic town houses. The noise she made here wouldn't be heard in the rooms the countess frequented. Landing on the second roof almost cost her the use of her left ankle. It turned wrong, but a moment's massage restored it enough for her to creep along until she found a trellis by which to climb to the ground.

Mattie sneaked out of the service area to a small passage between two houses. Speeding into the night, she thought about banging on one of the doors of the Georgian houses along the street, but it would take too long to explain that she wasn't a madwoman and even longer to persuade the occupants to allow her to telephone the police. If they had a telephone. The surest, fastest way was to sprint across the streets of Mayfair to Spencer House.

She arrived in St. James's Street gasping for air. Bursting into the house past a startled Wynkin, she almost ran into Narcissa and her mother dressed in evening gowns and wearing worried frowns.

"Mattie, thank God!" Mrs. Bright cried. "Where have you been? You're a mess. What have you been doing? We're going to be late for the New Year's ball."

"Not now, Mama." She grabbed Narcissa and shoved her toward the telephone near the stairs. "Call Scotland Yard. Tell them to send Superintendent Balfour to the Countess of Ixworth's house. She's the blackmailer."

Narcissa picked up the telephone and gaped at her. "Blackmailer?"

"No time for questions," Mattie called as she raced upstairs. "I'm going back."

"Mattie Bright, you come back here this instant and tell me what's going on," Mama shouted.

"Later," Mattie said as she vanished into her room.

Rushing to the armoire, she dug in the bottom of it and pulled out Papa's old Colt revolver. She loaded it with shaking fingers, stuffed cartridges into her pockets, and hurtled out of the house to the stables. While the coachman guided the carriage into the street in preparation for driving to the Prince of Wales's ball, Mattie jumped into the Panhard and started it. Gunning the motor, she hurtled out of the carriage house, startling the horses and grooms.

The journey back to the countess's house was the fastest she'd ever driven. Careening down Park Lane, she nearly overturned at the sharp corner at Oxford Street. She sped up into the turn and nearly crashed into a cab. As the car swerved to avoid it, she whipped the wheel around, went several blocks, turned, then turned again, and she was there. Without thinking, she killed the engine, jumped out and stormed into the house.

The foyer was brightly lit and crowded with the countess's New Year's guests. Mattie shoved aside a pompous barrister and an elderly baronet, grabbed Rose Marie's arm and spun her around. She cocked the gun and pointed it six inches from the woman's head.

"Where is he?"

Silence had fallen, except for some young fop who piped, "I say!"

Mattie's eyes never left the countess's. "I know they've gone to the docks. Which one? You have until the count of three."

Rose Marie cast a scandalized look at her guests. "Dear God, she's mad. Someone stop her."

"One . . ." Mattie said with icy calm.

"General Urqhart, do something," Rose Marie cried with an innocent flutter of her hands.

"Two, three." Mattie shot a vase behind the countess.

Women screamed, and the men backed away from her.

"She's insane," the countess said.

"I haven't got time for your stage performance," Mattie said. "So I'll just have to convince you I'm serious."

She turned and walked away from Rose Marie. Facing her, she aimed and fired again, hitting the marble tile at her feet. This time Rose Marie's facade of ladylike panic vanished. She yelped and hopped backward. Then she rounded on her male guests in fury.

"One of you cowards do something, damn it!"

"The next shot will hit your pretty little toes," Mattie said as if the countess hadn't spoken. "Which one do you want to lose? Aw, heck, even my aim isn't that good. I'll just settle for what I can get. I'll count to three again. This time you better believe me. One, two, three." Mattie smiled the smile of a hangman and aimed. "Say good-bye to your dancing days."

"No, I'll tell you!" Rose Marie cried.

Mattie kept the pistol aimed at her feet. "Spit it out."

"They're going to the Limehouse Reach, near the West India Docks."

"Good. Now come with me."

Mattie forced Rose Marie to the motorcar, where she retrieved a length of rope from one of the tool baskets strapped to the side of the vehicle. Knotting the rope around her wrists, she tied the countess to the frame that protected the front passengers from the engine. With the guests watching from the front steps, she slid into the motorcar, put the gun in her lap and roared down the street. The countess screamed as the Panhard zoomed faster and faster, but Mattie ignored her. While part of her mind concentrating on driving as fast as she could without crashing into a coach or hansom, the other part was racing, trying to decide which road Gamp would have taken.

"Did they go in your carriage?"

"We're going to crash," the countess whined, her eyes closed.

"Answer me. I can drive with one hand and shoot your fingers off with the other."

"Yes, yes they took my carriage."

That meant they would try to blend in with the traffic along Oxford Street, probably until they got past Cheapside. But what if they took Regent Street south? No, Oxford was the more direct route, and they wouldn't want to waste time. They knew she would bring the police after them and that their only chance was to kill Cheyne and vanish. That way the countess could deny everything, and with no witnesses, it would be a case of Mattie's word against hers. Mattie jerked the wheel to avoid an empty freight wagon, and Rose Marie screamed again.

"Shut up. I'm trying to concentrate."

"We'll be killed!"

"If they hurt Cheyne, I'll kill you myself."

They passed Totenham Court Road and veered

around a town coach, then a brougham. Mattie's heart screamed with frustration as she pulled the brake to avoid crashing into a knot of vehicles in the middle of the road. London traffic. She eyed the curb and released the brake. Bumping onto the sidewalk, she sent pedestrians fleeing as she rounded the obstacle. In seconds she was in the street again and joining a line of carriages and carts. She wanted to howl when it stopped. Then she spotted two men clinging to the back of a carriage like footmen. Only they weren't in livery. One of them turned.

"Insect Eyes!"

"You are mad," the countess said as she tugged at her bonds.

Ignoring her, Mattie pulled the brake, grabbed the revolver and sprang out of the Panhard. Oblivious to the cries of coachmen and cab drivers, she left the motorcar sitting in the middle of the road and ran silently down the line of vehicles. She was on the ruffians just as Insect Eyes noticed her. Mattie stopped, fired her gun in the air, and then pointed it at him.

"Run, unless you want the next bullet."

They ran. So did the driver. Mattie went to the door of the carriage and pointed the gun again.

"Come out of there, Gamp."

"You go away or I'll do for your young laddie here! He's still sleeping, and it'll be easy."

"Touch him, and I'll shoot you where it'll hurt most," Mattie growled.

Gamp stuck his head out the carriage window.

"I got me gun aimed at him right now, missy, so you just—"

Gamp screamed and disappeared. Mattie ran to the carriage, but dodged sideways when the ruffian shot out of the vehicle, propelled by Cheyne's boot. Gamp fell on the road and scrambled to his feet. He snatched Mattie's gun and brought it up, preparing to fire it in her face.

As Gamp aimed the revolver, Cheyne caught him by the back of his collar. He swung him around and delivered a powerful punch to the man's jaw. Tearing the gun from Gamp's hand, he followed with a jab to his gut. Gamp plummeted to his knees. Another blow to his jaw knocked him out at Cheyne's feet. At that moment a policeman arrived, and Superintendent Balfour.

Breathing hard, Cheyne handed the gun to Balfour. He looked at Mattie, who was incoherent with relief; he glanced at the countess in the motorcar down the street. "I guess that infernal machine is good for something."

Suddenly the city erupted with the peal of bells, fireworks, and cannon shots. The people in the streets began to cheer. Big Ben tolled in the twentieth century, and Mattie burst into tears and threw herself in Cheyne's arms. He hugged her tightly and buried his face in her wild hair. She listened to his soft voice reassuring her, but her body was reacting to the events of the past few hours. With hundreds of people around them, she clung to Cheyne. Her knees wobbled, she trembled all over, and she couldn't stop sobbing. Cheyne lifted her in his arms and kissed her through her tears. Mattie felt her trembling subside as he kissed her.

Cheyne lifted his head and smiled at her. "Happy new century, my love."

Mattie buried her head in the crook of his neck, and he lifted her into the carriage. Climbing in after her, he held her until her sobbing ebbed. Balfour stuck his head in the carriage and demanded an explanation. Murmuring reassurance to her gently, Cheyne left to deal with his friend.

Someone shoved a glass of water in her hands, and she gulped it down. She sank back against the seat, her eyes closed. The din around her faded for a while as she lapsed into a dazed stupor. The only thing she'd ever killed with a gun was a rattlesnake, but she'd been prepared to drill holes in Rose Marie Seton, body part by body part, rather than let Cheyne die.

Cheyne reappeared, climbing into the carriage. He held her close, rapped on the ceiling, and ordered the coachman to drive to Spencer House.

"We've got a police constable for a driver," he said. "Balfour is taking Rose Marie to the Old Bailey and he's arranged for your motorcar to be driven back to Spencer House."

Mattie gave him a watery smile, then sobbed. Cheyne pulled her into his lap and stroked her hair.

"What's this? Mattie Bright, frontier markswoman, in tears?"

"Land sakes, I hate this," she said between sobs. "I

can do almost anything in a crisis, but afterward I'm a mess." She dabbed her eyes with the hem of her skirt and sniffed. "If you kiss me, I won't be able to cry."

Cheyne kept her from crying all the way home. To her relief, he dealt with her mother as efficiently as he had Gamp and the police. Narcissa helped her to her room and ordered a bath and a toddy. She almost fell asleep drinking the milk laced with brandy and something more powerful. Her eyes were closed by the time she crawled between her bedcovers, and by the time her head was on the pillow she slept.

21

❧❧❦❧❧

The Painted Room at Spencer House was one of the most famous neoclassical structures in Europe. White Corinthian columns and pilasters separated the spaces, each gilded to match the frieze of rose wreaths and garlands of flowers above them. A quiet green served as the background for exquisite paintings celebrating love and marriage. The frieze at the chimneypiece copied an ancient Roman painting, the *Aldobrandini Wedding*, while a circular grisaille panel depicted a Greek wedding once found on the Acropolis.

The ache in his head having dulled, Cheyne paced across the floorboards while he waited for the butler to tell Mattie he was here. He sank onto an eighteenth-century chair upholstered in green silk a shade lighter than the walls, then rose and paced to a window. He stared out at nothing in particular and wondered how he'd survived the past twenty-four-hours. Oh, not the abduction. How had he survived Mattie's rash conduct, her irresponsible disregard of her own safety?

"God, where did she get that revolver?" he asked himself, not for the first time.

She couldn't go on behaving so madly; his sanity depended upon making her see that she couldn't take such risks. This was all part of the same difficulty— Mattie must see that he, as her future husband, should be the one whose judgment and wisdom guided her. He loved her; he was, after all, older and more experienced in the world.

He would approach the subject with subtlety and lead her to see the overwhelming sense of his position on the matter. Subtlety was essential, however, or she'd balk and lose her temper. God knew he'd had enough of fighting for a long while.

But first he had to do something he'd been avoiding for too long. He had to tell her the truth about his birth. She'd accepted him without knowing about his real father; he wouldn't allow her to go through with the marriage without revealing the stain on his heritage.

Cheyne was gazing at a circular panel depicting sacrifices to Cupid when Mattie came in. She was wearing a simple black skirt and white blouse, and she'd gathered her hair at the back of her neck in a ribbon. She stood for a moment looking at him with uncertainty, but Cheyne was already grinning at her foolishly.

He opened his arms, and she flew into them. He

swung her around, set her on the floor, and kissed
her. It was a while before they broke off, each
flushed and reluctant to speak. Cheyne cleared his
throat and set her from him.

"You're better this morning."

She squeezed his hands and smiled. "Now that
you're here, honey."

"Is that what you're going to call me? Honey?"

She nodded. "When we're getting along."

"And when we're not?"

"Don't know."

"Given your unique vocabulary, I shudder to
imagine."

"Tell me what you've found out," she said, leading him to a sofa.

He sat beside her and began. "I visited our friend
the countess at the Old Bailey last night while Superintendent Balfour was taking her statement." He
picked up Mattie's hand and kissed it, gazing into her
frank, dark eyes. "We were all deceived, my love.
Somehow she concealed a festering resentment of
us, everyone in Society."

"I don't understand," Mattie said. "I know she
wasn't of high birth, but neither am I."

"But you're an American. Believe me, it makes a
difference. You Americans derive your sense of
worth from what you do more than who your family
was. In England birth is everything. Ask Wynkin,
and I'm sure he'll tell you he knows his place. He'd
be the first to tell you if you forgot yours, too. And

poor Rose Marie was born the daughter of a tobacconist in Cheapside."

"But she seemed so content."

"She was when she married the Earl of Ixworth at sixteen, but twenty years of snubs, sneers, and insults poured acid into her character. It's frightening, Mattie. I think she remembers every condescending look, every invitation omitted, every sly remark she's overheard."

"Land sakes," Mattie breathed. "I knew she was still trying to get herself accepted into the highest circles, but to dwell on such things seems, well . . . isn't she a bit touched?"

"Unbalanced, yes. You should have seen her." Cheyne began to describe the scene. "They took her to Scotland Yard and put her in a room reserved for prisoners of high station. After I related what happened to one of the officers I was allowed to see her briefly."

He'd opened the door slowly, still dazed by the idea that a lady of Society, however tenuously accepted, was the blackmailer. When he came in, Rose Marie whipped around to confront him, and Cheyne was startled into silence at the sight of her. Rose Marie's hair was matted in places and had fallen from its perch high on her head. Pins and cushions used to make it stand out from her head were caught in its tangles. Her gown of royal blue damask and gold mousseline de soie was soiled and the hem torn where she'd stepped on it.

He opened his mouth, but she backed into a corner pointed a finger and hissed at him in an East End accent he'd never heard before. "You sorry sod. Ruined everything, you did. You and your filthy-cheap little heiress."

"Rose Marie, why have you done this?"

"Why? Why, he asks." Her eyes narrowed to glinting slits. Then put her hands on her hips and began to pace, eyeing him all the while. "Never good enough for them, was I? Couldn't make meself into a lady long as they remembered me origins, could I? You know how hard I tried? For years. Years, and years! But it didn't do no good. All I got was nasty remarks and slights and insults. Did you ever make a call and have every lady in the parlor excuse herself and hurry away like you was a plague carrier? No, I didn't think so."

"But you drove Juliet Warrender and the others to their deaths," Cheyne said quietly.

"Weak, that's what they was. What was a bit o' tin to them? They could spare it. Serves them right for pretending to be so high and refined when they was just as common as me. Gawd, what hypocrites."

Rose Marie came to a sudden halt nearby and stared at him, her head cocked. "All them years of suffering, I kept silent. Ixworth left me with nothin' but debts. I thought, let them give it to me. Teach 'em to be charitable." Her voice rose to a harrowing bellow. "I hate them! It eats at me, like a parasite in me gut, and nothing helps but getting even."

"So you evened the score."

Rose Marie smiled at this, and the smile turned into a chuckle, then a laugh that burst the confines of control. She laughed so hard she doubled over. Cheyne shook his head and left as Rose Marie's laughter turned to shrieks.

He sighed and smiled sadly at Mattie. "That's the last I saw of her. They called a physician."

"How terrible," Mattie said. "The poor thing should have gone somewhere where she was better received instead of staying here."

"Perhaps, but when the earl died, his estate went to a nephew, and her dower wasn't enough for the manner in which she'd lived. So the blackmail served two purposes. Lately, though, she must have been losing control, deteriorating in her judgment, because she began asking for larger and larger sums. Finally she drove several of her victims to destruction, and that was her downfall."

Mattie shook her head. "To allow rejection to eat at you and govern your whole being . . ."

"At least we've stopped her, and I bring Superintendent Balfour's thanks for your help."

"Tell him he's welcome," Mattie said.

Cheyne felt his hands grow cold. The time had come for the truth. With an effort he dragged his gaze from her slender neck and the delicate line of her jaw.

"Before we go on, there's something I must tell you. Something about my father."

"Lance was telling me not long ago that you two don't get along."

"No," he said, forcing himself to look at her. "His Grace and I never agree on anything."

She turned to him, her expression grave. "I know all about your father."

"He told you? But he doesn't know. Nobody knows the truth."

She frowned and said, "It's obvious. Two more different people couldn't be found. I'm sorry the duke is so intolerant. It must have been terrible to grow up with someone like that hounding you all the time."

"Oh." He avoided her eyes.

"What's wrong?"

"Nothing."

"Land sakes, Cheyne. It's got to be something. This is the first time I've ever seen you afraid to look at me." When he remained silent, she spoke again. "It's your pa. The minute you mentioned him you got all stiff and reserved. Lance told me what he did to you, the bastard— Oh, I'm sorry."

Cheyne looked at her then, smiling with his teeth clenched. "Right word, wrong man. I'm the bastard."

"You can be a trial, but I wouldn't call you that."

He held her gaze and forced himself to continue. "You don't understand, Mattie. It's the most accurate description of my birth." He didn't breathe while he watched comprehension dawn in her eyes. Something dark and indefinable stirred in them. Then, to his amazement, she shrugged.

"I bet you're glad of that."

He stared in disbelief. "How did you know? I should be ashamed. I am ashamed."

She leaned to him and put her hand on his coat sleeve. "You can't help what your parents did. Besides, I wouldn't want Bracewell for a father even if he were a king instead of a duke. It must have been a relief to know you didn't have his blood in you."

"It was." He went on to tell her about his real father.

"Will you play for me?" Mattie asked. "I can't think of a better way to celebrate the new century."

Cheyne smiled and kissed her hand. "First I want to thank you for saving me from becoming a floater."

Shuddering, Mattie said, "Don't talk about it."

"Now you know how I feel when I see you taking risks, like when you wanted to deliver the blackmail money."

Mattie sighed.

"Having to watch helplessly while the one you love walks into danger . . ." Cheyne said, watching her out of the corner of his eye.

She turned suddenly, and her eyebrows came together. "What are you getting at?"

So much for subtlety. "Mattie, you must realize that between a man and a woman sharing their life together, there must be a division of responsibility."

"Uh-huh."

"Since I'm older and more experienced, more knowledgeable in the ways of the world—"

"And you're the man."

"And I'm the man," he said, not liking the way

she had crossed her arms over her chest. "We must come to an agreement. I love you, and I want us to share our decisions, but my opinions and decisions must be the final ones."

"Is that so?"

He grasped her wrists and pulled her arms so that they weren't crossed. "Yes, that's so. After what happened last night, I'd think you'd realize you need someone to advise you on how to moderate your conduct."

"Anything else?"

"Only that this blackmail case is the only instance in which you'll become involved in my business affairs. I'll not have you taking chances with your safety again."

"I see."

Mattie freed her wrists and clasped her hands in her lap, but Cheyne wasn't fooled. Her black eyes glittered like jet in sunlight.

"Now, Mattie, don't lose your temper. Try to think about what I've said logically."

"As opposed to how I would as a woman?"

"I didn't say that!"

When she jumped up and faced him, he swore silently.

"Of all the uppity, high-handed—"

"There you go, losing your temper," he said.

She calmed immediately. Walking away from him, she turned and paced back, slowly and deliberately. "What do you know about ranching in Texas?"

"Nothing, of course."

"Then perhaps you'll allow me to make decisions regarding my property there."

Cheyne was beginning to wish he'd never brought up the subject. "Yes."

"Know anything about steel and coke?"

"No."

"Then, if you don't mind, I'll keep on running that side of my investments, too." She sank to the couch and draped her arm along the back. "I know you don't drive a motorcar, so I think I can be trusted to do that on my own. Can you have babies?"

"Don't be ridiculous."

"Well, then, I guess you'll just have to rely on me for that, too. Let's see, what else is there?" She tapped her cheek with a forefinger. "Oh, yes. I don't really care who manages the household. Do you know how to cook and clean and how to—"

"Mattie Bright, that's enough."

Hopping off the sofa, she swept a graceful curtsy. "Oh, I beg your pardon, my lord. Sorry to offend, my lord. Will you be choosing my wedding gown, my lord. My trousseau? The dresses I wear each day?"

Cheyne rose. "Stop it." Something in his tone must have warned her he'd reached the limit of his patience, for she complied. "I'm simply trying to avoid future misunderstandings. You know I'm not the kind of man to tyrannize over a woman."

"You just tried," Mattie said with a sneer. "I'm right tired of trying to be something I'm not, Cheyne Tennant. For a long time now I've tried to be sweet and gentle and good-tempered, but it just isn't in me." Squaring her shoulders, she said, "You'll just have to put up with me like I am, and you're not going to order me around all the time."

His patience evaporating in the heat of frustration, Cheyne stood toe-to-toe with her. "Damn it, woman, I like you the way you are, but someone has to be in charge."

"I'm glad you like me the way I am, and no, they don't," she said.

Cheyne glared at her, noting the way she raised her chin and looked him in the eye with all her American determination. How was he going to break this stalemate? Then an idea occurred to him, and he allowed his glare to fade. Summoning the smile that had cut through the jaded defenses of more experienced women, he lowered his voice.

"We shouldn't argue, my love."

"You started it," she snapped, giving him an uncertain look.

"I'm sorry." He kissed her hand, turned it and kissed the palm, then the inside of her wrist.

Mattie shivered. "I'm sorry, too."

"I love you, my midnight sun." He kissed her other wrist.

"I love you," she said unsteadily.

"I want you to be happy," he murmured as he drew her close and breathed into her ear.

Mattie swallowed and clung to him.

"I want you to be happy, too."

Cheyne smiled into her hair. "You do?" He

trailed his fingers down her spine and pressed her hips into his.

"Of course."

He kissed her, a long, deep, lose-yourself kiss.

"I'm desperately unhappy when you endanger yourself," he whispered.

"I'm sorry."

His mouth kissed its way from her cheek to her throat. "I beg you not to do it anymore."

"What?"

"Endanger yourself."

"I—I won't."

Smiling in triumph, he moved with her to the sofa, bringing her beneath him. She wrapped her arms around his neck and pulled him into a kiss that drove him into a frenzy of arousal. He felt Mattie's hands on his buttocks, shoving him against her, and he let out a gasp.

"Honey."

"Mmm."

"We made a decision."

"What decision?" He was struggling with her skirts.

"Just now, we made a decision." She nibbled at his neck, which made him jerk and almost toppled him from the couch.

"A decision," he repeated mindlessly.

The nibbling stopped and she grabbed the hair at the back of his head. "Yes, a decision. You decided to persuade me. And I decided to let you."

He stared at her, fighting to concentrate on her

words rather than her body. At last her meaning penetrated his overheated brain.

"Hell, Mattie."

In an instant she bucked, and he toppled to the floor. Propping himself up, he glared at her. Mattie giggled, jumped up, sat on top of him and tweaked his nose.

"I think it's a wonderful way to make decisions."

"I don't." He'd never win an argument with her if she turned his own weapons on him.

Resting her arms on his chest, she grew serious. "I have another suggestion."

He raised a brow.

"You take the lead in things you know about. I'll take the lead in things I know about."

"That seems appropriate." He knew more things than she did. At least, he thought he did.

"And nobody calls me Lady Cheyne. This is the twentieth century, and we don't need titles."

"Will Mrs. Tennant do?"

She kissed him. "Yes."

She lifted her head, and he smiled into her black eyes.

"So, I'm not a barbaric colonial anymore?"

He held her tight and rolled over so that she was beneath him. "Haven't you been listening, Mattie Bright? You're my midnight sun."

© Steve Lewis

About the Author

SUZANNE ROBINSON has a doctoral degree in anthropology with a specialty in ancient Middle Eastern archaeology. She has now turned her attention to the creation of the fascinating fictional characters in her unforgettable historical romances.

Suzanne lives in San Antonio with her husband and her two English springer spaniels. She divides her time between writing historical romances and mysteries under her first name, Lynda.

Look for these other books in the
MEET ME AT MIDNIGHT series

Midnight Mistress by Ruth Owen,
on sale January 2000

A Kiss at Midnight by Shana Abé,
on sale February 2000

Turn the page for sneak peeks at these
enthralling romances.

MIDNIGHT MISTRESS
by Ruth Owen
available now from Bantam Books
"Ruth Owen writes with a wonderfully
original voice."—Joan Johnston

*As a dazzling New Year's Ball marks the final moments of
1799, a wharf rat captures the heart of Juliana Dare, only
to betray her years later. When he reappears as a mysterious privateer, he must stop Juliana from revealing his true
identity—even if it means risking the temptation to revive
their long-ago passion.*

Four years had gone by, four years that had changed
her from an impressionable girl to a cultured and cele-
brated woman. And yet, as she watched his mouth
curve into a ghost of his laughing smile, and felt his
hand possess hers with its surprising strength and more
surprising gentleness, she felt the years drop away. Once
again she was sitting beside him in her father's moonlight garden, listening to him profess his undying devotion, her heart so full of love for him that it nearly
made her weep.

But his voice shattered the spell. Rough and ragged,
it was as far from Connor's light, breezy lilt as night
from day. Juliana's spine went stiff as she recalled the
rest of her memories, none of them tender in the least.
The man was *beyond* redemption. He should have
appeared contrite. Or made at least a half-hearted

attempt to pretend not to know her. Instead, his pale eyes took in every detail of her form, then met her own with a bold, completely unrepentant familiarity.

All at once she was glad that Renquist had dragged her here despite her protests. It gave her an opportunity to tell Connor Reed exactly how much she despised him. She squared her shoulders, intending to deliver a set-down so brilliantly stinging that it would be repeated at garden parties for months to come, but Morrow spoke first.

"Why, do you know our Lady Juliana, Captain Gabriel?"

Gabriel? Juliana glanced around as she wondered if another naval officer had joined them. But the Earl still looked straight at Connor. "But Lord Morrow, his name is not—"

"—not one the lady expected to hear at tonight's party," Connor finished quickly as he stepped between them. "We have known each other for years, but I fear my identity is as much a surprise to her as it is to the rest of you. I can only plead that I was under orders not to tell a soul. Come, forgive an old friend his deception."

Connor met her gaze, his icy eyes bright with unspoken warning. But if he thought a mere look would silence her, he was very much mistaken. Four years of anger boiled up inside her, four years of buried humiliation. *"Friend?"* she repeated, seething. "How *dare* you? How dare you even speak to me after what you did? I'll have you in irons—"

Her words ended in a yelp as Connor neatly tromped on her foot.

"Heavens, look what I've done," the captain said, though to Juliana's ears his distress sounded as false as his name. "Lord Morrow, could you fetch a doctor? I fear I might have injured this poor lady."

The poor lady feared it as well, but she wasn't about to let Connor get the upper hand. Balanced on one foot and biting her lip against the pain, she growled, "Reed, you slimy son of a—"

"And delirious, too," Connor interrupted. "She believes I am someone else. Quick, Morrow. Fetch the doctor!"

The earl lord scuttled off to find help. Juliana turned to the rest of the crowd, determined to tell *someone* who this man really was, but Connor scooped her up in his arms and carried her behind the curtain. He called over his shoulder to the people who hovered nearby, saying that the lady needed some breathing room. Alarmed, Juliana saw the crowd back away before the heavy curtain fell behind them and blocked her view.

Beyond the curtain was a narrow, deserted hallway that led to the back of the house. Connor carried Juliana to the servant's stairs, where he deposited her on the bottom steps. "Did I hurt you?"

" 'Tis a bit late to be asking that," Juliana fired back, barely able to speak. She'd thought his spurious actions of four years past were beyond compare. Apparently she'd been wrong. He'd compounded his already unforgivable behavior by stomping on her foot, sweeping her up, and carrying her off like a common barmaid. Had the man no shame? She bent forward and nursed her injured foot, burning with an emotion she told herself was simple fury. "I would not be surprised if you have crippled me for life."

Connor's hard mouth ticked up. He'd wounded her pride, but nothing more. "No doubt," he agreed as he sat on the step just below her. He drew up his knee and leaned back against the wall, taking an unaccountable pleasure in watching her fuss over her abused foot. "It is your own fault. You should have heeded my warning glance."

"Captain *Gabriel's* warning glance," she corrected. "Where did you come upon such a ridiculous name?"

"It suits my purpose as well as any. Here, you are only making your foot worse by doing that. Let me."

Before she could protest he took her foot, stripped off her flimsy slipper, pushed her skirt up to a scandalous height and started to massage the injury. Juliana wanted to jerk away, but she couldn't deny that his ministrations made her feel better. Much better. His strong, gentle hands seemed to magically draw the pain from her body. Anger and propriety told her to pull away, but her practical core reminded her that if she did so, she would be the one in pain, not Connor. With great reluctance she allowed him to minister to her ankle. At least, she told herself it was with great reluctance. "I am allowing this only because I fear permanent injury."

"Of course," he said as a hint of his old humor

crept back into his voice. "You were not so angry the first time I stepped on your foot. Do you remember?"

How could she forget? She had been ten and Connor fifteen when her father had put into the Indian port of Bombay for repairs on their ship. Bored by the stuffy English children she'd been sent to play with, she'd stolen away to explore the back streets on her own. Wide-eyed she'd wound through the narrow alleys, piling wonder on wonder as she took in the festive sights and rich, mysterious smells of the exotic Hindu City. Somewhere in the midst of the adventure she'd come nose to nose with a hissing cobra. She'd stood transfixed in horror as the creature gracefully rose up and unfurled its killing hood.

Then, out of nowhere, Connor appeared. He put himself in front of her, inadvertently stepping on her foot while driving the snake into the shadows. Afterwards it did not matter to Juliana that her toe was black and blue for a week, or that the cobra turned out to be a harmless family pet, or that her father had to bribe the owner to keep Connor from being handed over to the authorities for reckless mischief. All that mattered to her was that Connor had again risked his life to save hers.

She shut her eyes, fighting a stab of pain that had nothing to do with her injured foot. "That was a long time ago, and it has nothing to do with your *cowardly* action tonight. Be assured that I still mean to tell everyone who you really are."

"Indeed," Connor commented, looking far too calm for Juliana's liking. "And exactly what will you tell them? That their guest of honor, one of England's most worshiped and triumphant heroes, is really a beggar boy who got caught with his hand in the till? Do you think Morrow or his friends will thank you for the knowledge? Do you think the highly placed officials who have spent so much time and trouble to bring me here will thank you?"

Juliana swallowed. " 'Tis the truth."

Connor leaned closer, his eyes narrowing. "No, my innocent, 'tis *war*, and truth is always one of the first casualties. The Admiralty wouldn't care if I had robbed a dozen men and murdered a dozen others. I am their victor, their conquering champion, their highly publicized and carefully promoted hero of the hour. The few who remember me in Whitehall have already been cautioned to keep silent about my past. If they'd known you would be here tonight you would have been told the same."

"I would not have agreed," she said, though her words came out weaker than she'd hoped.

This time Connor's smile was as cold as his eyes. "You *will* agree. Not because it is right, but because no one wants to hear anything else. They don't give a damn about who I was—they only care that I am winning battles in a war where others are winning too few. Right now England needs all of her heroes, Juliana. Even tin-plated ones like me."

She wanted to tell him he was wrong. She wanted to scream it. But his winter gaze bored into her, freezing her speech, her breath, her thoughts. She looked in his eyes for a trace of warmth, for the bright humor that had once overflowed from his soul like water from a day-spring. She saw only ice and desolation. For the first time she looked at him without the memories of the past, seeing the harsh, unforgiving set of his jaw, the bitter line of his mouth, the red, livid scar that cut his cheek from his left eye to his throat. She wondered how he'd gotten that scar. She wondered if he'd killed the man who gave it to him. If he'd killed . . .

This man wore Connor's face. He had Connor's memories. Once he'd even borne Connor's name. But the pitiless eyes that riveted hers were the eyes of a stranger. Suddenly she was aware of the strength in the hands that held her foot, how they could snap her ankle like a bit of kindling. She was alone in a deserted hallway with a powerful, dangerous man, out of the earshot of anyone who might help her, and incapable of running away. She was at the mercy of a man who had no mercy.

"My dear, there you are!"

Commodore Jolly bounded down the hallway with Meg, Morrow, Renquist, and a man carrying a physician's satchel. Relief poured through Juliana, until she remembered her immodest pose. Hastily she pulled back her foot and was surprised to find the slipper already back in place and her skirt discreetly arranged around her ankle. She glanced at Connor, but he was already on his feet with his hands clasped behind him.

Meg reached her first. "You poor darling. Are you all right?"

"I am fine," Juliana assured her, and circled her much improved ankle as proof. "Captain Re . . . that is, Captain Gabriel was most helpful."

Was that a flicker of gratitude she saw in his eyes? She couldn't be sure, for no sooner had the words left her mouth than her view of Connor was blotted out by the round-cheeked face of Lord Renquist. "My deawr, I was so dweadfully wowwied for you."

"So was I," Mr. Hamilton stated emphatically as he pushed in beside Lord Renquist.

"And I," chorused another one of her suitors.

Suddenly the narrow hallway was stuffed with people. Juliana pressed back against the stairs, struggling to find the grace to deal with both the embarrassment of attention, and with the less than gentle ministrations of the physician. She tried to catch a glimpse of Connor, but he had disappeared. A few minutes later she heard someone in the crowd mention that the captain had left Morrow house entirely. The man had gone without so much as a by-your-leave. Not that she expected one. Not that she *wanted* one.

Finally, with the commodore's assistance, she was able to make her way through the bevy of ardent suitors and limp to the carriage. She settled against comfortable brocade cushions, with the concerned Jolly sitting across from her and Meg's arm clasped protectively around her shoulders, and watched as Morrow House faded into the shadows. The pain in her foot faded as well—by morning it would be quite fit to walk on.

In time, she told herself, this night would become no more than a curious memory in an otherwise sane and pleasant life, a life that did not include the disreputable Connor Reed. He would return to the sea, and she would return to her parties, picnics, and country weekends. Their worlds were as far apart as heaven and Hades. It was highly unlikely that she would ever see him again.

She clutched the carriage's door handle, determined to take pleasure in the thought of never seeing Connor again. Just as she was determined to ignore the tight, twisting ache that had suddenly surrounded her heart.

A KISS AT MIDNIGHT by Shana Abé
On sale February 2000

Ancient law proclaims that, as the year 999 draws to a close, the land of Alderich will be wrested from the Rune family by the clan of Leonhart. But when Rafael Leonhart kidnaps the beautiful Serath Rune for ransom, he falls under her spell . . . and the conquest he desires most of all is the heart of his alluring captive.

He had been waiting for her too long.

To anyone else, the passing time had been no more

than a day and a night, camped out in the woods surrounding the convent, a quiet scrutiny of the situation before the attack. Just a day and a night, and then
suddenly the girl was there, and she was theirs.

But to Rafael of Leonhart, the waiting time had
been years—thirty-two of them to be exact, the sum
of his entire life.

Thirty-two years of waiting to gain access to this
girl and steal her away to suit his needs.

Thirty-two years waiting for the turn of this century, when the land of Alderich and the castle, and
the wealth they represented, would become his. And
now this granddaughter of his enemy would ensure
it for him.

So while his soldiers had remained in the woods
with him for that day and night, had met with him and
discussed how best to breach the walls of a holy sanc-
tuary, most of them felt mere hours slip by. But Rafe
had felt his lifetime come sliding to a sudden and final
countdown, each second bringing sharp anticipation.

He had Serath. Rafael broke into a fierce smile
that no one could see, unable to help himself. He
had her. And so he had Alderich.

"This way, my lord." His cousin Abram took the
lead momentarily, showing Rafe the correct path
amid the autumn grasses.

The woman in front of him started at the words.
She turned her head to see Abram, who spared her
only one quick look before turning away.

Rafe followed the faint trail, pushing his mount

to a gallop as they entered the smoothness of a valley. Serath's black hair flew up with the new wind, brushing against his chest, curling along his neck with surprising softness. Rafe ignored the sensation, concentrating on the land ahead of them.

Rafe slowed his steed, waiting for the rest of his men to catch up, and the figure in his arms shifted and then somehow there was nothing but empty space where a warm woman had been. It happened so quickly that it took him several seconds to comprehend it—as if she had transformed into the very air before him.

Dammit! Rafe reined in completely, looking left and right before catching sight of her running through the trees, swift and nearly gone already.

"Where did she go?" one of the men asked, dumbfounded.

He didn't bother to answer, though several others did, shouting and pointing at the diminishing shape. Rafe was already lunging after her, his stallion picking his way through the trunks of the trees with surety. She would not be able to outrun a horse.

At last Rafael dismounted, walking away from his soldiers, his steps slow and sure on the mossy ground.

He stopped, closing his eyes, listening. The obvious came to him first: men behind him, completely silent now but for the creaking of saddles . . . the bare, metallic clinks of shields and swords against chain mail. Horses, a few shifting with impatience. Wind through pine needles, a ghostly murmur of sound . . .

. . . faint breathing. Muted, nearly imperceptible. Off to his left.

Pure relief made him release his own breath, close to a sigh. Rafe opened his eyes and found her immediately—or rather, found the spot he had figured to be just another bramble of bushes, exactly the same as the multitude of others that dotted the forest floor. He walked past it, the relief becoming close to exhilaration, then stopped again.

"Serath," he said, not raising his voice. "It was a good effort, my lady, but now it is done. Come back. My patience is ended."

And since she did not move, he reached through the brush and grabbed what was there—a mass of cloth, the woman beneath it erupting from the branches and dead leaves with complete and sudden fury, striking at him, struggling as he wrapped his arms around her and tried to contain the unexpected strength of her. It was a strangely silent battle, no sound from her other than the raggedness of her breathing, and his own harsh gasp as she landed a blow to his cheekbone.

"Enough!" Finally he had her restrained in front of him, her arms pinned, her tousled head held just below his.

"Enough," Rafe said again, more subdued, and held her there until she was still at last, that blanket of silence about her shrouding them both.

There were leaves in her hair. They stood out against the black even in this dim light, papery ovals, a few twigs enmeshed in otherwise glossy locks. Her panting was slowing but the heat of her body seemed to grow against him, uncomfortably warm.

Rafael scowled again, fighting the unexpected appeal of this, a soft woman so near.

"Will you obey me, Serath Rune?" he asked her, his voice rough.

Slowly, slowly, he felt the tension from her body begin to fade, begin to melt, ever so slightly, against him. His own body responded with a completely unwelcome rush of hunger for her, for the sweet curves and ebony hair and the scent of some unknown spice that haunted her.

This was bad. He could not allow himself to feel for her, not even this basic, overwhelming lust. He could not allow anything so petty as passion for a woman to disrupt his plans, no matter how fair or enthralling she was.

"Will you obey?" he asked again, gritting his teeth.

And at last she nodded her head, just once, a short jerk. He turned her around in his arms, not releasing her completely, because he didn't trust a nod.

Her head lifted; she shook away the curling strands of hair. Rafael found himself staring into a pair of blue eyes pale with moonlight, a face of such delicate and unlikely beauty that it left him winded for a moment, mute himself.

I know you, Rafe thought, shock running through him.

Aye, there was a profound and telling recognition in him at the full sight of her, those eyes, that look. It was as if he had just discovered a part of himself in this person, a missing part that only now pained him for its loss.

He stood there gaping at her, knowing how inept it seemed, unable to help himself. She was a vision from a forgotten youth, a young woman with a face of timeless sorcery, dark brows, perfect nose, full lips, eyes surrounded by thick, black lashes. Her skin was utterly colorless in this light, her gaze the color of silver on heaven. She was the sun and the moon together, she was smoke and desire made real.

She had the face of an enchantress, yes, but the blue of her gaze told him something more: she had pride, and spirit—and what might have been fear. Rafe fought his reaction to that, the desire to comfort her.

He became suddenly, acutely aware of his hands on her, the burning heat of his palms against her upper arms, where he held her. The firm but giving flesh of her, so close her body nearly brushed his. He felt a kind of insanity from it, realizing all at once that here in his grip was more than a prize he had won; this was a woman, warmth and familiar succor, and he wanted nothing more than to pull her the rest of the way to him, to feel the whole of her pressed to his body. To bury himself in her.

It *was* a spell—a mortal spell to be sure, but a terrible and disastrous one, and Rafael of Leonhart was, for the first time in his adulthood, helpless to combat the emotions that raged through him.